THE TRANSFORMATION: GTE 45

BY FAREN SIMINOFF

Published by Starry Night Publishing.com

Rochester, New York

Faren Siminoff

THE TRANSFORMATION: GTE 45

Abbreviations Key

BoT: Board of Twenty

CCU: Consolidated City University

CRS: Church of the Revealed Saints

CSA: Corporate States of America

EASY: Entertainment, Arts and Sports (classification)

FAP: Founders Action Party

GTE: Great Transition Era

JC: Job Creator

MTC: Metropolitan Transit Company

POL: Politician

PROFFIE: Professor

SAT: Skills Assessment Test

SM: Social Media

STD: Scholastic, Training & Development, Corp.

WE: Wage Earner

Chapter 1: Paul

New York City, The Platform [GTE 45]

Paul stood on line waiting for the train to pull in. Another long day ahead of him and already the sweat was running down his spine, soaking the back of his collared shirt. He'd be drenched by the time he arrived at the office. He was heading out despite still feeling sick, even after two days at home. Of course, he tried to get an extension of his out days. Yesterday he had even pulled up Patient Centered Solutions on his Palm Pad, which he visualized through his Third Eye.

"Do you want holographic communications?" it asked.

"Yes."

"Ok, hang on. Your holographic communications will commence in twenty seconds."

Paul blinked as he listened to the countdown to visualization. He reached for a packet of C-juice, took a sip and focused on the image that appeared.

"Patient Centered Solutions," the computer generated hologram chirped reaching out to Paul as if to pat him reassuringly on his arm. "How may we provide for you so you can get on your feet again?"

"I've been sick- actually in bed for two full days- I can barely move, have a one-hundred degree fever. What's wrong with me?"

"Would you like to see a female or male doctor?"

"Female"

"Ok, I have registered your symptoms, placed your order, and put you in the cue. A doctor will appear in a moment. Do not disconnect your Palm Pad or you will lose your turn on line and be charged for the visit. Do you understand?"

"Yes," responded Paul.

The image flickered off almost immediately replaced by a female holo dressed in a white coat with a stethoscope slung around her neck.

"What's your problem?" the holographic doctor sternly inquired.

"Like I told your Intaker, I've been in bed for two days, can hardly move and have a one hundred degree fever. What's wrong? What should I do?"

"Don't worry I am trained to assist you and resolve your problem quickly. Place your hand on your Palm Pad and give me a moment."

He did as he was told.

"Ok, you can remove it now." She looked down at the results then back up at him. "You have a simple virus. Nothing to complain about. It will resolve on its own."

"How long? What should I do?"

"Take two Ibuprofens, drink lots of C- juice and I strongly urge you to get out of bed and go back to work."

"That's what I've been doing. It's not helping. How can I go to work with this fever?"

"How much out-time do you have?"

"None left."

"Hmmmm…. I see. Any vacay time?"

"All done. Used up."

"Hmmm…I see. Well, there's nothing left for you to do than return to work. Take two Ibuprofens, drink lots of C-juice and go to work. It will pass."

Another pause. The holo doctor looked him squarely in his Third Eye, asking in a disdainful tone, "Is there anything else I can help you with?"

He should have just ended the convo there, but Paul persisted. "Well, I've been doing all that. I thought if I could stay home a few more days and rest up I'd be really fit for work again. I think I need a prescription for a medical emergency extension. Could you do that for me?"

The Hologram answered crisply, decisively, "Your condition does not meet the medical criteria for that prescription. I suggest you get your lazy ass out of bed and go back to work unless you want to find yourself in the Projects."

Connection ended.

The next day Paul had no choice but to drag his sorry self into the street and down to the subway. There was nothing he wanted more than to turn around, crawl back up the four flights to his micro-apartment and get into bed. But despite the fever, he simply had no more out-days left in the current fiscal cycle, which made his bed not a refuge for the infirm, but a potential one-way ticket to the Projects. The very thought made his fever spike.

Sure he had been unlucky this year. Problems and illness had shadowed him. Sometimes he asked himself if this was a manifestation of God's will, bad luck, or something else? And what if it were God's will? He simply wouldn't or couldn't contemplate its implication. So he scratched that off his list. And, as he well knew, explanations, justifications were unacceptable. Bad luck was frowned on, dismissed, and derided. No excuses here and the two out- days just taken was it. He had now used them all. Any overage would result in lost credits and even, *Oh horror*, he thought, *please Sainted Darwin, don't let this happen to me. Don't let them terminate my contract.*

Termination was a serious matter in the Corporate States of America. Sixty days of WAGE EARNER, "WE" benefits, then he'd have to dip into his meager savings or lose his apartment. And how long would the few thousand credits he'd put aside last him? Three months? Oh, if only he had listened to the mantra of Trudy Evermore, the screen goddess of personal finances, "More is more, more is more."

He should have listened. *Yes, I wanted to listen. I wanted to follow her advice,* he thought, but there always seemed to be something he absolutely had to do or buy. So he squandered his precious credits on a dinner here, a new shirt there, and so many other seemingly small items. Sheer frivolity, but it all added up.

Is it really my fault with so many temptations emanating from every wall - screaming at me, beckoning me quite literally to, buy, buy, buy, and buy some more.

His screen, in the third dimension mind you, showed him things and places he could only imagine owning or visiting. Of course, there was his U-R-DARE that permitted him to feel as if he were actually being, doing, wearing, driving, flying, or anything else imaginable. Who could possibly resist? How to keep those credits securely banked for a rainy day? It seemed almost impossible!

They drained out of his bank account like water running into a sewer. But one thing he was sure of: those little U-R-Dare breaks, along with those small purchases, kept him and the rest of them going. Then, as if his thoughts had strayed into dangerous territory, he reminded himself that consuming was every MAKER's patriotic duty; a public good. He reached back into his memory pulling up a download on this topic from his Learning Center's American History class. Yes, now he remembered. It was President George W. Bush, that great visionary who wisely instructed Americans to, "go shopping," fresh off the 9/11 attacks. To do their duty to stand up to the terrorists by buy, buy, buying. After all, America was created for the "pursuit of happiness" and, as told in the *Book of Darwin,* one of the things that separated us from the apes and other animals was our capacity to shop and consume, and consume, and consume. It was the foundation on which the nation's economic success rested; indeed it's a hallmark of our humanity. So, of course, he was obligated to buy, buy, buy and buy some more. Of that, he was certain.

Chapter 2: History

Excerpt from an official history: *The Restored History of America from 1492 to the Great Transformation,* Chapter 25, The Beginning of the End of the USA

The beginning of the end of what was once known as the United States of America came when Franklin Delano Roosevelt took possession of the presidency during the Great Depression. Although it would not be apparent for many years to come, that event opened the door to anti-American forces. Through their chosen leader they seized power and began to dismantle the most successful economic system the world had ever known: American capitalism. Lionized until the end of the twentieth century as the savior of American capitalism, FDR's so-called "New Deal" nurtured a culture of dependency and demonized the Job Creators- our beloved "JCs." By 1964 President Lyndon Johnson's "Great Society" had completed America's transformation into a nation of "TAKERs" not "MAKERs."

Under LBJ's leadership millions of uneducated immigrants flooded into the country lowering wages and snatching the bread from the mouths of hardworking MAKERs. Not content to stop there, onerous job-destroying regulations and taxes were heaped onto businesses, all for the sake of "safety" in the workplace, the environment, and to pay for the ballooning welfare state.

By the end of the 1980s the handwriting was on the wall as cracks began to appear in the fifty-year old welfare state. The country was weak and vulnerable to attack. The first assault on fortress American slammed it hard when in 1983 a U.S. Marine barracks in Lebanon was attacked butchering two hundred forty-one American soldiers.

The response by President Ronald Reagan [Sainted be his Name] was swift and deliberate. He called out the cowardly Democratic controlled Congress to more fully fund anti-terrorist activities, only to be turned down. The ramifications would be far-reaching and not fully understood until the infamous 9/11 attacks.

From the moment Reagan became governor of California in 1967 he labored in the wilderness to stem America's decline. The turning point came in 1981 when the Air Traffic Controllers' union, PATCO, went on strike. Well paid and pampered they demanded over-the-top pay increases along with a reduction in work hours. Reagan held firm against their outrageous demands and the PATCO workers walked. The media predicted the government would quickly capitulate. President Reagan did not. He broke PATCO and fired the traitors.

"Help," as the Gipper promised, was truly "on the way." Little by little the Republican Party pried the Wager Earners [WEs] away from the Democratic Party and back to the party of Lincoln. From a small trickle to a flood, WEs joined the Republican ranks and the movement to reclaim America began in earnest. And while Reagan, like Moses before him, did not live long enough to see the "Promised Land," his actions paved the way for, "The Great Transformation" and America's return to its former glory.

Excerpt from an unauthorized history: *What Really Happened to America from 1492 to the Great Transformation* [accessed by a special password]

On October 19, 1929 the stock market crashed worldwide followed by the collapse of the American banking system. By the time Franklin Delano Roosevelt took office on March 4, 1933 stocks had lost 80% of their pre-crash value, over half of the banks in the United States had failed, while 30% of the workforce, roughly 15 million people, were unemployed. The nation's Wage Earners were on their knees while American capitalism stood on the verge of total collapse.

FDR's New Deal rescued American capitalism by finally extending full participation to the Wage Earners by welcoming labor unions and creating an economic safety net, all, which imbued working people with dignity and the hope of a better future for themselves and their children. Via careful regulation FDR resuscitated the American capitalist system ushering in a "golden era" for American businesses both at home and abroad. By the close of World War II, the USA was an economic and military juggernaut.

Not all benefited from the New Deal or the prosperity, which washed over post-WWII America. Large swaths of the population were discounted, left behind. African Americans, women, and other minorities were not fully embraced by FDR's renaissance. It was left to the modern-day Civil Rights movement, spear-headed by African Americans, to pave the path towards that "more perfect union" not only for blacks, but all minorities. A series of U.S. Supreme Court decisions, along with President Lyndon Baines Johnson's "Great Society," gave legal legs to this push forward. The United States of America was poised to fully realize its great experiment begun in 1776. But then, in 1980, it was derailed.

In that year, on the heels of political scandal, an oil crisis, rising inflation and cultural rifts, Ronald Reagan was catapulted into the presidency ushering in the "Reagan Revolution." Within a year of taking office Reagan broke the PATCO union. From 1981 going forward, unions were hard pressed to retain membership as each succeeding administration refused to protect workers' rights to organize, turning a blind eye to their evisceration by the private sector. By the early decades of the twenty-first century the unions made their last stand within the public sector. The last to fall were the teachers' unions.

Pity the average person on the street who never connected the dots between the existence of unions and their own earning power. They never understood that as unionization declined, so too did the wages and benefits of all employees, union and non-union. Yet, how can they be blamed?

By the early twenty-first century the corporate stranglehold over the media was complete. Americans were fed a regular diet of "blame the unions," "blame the poor," "blame African Americans," "blame the immigrants."

The corporate media did their job. They extolled the virtues of the so-called "Job Creators" and demonized those who were still striving to make it. They lauded those who sat on their rears moving money around like croupiers moving chips in a casino and diminished the worker who toiled every day, stood on his feet, made the wheels move, taught our children, picked up our garbage, delivered our mail. For all the JCs' talk against socialism, handouts, moochers, redistribution of wealth, keeping government out of the way and blah, blah, blah, they benefited more from all these things than any other group. Corporate welfare was the real government handout.

The Beltway Bandits siphoned off money that could have been used for the public good and, thanks to tax loopholes and laws that taxed the JCs' income stream, those so-called "capital gains" at less than half the rate the top Wage Earner paid, most of the money not only flowed to the top but stayed there.

Yet, despite the clear handwriting on the proverbial wall, the typical American remained locked in an almost perverse state of denial. They gobbled up the message that their problems were due to corrupt unions, the welfare moochers, and excessive regulations tying the hands of business, along with illegal immigration.

"Oh," moaned so many, "if we could only get rid of all these things our lives would improve!!!"

They mouthed the mantra the JCs placed in their mouths: "Why should unionized workers have wages, benefits and working conditions I don't have?" They never asked: "Why not me too?"

By the early decades of the twenty-first century, the remnants of the middle and working classes were simply scrapping over the crumbs, eyes cast perpetually downward towards the bottom of the economic ladder.

Chapter 3: Paul

Dream No More [GTE: 32]

Long ago, when Paul was a boy, his grandmother told him there had been a time when young people were permitted to "explore their dreams." He must have been all of sixteen when she let that tidbit drop from her mouth giving little thought to the fact that the idea bordered on heresy. At the time, he hadn't really comprehended what a dangerous notion she was voicing. Still, even as half-baked as he was, he instinctively knew enough to respond with a mixture of disbelief and even horror.

"What," he asked his aging grandparent, "does that really mean, anyway, 'to explore your dreams'?"

"Well," she responded eagerly, "in my day after you graduated from what we called 'high school,' you could have chosen what you wanted to do. Gone to art school, or just explored your interests by taking General Studies, what used to be called the Liberal Arts. I remember some kids even took a year off after high school just to travel around to see where it all took them. In my day you could have explored your dream of being an artist."

Then, as she often did when thinking about the past, she got this dreamy look on her face and half-whispered as if speaking to the air, "Wouldn't that be a great opportunity for you?"

"Granny, what are you woofing about?" he challenged her. "A dream is just that, a dream. Why would I aim for something that disappears when I wake up? No, I am going to follow the occupational track my SAT will lay out for me. That's what leads to security. Following dreams only results in unemployment and reclassification to, to…" his voice trailed off.

"That's ok," she hissed, "just say it!" But he remained silent.

"Hmmuph," she intoned, "Let me voice what you are thinking. Reclassification to TAKER - a 'TAKER'! I know that's what your grandpa and me would be but for your Mom and Dad. I know otherwise we'd be in the Projects."

She stopped. Then her voice drifted back to a past long gone: "It wasn't our fault. We worked hard. We could have continued to contribute if they'd only let us. But they called us 'TAKERs,' cut our jobs and we were left to drift."

Paul had heard this all before, but said nothing. She continued, "You know Paul, your grandpa was a good layout man at *KnewsDay* but they got rid of him and all the older workers- just cut them all. 'Too much money,' they said. At first they hired younger, cheaper workers- no benefits at all-but then the greedy SOBs decided even that was too much. Top management said it cut into their profits. I guess they weren't content making forty times more than the average worker, weren't content with their mansions and Beemers... always wanted more..."

"But Granny," Paul gently reminded her, "Trudy Evermore says 'more is more,' so what could be wrong with that?"

She ignored that comment, swallowed hard and continued, "Anyway, they finally cut even those jobs; sent the whole shebang off to Bangladesh. Those poor bastards. They paid them just $1.00 a week. After your Grandpa got the shaft it was my turn. The 'Great Fiscal Crisis' gave the legislature its excuse to abolish collective bargaining along with tenure. Eventually, all the full-time teachers were fired; either replaced by temps or some returned on yearly renewables at half the price. Of course, no one in New York State could believe **our** state's progressive governor – Governor Lakeside- would do something that was so anti-labor. He was a Democrat after all. His daddy trusted and beloved by the working people had been governor before him. He was to the governorship born; he'd never betray us like that, well, would he, could he? 'Course not! We thought only the Republicans did stuff like that, but they were all just cut from different sides of the same cloth. More fools we."

Paul rolled his eyes. The "Leftovers"- that's what his generation called so many of them, because here they were, after so many years, still whining, still blaming others. It was an old refrain.

"At half the cost," Paul parroted. "Sounds pretty smart to me," he confidently proclaimed.

He tried to further school her. "Gran, it was just that people weren't properly trained. Those of you born in the late twentieth century just got left behind. It was sad but life is soooo much better now. We have security. The Corpus has secured it all for us. Life is good. I just don't know why you can't see that."

But old passions and frustrations bubbled to the surface. The older woman rallied to challenge him.

"What they did was wrong and what they're doing now is wrong. It's plain immoral. You're a talented boy. You should have options and the chance to succeed or fail. The opportunity to explore your dreams, to spread your wings and soar instead becoming a soulless automaton like the rest of 'em."

He moved towards her, gently taking her hand, "Well, if that were true, why did so many of your generation become TAKERs? Or spend most of their lives drifting from job to job?"

He paused. She looked down, her hand limp in his. He continued, "There's no more guesswork. No more wasted time or resources [he shuddered at that thought]. We know where our lives will take us. It's all laid out in our occupational track. We don't need to worry anymore like you and grandpa did. The bad old days are gone."

He finished by giving her: *I love you but you are so misguided* look. She was his grandmother after all. Of course, he loved her, but like many of his generation he also pitied her as a Leftover. He couldn't understand how, after so many decades, she continued to be so misguided, so haunted by remembered promises from false prophets whose voices had, for a time, misled the American people.

The elderly woman winced at that look. She knew what it meant. He clearly hadn't understood a word she said to him. Giving up, she shrugged turning to the wall screen where an attractive girl with pretty teeth was hawking the latest whitener promising the viewer that brighter teeth would not only make you look younger, but ensure a longer working career.

"No one wants to have unsightly people around them at work," she intoned while keeping a wide grin plastered on her face. "No," Grandma repeated, "No one wants to have old people around them at work, they are depressing to look at, they smell bad, and are too expensive to maintain…"

Paul, like the rest of his generation, had been schooled from a young age to address the lingering discontent and wrong thinking of that Leftover generation. They were the last Americans who had the misfortune to live out much of their adult lives before the *Great Transformation.* The Leftovers were dreamers, wanderers; a group looking for something they referred to as "self-fulfillment."

They babbled on about how their parents spent weekends on the soccer field with them, gave them music lessons, or dance classes, all to let them "explore their interests."

Even worse, these poor fools were led to believe they could all be "winners," which was reinforced by receiving accolades and trophies for merely "trying."

No wonder my poor grandma thinks the way she does! What a sucker she was to have ever bought into such garbage.

Paul understood that the Leftovers never imbibed the lesson of relevant skill set acquisition or that America's business was business as proclaimed by the great Henry Ford, one of the true prophets of the twentieth century. So, if America's business was business, didn't it stand to reason, "We the People," were put on this earth to fulfill that purpose? Of course, the WE were always contemplated as being central to the American journey. Just look at how our revered Constitution begins: "WE the People," meaning "WE" as in the Wage Earners. Front and center again Paul thought while giving himself a silent pat on the back for his insight.

The debate about the role of business in American society was now long over. Business, everyone agreed, was the heart and soul of a healthy and prosperous society. It was clearly counter to everyone's interests for the Job Creators, the "JCs," to hand over all their money to the government instead of doing what they did best: create jobs. As the revered *Great Transformation* President Cross liked to say, "We can't help the WE by taxing the JC." And, as he slyly pointed out in his famous speech introducing the new permanent classifications or tiers to the American public, "It is not a coincidence that the initials for our "Job Creators" is "JC" just like that of our Lord and Savior. Amen!"

Once Americans had accepted these two simple bedrock principles, a sound economy and a stable society was all but guaranteed. Everything else – people and things- simply fell into place. And if you didn't learn this lessons or if you failed to follow the occupational track assigned by your objective Skills Assessment Test and become a full MAKER, a genuine Contributor, well then, you were reclassified as a TAKER and sent to the Projects. It was that simple.

A TAKER! TAKER! The most feared classification in America. For the vast majority of sensible, normal Americans such a fate was unthinkable, inconceivable. So when his grandparents waxed prosaic, as they did from time to time, about how great things used to be before the *Great Transformation*, he could only pity them for having been born during such a dark period in America's history. Paul, on the other hand, lived in an enlightened society and for that he counted his blessings.

Chapter 4: History

Excerpt from an official history: *The Restored History of America from 1492 to the Great Transformation*, Chapter 28, Reorganization

One year into his presidency, during his first State of the Union address, President Cross proposed the establishment of a Constitutional Convention; something that had not occurred since 1787.

"My fellow MAKERs. These are momentous years, critical for our nation's future. Do we move forward with the changes wrought by the Great Transformation or do we leave the job unfinished? Do we bravely forge ahead and complete the task or do we listen to the naysayers and slide back into chaos and failure? I say we dust off the old militia coats donned by our forefathers so long ago and renew our revolutionary fervor for change. I say we do what Abraham Lincoln exhorted us to do so long ago and forge that more perfect Union." [APPLAUSE, APPLAUSE]

"A more perfect Union you might ask? How so? Hasn't the big story since Lincoln's day been our march towards inclusion, perfection of our union? Blacks, Latinos, Women, Gays, now woven into our great American tapestry.

Yes, great progress has been made. Yet one group has not received the blessings of inclusion. There still remains amongst us an excluded, persecuted, scapegoated group: the Corpus. Yes, yes, we all accept that corporations are vital to our success, but full integration? True personhood? No, not yet. That hill is still left to climb. So, progress yes, but mission accomplished? No. So let's grab the reins of change and ride it into the future- our FU--A-TURE!" [THUNDEROUS APPLAUSE]

"Today, we embrace anew a long forgotten paradigm espoused by our greatest founder, Alexander Hamilton, the first Secretary of the Treasury, author of the Five Reports, and founder of the Bank of New York. So, at the risk of boring you all [loud guffaws from the audience] let's review a little history." [groans from the audience but Cross continued]

"In his Five Reports to the Congress [Cross, crossed himself intoning hallowed be these] Hamilton laid out a plan, guidelines, for the Corpus' full integration as the fourth branch of government. He knew that the 'WE' in 'WE the People' referenced this nation's 'Wage Earners.' He understood the promises contained therein could only be fulfilled with the Corpus' full integration. But even then, the forces of darkness were conspiring to prevent this. Yes, it was a vast conspiracy from beginning to end to exclude the Corpus."

[He picked up a sheath of documents and began waving them as he spoke]

"These documents were hidden in a vault in the Capitol's basement and verify the original intent of the Founders to include the Corpus. It details the conspiracy, beginning with the killing of Hamilton in 1804, through Lincoln's assassination by the Radical Republicans – y'all still don't think John Wilkes Booth did it do ya? - from the two Roosevelts to Lyndon Johnson and ending with the last Democratic president in the twenty-first century to keep the Corpus OUT and the WE down and out! But finally, after centuries of struggle, the truth is revealed.

What I am proposing is the full implementation of the blueprint laid out in the Constitution's Preamble and in these documents long hidden from us. Hear it again as if for the first time: WE the People of the United States, in Order to form a more perfect Union, establish Justice, insure domestic Tranquilly, provide for the common defense, promote the general Welfare...

It's all there. Are we supposed to believe the Founders had no plan to secure the 'general welfare'? What rubbish! So, now say it with me. What was the Constitution supposed to secure?"

[The audience rose, screaming in unison: "THE GENERAL WELFARE!!!!"]

"That's correct ladies and gentlemen. And who was supposed to guarantee that? Come on! Come on now! Rise, I say rise to your feet and say it with me!!!!"

[The audience rose as one bellowing: "THE CORPUS!!! THE CORPUS!!!!"]

"What," Cross continued after the crowd had quieted, "would our forebears, the Founders, do if they were here today? The answer: a Constitutional Convention. That's what they did when the nation came near to collapse under the unworkable Articles of Confederation. Our Founders discarded that document and replaced it with our revered United States Constitution. So now, following in the footsteps of our forefathers, I am calling for the same."

[The audience gasped]

"But there's more. Now stay with me for just a few more minutes. To mark this new resolve I also propose we rename our great country. Rename it you ask? You shake your heads in disbelief, 'No, that's unthinkable!' Yet, think again. Rebirth is symbolized by baptism, a new name. We, as a nation, as a people, must be born again. With this in mind I propose we bear the baptismal name, The Corporate States of America! We will be the CSA"

We don't know if President Cross had more to say. If he did it was drowned out by the roar of "CSA, CSA, CSA," that came from the assembled politicians and leading JCs. Within the month a Constitutional Convention was convened and three months later the USA was rechristened the CSA.

But that wasn't the only change wrought by the Convention. While much of the old constitution remained, a number of forward-looking amendments were considered and approved. Most importantly, it provided for a fourth branch of government, the Corpus headed by a self-selected "Board of Twenty" and its CEO. It was this entity that was the legal embodiment of all American corporations, empowered to represent American business in the public and political sphere as well as formulate policy on their behalf.

Once convened and given an official position within government, the Corpus' Board of Twenty promptly divided the country into efficient economic zones each under the direction of a holding company.

Finally, in that same year, now known as Great Transformation Era, "GTE," 1 the "Makers' Relief Act" formally classified every MAKER. This seminal legislation provided a weary nation with the guarantee that going forward each individual's station in society would be based on objective, measurable criteria; all assessed and assigned to their appropriate occupational sphere. Within a few years a fading, lackluster USA was transformed into a vibrant economic powerhouse; the new and improved CSA was here to stay.

Of course, there were the naysayers, the whiners, the grumblers and the malcontents. Even in the face of success they simply couldn't or wouldn't accept change. A lawsuit was brought to turn back the hands of progress. But, thank the Corpus, in GTE, 3 the Supreme Court had the good sense to reject their petition. In a 5-4 opinion they upheld the Makers' Relief Act:

"...Petitioners object to the new classifications provided for in the Makers' Relief Act: MAKER and TAKER. We note that MAKERs are further tiered into two basic categories: WAGE EARNER and PROFESSIONAL etc. Subcategories have also been provided for: JOB CREATOR, POLITICIANS, FLIPPERS, FABRICATORS and the like. None of these violate the CSA Constitution and certainly not the 13th Amendment, which has been retained... no one is compelled to accept employment. No one is forced to be a Contributor. Such an imposition would, in fact, be an affront to the 13th Amendment. However, individuals who voluntarily choose to opt out also willingly accept a designated position as much as employment confers a certain status in society; both the former and the latter are freely assumed. The consequences of that exercise of free will falls on the shoulders of the individual... and, contrary to Petitioners' ludicrous assertion, neither classification as MAKER or TAKER can be analogized as a 'badge or incident of slavery.'

Respondents have convincingly demonstrated that the new classifications are free from bias; no protected classes are impacted.... Judicial notice is also taken of the fact that wealth, occupation, and education have all, throughout our history, served as determinants of an individual's social and economic standing. This has been the de facto reality of America since its inception.

The new classifications are, contrary to Petitioners' assertions, a great leap forward towards removing those discriminatory elements that have, since our great nation's inception, hampered individual progress. Indeed, for the first time in our nation's history, these new classifications actually bulldoze those historic barriers providing society with the tools to implement full inclusion based solely on individual aptitude and merit, paving the way for a truly equitable society... This Court not only rejects all of Petitioners' arguments, but also reminds the public that while the Constitution guarantees the 'right to pursue happiness' it is no guarantor of it. Its obtainment rests squarely in each of our hands."

Chapter 5: Paul

WHAT'S AN EASY? *Entertainment, Arts and Sports.*
EASYS are comprised of career artists, curators, actors, directors, athletes, coaches and like skilled individuals. They take the lead in designing or actuating society's games, entertainment, and decorative arts. While most operate behind the scenes some obtain "star" status and grace the cover of our mags, screens, and even perform in- the- being. ***[GTE, 45]***

Sometimes, when Paul was feeling down, when he felt that life was simply unbearable, he would put on the U-R-DARE and let it transport him to places he could never travel to in- the- being. His absolute favorite location was Tahiti. He went there so often it felt like a second home; the fantasy played itself out with little variation. That was part of its gracia, grace, and comfort; knowing exactly what would happen. The perfect vacay. On arrival, [of course, he travelled first class] Paul always he stepped off the plane where he was greeted by a lovely, young, soft-looking woman. She'd immediately remove his hard plastique shoes and ever so gently slip a comfortable pair of soft leather sandals onto his feet beckoning him to follow her.

"What about my bags?" he always inquired.

"Please, not to worry, these will be waiting for you in your villa." Then she'd smile at him, her JC- like teeth straight and white, gleaming, so attractive, so inviting. He always grinned back at her while she ran her tongue over those pearly points of light, motioning him to follow. But sometimes, a disturbing thought marred the welcome: those teeth seemed too bright, too perfect and once, just once, for a moment, that lovely, welcoming Tahitian seemed to transform into a giant shark causing him to instinctively jump back from her, actually falling backwards over his sofa. But then, the vision passed, and he was once more ensconced in the bosom of his favorite fantasy. He sighed, relieved to be released from that unbidden vision and gave himself up to the U-R-DARE.

Always the same.

In the CSA familiarity bred comfort, security.

Each time Paul arrived she led him to the nearest beach and then simply disappeared. "Odd," he sometimes thought, "I never know her name." But no matter, there were so many people that flashed in and out of his existence without a name that it didn't matter to him. All he cared about was getting to the moment when he dipped his toes into that crystal clear water to forcefully declare:

"This is the most beautiful place in the world and I should know since I have been everywhere!"

He'd stand in the water, travel pants pulled up to his knees, dress shirt sleeves rolled up, a pair of snazzy sunglasses perched on his nose, looking out over an indescribably beautiful landscape. He never remained alone for long. Another magnificent Tahitian woman wrapped in a bright scarlet sarong would hand him a drink in a cool translucent pink and green glass, kiss him square on the mouth asking, "Why have you stayed away so long?" As always, he smiled the smile of recently ingested crispy poppy treats before melting into her.

Now, standing on the subway platform, sweating his brains out in that dank underground holding pen where he, along with his fellow perspiring travelers looked more like steer being led to the slaughter than the privileged sojourners in his U-R-DARE fantasy, it suddenly occurred to him that the woman in the sarong was straight out of an old painting by Paul Gauguin he had caught a glimpse of in the big art museum on Fifth Avenue. He had only visited that cathedral of the fine arts once when he was sixteen and that was years ago with his Learning Center's art class.

"Why," he asked himself, "have I never noticed this before?"

He never forgot his first and only trip to the D. Khoke Metropolitan Museum of Art. It was one of the most memorable events of his life. His Content Facilitator, Assam Handler, had pointed out the works of Paul Gauguin and that name had simply stuck with him. Maybe it was because the artist's name was so similar to his own- Paul Gaugin. He was so surprised when his Content Facilitator spoke the artist's name.

"Why, it's just like my name only it has an extra 'u' in it," Paul had blurted out.

"Ha, ha," his Content Facilitator chuckled while acknowledging the resemblance. "Don't get too taken with the likeness between your two names. There couldn't possibly be any relationship. If Gauguin had been alive today he would have been an EASY and a top EASY at that. Not one of those fly by night types that burn out and then have to be sent to the Projects."

At that pronouncement, Handler turned to a nearby painting, paused for a moment, pointed at it like one of those prosecutors on EYE- TV and with a stern gaze trained on each of his students, admonished them to take note of what he was about to tell them. That tone was his eager students' cue that he was about to impart the fieldtrip's actual take-a-way. Their Palm Pads snapped open to record the pearls about to drop before their swine.

He swiveled away from the Gauguin canvas to another canvas almost adjacent. "Look at this!" he commanded as he pointed to it. "It's called, 'Starry Night.' Note the uncontrolled, almost savage brush strokes. The wild swirling of the sky as it overtakes the moon threatening to do violence to the town below. It's the creation of a long dead EASY, Vincent Van Gogh. He was a genius but led an abandoned, undisciplined life…"

He paused making a kind of clucking sound indicating his sharp disapproval. His young charges listened intently; their Palm Pads opened, recording every word.

"Well, where do you think this led?" he queried sharply but he didn't pause for an answer. "It led," voice rising to a crescendo, "to a disordered mind. It LA-Ed to his cutting his ear off and ending his days in what was then a facility for the insane!"

At this, some students gasped, others grimaced, while a few even put a hand to their ear as if to protect themselves from the same fate.

Having elicited the desired reaction he smiled wryly continuing, "If he had been alive today he would have been sent to the Projects. Talent without restraint, without a productive goal, without contribution, is of no benefit, not to the EASY and certainly not to the Corpus."

He stopped for a moment before continuing, "So, don't forget that no matter your classification nothing is guaranteed. It all hinges on hard work, discipline, hard work, and more discipline, which leads to high yield profits. That's the only way to avoid the Projects. Even a JC can be sent down...no single individual is too big to fail. Only the Corpus doesn't die. Only the Corpus is too big to fail. Don't forget that now ...or ever."

He paused again assuming a reverential stance swiftly crossing himself. As he did so the assembled students intoned the CSA's sacramental mantra, "Blessed be the Corpus that bestows on us the promise to do **good** by doing **well**, Amen."

He looked his young charges in the eye, holding each and every one for a few seconds to make sure all had drunk sufficiently from the sacred chalice of truth just proffered. The group stood looking sufficiently chastised and scared, the Content Facilitator quite pleased with himself. *After all, what else could these kids really take away from this little field trip to the museum?* He knew that most of his young charges would never again walk these corridors in- the - being.

He had a point. Most of them would never again, physically that is, step foot in this or any other such cultural institution. They might make virtual visits but a flesh and bone, in –the-being visit was not in the cards for most of these soon-to –be officially classified WEs. Actual in- the -being visits to any site of artistic and cultural interest or sporting event was something open only to the most accomplished EASY, high-ranking PROFFS, GODSTERS and, of course, JCs. It was not that WEs were banned from such places- anyone with the credit could buy a ticket to attend a live baseball game, a play, or museum - it was simply that a WE typically had neither sufficient funds to pay for such jaunts nor the time. And it was just this fact that most disturbed Handler. *Why was this field trip scheduled anyway? How could he justify it? Account for such an extraordinary and unusual expenditure of resources?*

So he did what any ambitious Content Facilitator would do, he turned what appeared to be an unnecessary trip into a profitable one. He transformed what was on its face a wasteful excursion into a value-laden, utilitarian expedition.

"Hah," he silently exulted! From the moment he saw this activity on his semester program he knew it was the doing of the head Programmer, one Jack Darkit. Surely it was Darkit who slipped this into his schedule to sink him.

Handler, a young, ambitious Content Facilitator, threatened Darkit. It was, to be sure, the nature of things. All Content Facilitators were potential Programmers. In the end, the only way to move up in the system was to become a Programmer. Most accomplished this by pushing a Programmer out. It was down and out or up and up. That was the system. It was God's design. No one questioned it. After all, these fundamental principles were all spelled out in the *Book of Darwin*. One of a child's first downloads was Darwin's seminal, "survival of the fittest."

"Survival of the fittest," muttered Handler as he thought about his rival's career.

Darkit was truly remarkable. At age sixty he had managed to command his position as Head Programmer for closing in on twenty years. He was, Handler begrudgingly admitted to himself, a master Darwinist. He hadn't stayed where he was all those years by being a soft- hearted sap. No, he retained his position by removing ambitious low-level Programmers as fast as he could. True, Handler was not an imminent threat. He was only a Content Facilitator, not yet even a Programmer 1 and Darkit, in all his years on the job, had never gone after a Content Facilitator. In Handler's case, however, he was making an exception. Darkit could sniff out a future threat like a dog can find a buried bone and Handler was that bone.

"I guess I should be flattered," Handler mused. In fact he had anticipated that at some point he would be a target, just not so soon.

"What's this?" Handler had demanded of Darkit pointing at his Palm Pad as soon as he saw the scheduled trip.

"Hmmm," responded Darkit without missing a beat, barely glancing at the Palm screen Handler shoved in his face.

"It looks like a field trip to a fancy museum. Expensive too," was the snarky response. "I hope you will be able to justify that expense or you might be missing a few credits from your account next month. Maybe a letter to your file as well."

"Don't think so," retorted Handler.

"Can't see how you'll justify the expense," Darkit responded, a slow grin spreading across his pale face.

Handler did not respond. He snapped the screen shut with a quick close of his hand, turned and left the Head Programmer's office more defiant than when he entered.

Now, sitting at his desk, inputting the trip's assessment matrix for the Evaluator, he couldn't help but chuckle to himself. He had fabricated the trip's added value practically out of thin air by turning that old Starry Night canvass into a cautionary lesson. Anyone, in any tier, could get on the on road to the Projects' gates. No one was exempt. Indeed, this was arguably the most important lesson a WE could learn: those who couldn't or wouldn't contribute to the Corpus, the indisputable heart and soul of the Corporate States of America, had no place within the ranks of the MAKERs and would shortly find him or herself standing before the Project's gates.

"Bless the Corpus," thought the Content Facilitator, "but I am good! I will go far!"

He instantly input the new lesson plan devised for the museum field trip into the Learning Center's central lesson plan programmer. That would stick it to Darkit! Not only was the Head Programmer unable to sink him with this little trip, but if his lesson plan was officially adopted it would help convince the Evaluator to renew his contract for the following semester. In fact, while most Content Facilitators lived in terror of the Evaluator, he couldn't wait for the feedback.

By the time Handler was done filling that lesson's assessment matrix, he was not simply pleased with himself, but positive he was firmly on the road to becoming a Programmer. After all, hadn't he managed to turn a sow's ear into a silk purse? *Ha, not only is my contact renewal a shoe-in, but I'll have that step-up in no time. I'll teach that asshole Darkit not to mess with me!*

Despite Content Facilitator Handler's admonition, and up until the time he received his Skills Assessment Test results, Paul remained fervently convinced there was a familial connection between that great, long dead EASY Gauguin, and himself. After all, he drew all the time and didn't his grandma tell him that her great-grandma was from somewhere in the South Pacific? Wasn't that where Gauguin went to paint?

He believed that like that other Paul, he could be a great artist. Blood would tell! Didn't Darwin speak of genetic predispositions?

One day his paintings would grace the halls of a famous museum just like that other Paul's; of that he was certain.

When he mentioned this to his grandpa, he was surprised by the old man's reaction.

"Paul, don't dream that dream," the old man cautioned.

"Why not," Paul asked. He was approaching his eighteenth year and awaiting his SAT results, which would surely catapult him into an EASY.

"It's not a dream. I don't dream. Dreaming is a waste of time. It just makes sense we could be related to Gauguin and just not know it. I have talent and our name is almost the same. Darwin, sainted be his name, [he intoned quickly] taught us that natural selection is what preserves the genetic advantages in a group that are then passed on to their offspring. That's why most of the JCs' kids become JCs. Right? They have this genetic advantage. I know it's no guarantee- but that's what our Content Facilitator told us- there's more chance when there's a predisposition. It's right there in the *Book of Darwin*. So, if [and I say if] we are really related to Gauguin, then maybe that gene for art is coming out in me! That makes sense, doesn't it? And don't forget granny was an art teacher, so obviously there's something genetic, right?"

At that, the older man gave him a stern look, but Paul persisted, "Well, it's possible, isn't t??" he pleaded with his grandfather. "Well isn't it? I mean, why can't something like that happen to us? To me?"

"My poor boy," his grandfather crooned passing his gnarled hand over his grandson's head.

"Listen to me boy. Your Grandpa loves you and is as proud as could be of you, but no how are you gonna' be a famous artist. It just can't happen. You just still don't know whatcha' up against. And anyhow, I thought you told your granny a while back you don't go in for all that dreaming stuff that Leftovers like us cling to."

Startled by this, Paul pulled back from his usually doting grandfather declaring, "You just don't know what you're talking about. I'm not dreaming like you and grandma did. There's an objective test that will prove it. All I have to do is wait for the test results. The test knows and the test places each according to his ability. Mine is to be a great artist and the SAT will prove it. All I have to do is wait."

"We'll see," mumbled the old man as he shuffled off to the small alcove that doubled as his and his wife's bedroom, "but hope, in this world, is a dangerous thing."

Chapter 6: History

Excerpt from an official history: *The Restored History of America from 1492 to the Great Transformation,* Chapter 50, Education Reform Takes Hold

The Great Transformation ushered in a new era of opportunity and prosperity for all. Central to this achievement was the reform of the American educational system. That system had collapsed under the weight of its own corruption. The reasons for this were self-evident: education was disconnected from workforce needs. Americans had been hoodwinked to believe it was all about "enrichment" and "self-discovery;" education became mere self-indulgence.

Nowhere was this problem more endemic than in higher education where the "liberal arts," an undifferentiated course of studies, was emphasized. As if partaking from a buffet, students took a few courses in humanities, social sciences, math and sciences. Today, we refer to these as, "smatterings."

That emphasis proved disastrous for both the individual as well as for the Corpus. As early as the 1980s, the American educational system was failing millions of young adults. Today, we understand that such an undifferentiated education is pedagogically unsound. If an individual's aptitude is, for example, fabrication, s/he doesn't need to study a subject like poetry. In fact, research has confirmed that imposing such studies on an individual without aptitude leads to anger, hostility, and even violence. Unprecedented rates of ADD, ADHD, autism, and all manner of psychiatric illnesses first seen in the late twentieth century, were caused by this misguided educational system. The result: America lost millions of potentially productive MAKERs.

Today we offer a revised version of these studies, exclusively at our elite institutions, reserved for students selected through a rigorous assessment process. After two years of this generalized exposure the student chooses a major. Two or more years follow of intensive field inculcation and qualifying exams, before these students move into their final professional training.

Reserving this directed version of liberal arts for these students has ensured such studies no longer degenerate into "smatterings," but form the foundation for specializations offered at our great universities.

We no longer believe that educators can spin straw into gold. At long last we are willing to sort the wheat from the chaff, guaranteeing society's resources are not wasted. Rates of violent crime and mental disorders have fallen dramatically. Under the Corpus' guidance, education is now a value driven rubric, with early and constant assessment at its foundation.

Darwin be praised! After centuries of striving, America has discovered the key to genuine opportunity and equality. The economy's most precious resource- human capital – at long last, can be put to its highest and best use. Capitalism and the nation are now secure.

Chapter 7: Paul

Face To Face With The Meritocracy [GTE, 33]

Multiple rumors, stories, and anecdotes reinforced the SAT's efficacy as the engine of opportunity and equality. Every WE Learning Center had its own account of a student plucked from its ranks by his or her SAT results. Paul's Center was no different. Its story went like this: One of their own had always been exceptional. Everyone said so. He was, no exaggeration, brilliant. He knew the entire Constitution by heart. He could explain why twentieth century America failed and how the Great Fiscal Crisis, along with the rise of the Founders Action Party ["FAP"], saved the country from ruin and returned it to its former glory.

This prodigy, no LOL, even understood that Darwin's true genius was not found in his hypothesis that we evolved from apes but, as Herbert Spencer gleaned from Darwin's writings, that life was truly all about the "survival of the fittest."

Our boy wonder's senior project focused on the import of President Andrew Jackson's coining the phrase: "To the victor belongs the spoils." His thesis perceptively observed that Jackson's pronouncement was nothing more or less than the anticipation of what science eventually proved: "winners" **should** "take all." Why? Because it's nature's way of assuring the fittest survive and thrive. His Content Facilitators praised him to the heavens; everyone had no doubt but that he would go far.

Absolutely no one was surprised when our budding little genius's SAT results affirmed what everyone already knew: he was special. Prediction? The SAT would provisionally classify him as a PROFESSIONAL and send him to one of the prestigious universities where he would explore his options before settling on a profession: lawyer, doctor, politician, the sky was the limit.

On the big day the Learning Center's administration was jubilant.

Euphoria!

Ecstasy!

Validation!

The SAT had indeed reclassified him as a PROFESSIONAL. Word was he was whisked off to one of the CSA's private, elite universities. Full Scholarship! Surely they would hear great things about him in the future, though no one, including Paul, seemed to remember his name or to have ever met the fellow. No matter. It was understood and accepted that student "What's-His-Name" was now far above their touch, never to be seen again in their realm.

But that was really beside the point. Student "What's-His-Name" was now the embodiment of the CSA's new covenant with the American people: a perfected meritocracy. Everyone and everything was in its rightful place. It was onward and upward for anyone who could earn it. This was America after all! Everything was possible again. Well, wasn't it?

Chapter 8: History

Excerpt from an official history: *The Restored History of America from 1492 to the Great Transformation,* Chapter 51, The End of Regionalism

The nation had always been roiled by regionalism, marred by localism, its seeds of animosity growing into the weeds of disunity. This has, historically, sapped America of its ability to coherently tackle its problems. The "Scattering," the next step on the path to becoming a full-fledged Contributor, has been instrumental in breaking sectionalism's grip.

After graduation from our Learning Centers graduates are, quite literally, scattered across the different regions of the CSA for finishing, permitting each MAKER to achieve his or her highest God given potential wherever that skill or ability is genuinely needed. For the first time in America's long history, the construction of a genuine national identity is at hand.

Chapter 9: Paul

Scatter Day! [GTE, 36]

Paul had a little set back in his Senior Year. What led up to it was his absolute conviction that he was not a WE, but an EASY. He fully believed this was his genetic destiny. He had placed his full faith and credit in the SAT confirming to all what he already knew. It was to be his savior, his way out. It would authorize his destiny and instantly whisk him out of the WE and into the EASY.

April 1 of senior year finally arrived— the day graduating seniors received their SAT results and occupational tracks were revealed; their future set in stone. No guess work. No doubt. In the CSA, everyone understood that unless you really messed up, you would soon be a full-fledged MAKER with all the attendant obligations and privileges. It was liberating!

As tradition dictated, the entire graduating class congregated in the Gathering Hall to collectively receive their SAT results. Immediately, they all began woofing the results to their families:

"I'm a Graphic Designer, going to Zone 6."

"A Computer Geek, Zone 1."

"A Service Rep, Zone 20."

"A Content Facilitator, Zone 15."

"A Sales Associate…"

In just two months each would be packed up and scattered to their assigned Zones for finishing - each according to his/her now determined abilities. The appropriate Career Centers awaited each. Some would spend one year, others up to four years, but the average was two years. First Responders, for example, were immediately assigned to their units. Some stayed in their home Zones, but most were sent out. The JCs, in their wisdom, realized there was an inherent danger in creating units of FIRSTERS, as they were affectionately called, attached to birth Zones. Indeed, the Zones and the scattering of all would-be MAKERs after graduation was considered by POLs and JCs alike as President Cross's most brilliant innovation.

Paul disregarded the barrage of incoming woofs he was receiving.

"Tell, me, tell me, tell me!" woofed his insistent mother.

"So, what's the assignment? Where are you going?" growled his dad, but Paul replied to no one. Only his Grandpa remained silent. He wondered why.

Paul simply refused to answer; he went dead. He even turned away from his classmates' and Content Facilitators' excited chatter. His reserve was noted.

"Paul," his best friend Alvin called out to him, "what's your assignment?"

"A graphic designer," Paul mumbled, quickly turning his back on his friend.

"Hold on," Alvin called to him stretching out his hand to catch his friend before he walked away.

"Get off me," shouted Paul, roughly brushing away his friend's hand, "leave me alone!"

What, they all wondered, *could have caused such an outburst?* Here they all were celebrating their Scatters, saying their goodbyes, sharing their destinies, yet Paul remained stubbornly silent and sullen. Most unbecoming! Shocking really!

"Oh look," Alana motioned to one of her classmates as he leaned over to peer at her Palm Pad screen displaying a map. "See," she exclaimed, barely able to contain her excitement, "I am going to Zone 15. I can't believe it! The SAT assigned me to the Maine Fishery Management Career Center. And after that who knows which Zone I will live in. Well, it's all up to me now, isn't it? 'Up and Up' as they say or 'Down and Out'! And I have no intention of being out! No TAKER time for me!"

Paul's classmates' jubilance appeared unending. Exclaiming and squealing, chuckling and gurgling, simply rejoicing at their imminent Scattering. But he had nothing to celebrate. He felt the room spin. His core was splintering. Everything he believed was now in doubt. How, he mouthed silently, could the SAT be so wrong?

He was an artist. In his heart, in his gut, he knew this was true. Didn't he always dream in color? About forms and figures and even the very images he would one day put on canvass? Hadn't he always drawn all over the walls of his room and then, when he'd filled up every blank space, his Grandpa would come in and cover the wall with some cheap leftover whitewash so he could start all over again. He remembered how his Grandpa assiduously collected that whitewash from the public service jobs he was required to perform so that he could continue to live in that little corner in his son's small home.

How could the SAT not know this? How could it have made such an awful, such a tragic mistake? He was meant to be a real working, creative artist, an EASY, and not some 3-D graphic designer. Somehow this mistake had to be rectified.

In the background the ceremony continued.

"Graduates," lauded the school's Executive Director as the roar of cheers from the assembled crowd answered that single salutation. Director Fizzle waited for the cheers to subside. She smiled down at them from the podium patting into place her carefully coiffed dyed blond hair and smoothing the Kelly green skirt that matched her jacket framed by generous amounts of piping. She had recently injected plastique filling into her nasal labial fold lines, which increasingly looked like trenches. Never a pretty woman, not even in her heyday, the result simply hardened her already severe but small rodent-like features into a kind of rigid mask.

After a few more moments of unabated cheering she raised her hand waving her mid-three fingers in a kind of up and down "now hush" motion, and the graduates quieted down. It was, they knew, time for one last speech, one last reminder of what they should expect and what was expected of them before Scattering.

"GRAD-U-ATES...," she called out again, "LETS GET READY TO SCATTER! [APPLAUSE, APPLAUSE] and loud calls of "WOOF, WOOF, WOOF."

Pausing, she looked up over the crowd, raised her palm outward towards the assemblage so that her Palm Pad screen popped open and began broadcasting across the group the words: **SCATTER TIME** and **CONGRATULATIONS FROM THE CORPUS**, in bright colorful letters which seemed to pop and explode into cascading stars, flashes, lights, and brilliant tones, setting off more applause and woofing.

Snapping shut the Palm Pad screen she intoned in a very matter of fact voice, "Last lesson," and instantly the room went silent.

"Graduates of Learning Center D11-718, congratulations once again. [Applause, Applause!] You have done your job. Learned the bedrock principles on which the CSA sits. Let's review together one last time. What are the lessons learned? First, all liberties are granted by the ALMIGHTY [the graduates crossed themselves as she said this]. Second, we bless the Corpus that now stands by those who help themselves [again the graduates crossed themselves]. It is the Corpus that sets the economic table, provisioning it with the most important dish there is: opportunity. But to eat from that dish you need to pay for the meal..."

Paul tuned her out even as the other graduates cheered. His obvious discontent did not go unremarked and Scattering Ceremony notwithstanding; it earned him a trip to Ms. Leavitall, the director of the Human Capital Unit. Human Capital tracked and assessed each student's skill sets and social proclivities. This unit also administered the SAT, reviewed the scores, and was the ultimate arbiter of a graduate's provisional classification and finishing assignment.

A woman like Ms. Leavitall was successful because she understood her job's bottom line: keep human costs down and maximize each individual's cost-benefit ratio. She, and others like her, did this by alerting her superiors at the first sign a student would not or could not be successfully situated due to mental or social impurities, such as a criminal disposition, mental defect, or even tendencies to rebel. These individuals would be appropriately reclassified. So, no doubt, she was important. She was, in a word, powerful. She could make you or break you. And the "woofs and growls" confirmed this.

Reclassification was no idle threat. Everyone seemed to know or know of someone who had been reclassified a TAKER, summarily expelled, and sent to the Projects. It was the Sword of Damocles hanging over everyone's head. It was the carrot and stick. No one, including Paul mired in all his disgruntlement, aspired to a life in the Projects. Naturally, a summons to Ms. Leavitall was no LOL.

He loped into her office looking scared and already remorseful before a word was even said to him. He sat down looking up at the

Secrey who, in turn, looked down at him from an elevated platform style desk behind a bulletproof plexiglass partition.

He didn't know her age- but then, that was the goal. Everyone did whatever it took to affect that indeterminate age where you weren't so young you could be disrespected or, so old it was, well, simply distasteful and time to cash out. No, it was best to always look like you were in the prime of life. Mature enough to have the type of experience needed to get the job done correctly and efficiently and young enough to be full of vitality and energy so as not to be a drag on or a burden to the company. What business could afford to carry a chronically sick associate for long? It adversely impacted the bottom line and forced everyone else to shoulder the slacker's work.

The Secrey wore two distinct ear-chips, two distinct third eyes, and one bionic arm. She was obviously a proficient multitasker; a skill highly prized.

"You can go in now," motioned Ms. M-tasker with a wave of her third arm, never taking her frog-eyes or hands away from her work.

"Oh, ok. In there?

"That's what I am indicating," she sang out.

Paul wondered if all secries spoke like this, were trained to appear and sound, well, all wavy, but sharply calibrated all at the same time. Or was it just her?

He moved through the opening panel and stepped into Ms. Leavitall's impressive office. All the furniture was of highly polished chrome metal, no cushions on the sofa or chairs, just metal as if to say, "You really don't want to be here long."

Ms. Leavitall rose from her chair. An impressively tall woman, [or was she wearing lifters? Well, no matter] she was dressed to intimidate. All in steel grey, high starched collars, dark steel grey hair spiked skywards, long acrylic nails in light grey. Even her makeup, all in shades of grey, tied her completely to her office. It was as if she and the office were one.

"Have a seat," she motioned to one of the steel, cushionless chairs.

He took a seat struggling to find a comfortable position. The spine of the chair stuck into his backbone causing him great discomfort.

39

"So, I hear you have a problem."

He was about to respond. He wanted to tell her that he was no dreamer and that a serious mistake had been made, but she quickly cut him off:

"Scattering is a tense and difficult time for some students. Playtime is over. This is your moment to face the real world. Paths are laid out. Friends say goodbye and sometimes, yes sometimes, dreams are shattered."

She paused, she smiled, she continued, "Yes, I used the word "dream" even though I am sure you will tell me you do not so indulge."

Paul vaguely nodded and she continued, "Everything in your file tells me you are by nature a 'dreamer.'"

Again she stopped speaking but this time staring at him so intently it was as if she were trying to extract something from inside him and his fear grew immeasurably. She smirked, seemingly pleased by his silence, his expression of desperation, recognizing that his would be an easy case.

"We appreciate that human beings with artistic proclivities are so inclined. We can't squash it. Indeed, we don't wish to. Simply redirect it so it becomes an asset, not a deficit."

She paused again, now looking him straight in the eyes. Holding his gaze for a few more moments before she resumed.

"Let's review your results and assignment. Let's redirect that proclivity before it becomes a real hindrance."

She clicked on a wall screen behind her that instantly displayed his data.

"Well, you have displayed a strong interest and aptitude for art since you were a child." Paul eagerly nodded his agreement.

"Let's look at these evaluations. Very nice, very nice. And see here," the cursor's movement rapidly drew his attention to a series of assessment results, "because you displayed such a high aptitude for art at your Learning Center, Evaluators added a special art tracker to your assessment package. Well done, I would say. Don't you agree?"

"Yes," assented Paul.

"So let's see the results of these."

With a single click those results posted on the screen. For the first time Paul noticed she had one of those special scanning eyes

40

which rapidly fed the results to her so that data digestion time was kept at a minimum.

"As you can see, you received high marks in reproduction abilities, color identification and use, as well as overall visualization. But," and here she highlighted part of the report, "while your aptitude for originality, creativity were above average, they were not outstanding and the same for trend-spotting ability."

With that she turned off the monitor, lights on, a bit brighter than earlier, as she prepared to deliver the conclusions.

"You see the Evaluators did their job. They identified your talent early and turned your case over to the Trackers, who followed you into your senior year. I also noted in the files a vigorous discussion about your SAT results and whether or not that, plus your other assessment results, warranted classification to an EASY. The answer: 'No.' Reason? You simply did not meet **all** the criteria to be an Art EASY. If the trend-spotting marks had been high and creativity outstanding then possibly... but without that there was no way the Trackers could responsibly make such a recommendation. It would not have made economic sense, not for you and not for the Corpus. You wouldn't want that would you?"

He meekly shook his head. She continued, "It would be unfair to the Corpus and, more importantly, to you."

She swiveled her chair round sharply and slammed the palms of her hands hard onto the desk for emphasis.

"You know, Paul, of all the EASYs, the fewest in number are in the pure arts. Few, even the very gifted, possess all the criteria to make it as an 'Artist.' So, don't feel bad. Indeed, we have high hopes you can emerge as a leading 3-D graphic designer."

Again, Paul nodded.

"Have I answered your questions? Your concerns?"

Paul nodded again.

"Good," she said looking at his still projected file. "I see you have been assigned to your local Career Center for finishing in 3-D design. That means the Evaluators think you have a promising career right here in the heart of the commercial media beast- New York City. That's why you stay local. No need to Scatter you afar because with your indicated talent you would certainly be brought back to New York City after your finishing. Waste of moving expenses and time."

That was it. It was done. She snapped the wall screen shut and his data disappeared.

"Do you think you are set now? Ready to be finished?"

"Yes, yes absolutely. Thank you so much for explaining it all."

It was over. He knew he was dismissed. He got up, turned his back on that steel grey room and on his dream.

NCC [GTE, 37]

Paul grew up in Nassau County, a formerly privileged bedroom suburb in the New York City metro area. Even before the Great Fiscal Crisis it had, for the most part, fallen on hard times. The crisis simply finished it off. By the time Paul was born it was nothing more than a vast expanse of cheap WE housing from which WEs daily trekked into New York City.

After graduating from his Learning Center Paul was assigned to his local Career Center, Nassau Career Center ["NCC"] where he was duly enrolled in the Design Department. Not art, but design. There would be no art classes for Paul.

During his two years Paul managed, for the most part, to excel with one tiny exception. He did, just once, deviate a bit. At the end of his second semester he asked his NCC Human Capital counselor if he could take a class on Impressionism offered at SBU, the only large university left in the area. He had his arguments all laid out in advance to justify the request.

"So, like I was saying Ms. Hockker, I went to an art museum in my senior year."

"In- the-being?" she interrupted.

"Yes, in- the- being..." but before he could proceed she interrupted again.

"Why in the world would the Program Unit approve such a trip? Holy President Cross, the expense! Whatever were they thinking at your Learning Center? Such a waste of credits."

Poor Paul, at that point he knew he had lost the battle but he persevered; like a soldier who volunteered for a suicide mission.

"Well, as I was saying, I was fascinated by the impressionist artists and I just thought this course being offered at SBU- it teaches how to paint in the impressionist style – would enhance my career trajectory and value. After all, the impressionists thought outside the box for their time and really added texture and dimension and since I am going into 3-D and, ummm, well…"

Ms. Hoccker certainly enjoyed watching him squirm; a small smile cracked open the vault.

"Oh, and I did my homework and know the course fee…I even saved up for it. I won't be asking for a handout! No, I am self-sufficient Paul Gaugin! I just need permission to take the class. That's what they told me. And look, see here," he whipped a folded form out of his pocket plopping it down on her desk, "you don't even have to go online to find the permission slip. I printed it for you. All you have to do is sign and I will actually give it to them in-the -being!"

Ms. Hockker looked down at the form and back at Paul. Again that quirky smile and for a moment Paul thought she would sign the form, but the smile quickly morphed into a sneer.

"Mr. Gaugin, what is your provisional classification?"

"WE"

"Yes, that's the acronym. And what, may I ask, does it stand for?

"Wage Earner," he dully intoned. He knew where this was leading.

"And please explain the training protocol."

"All individuals, regardless of their parents' classification are presumed a WE unless rigorous assessment proves otherwise. All individuals attend their local Learning Center. Each person's ultimate classification depends on a combination of things: his innate abilities, willingness to work and improve, and the results of the SAT. In his Learning Center senior year he will take the SAT. If he remains classified as a WE then the SAT plus the final career path recommendation from his Human Capital Unit based on years of assessments and observations, in addition to the SAT, will recommend a career path and he will be assigned to an appropriate finishing center. "

"And what were you classified?"

"A WE."

"And where were you assigned?" she continued.

"Here, to NCC."

"And what degree will you obtain if we permit you to stay?"

"A Vocational Entrepreneur Degree – a VED- which certifies me to be a 3D-Graphic designer."

"And when you graduate?" she persisted. [God, she was intent on torturing him.]

"It is up to me to secure a short-term contingent or, if I am highly enterprising, a long-term contract, and keep myself gainfully employed."

She nodded her head approvingly.

"And do you doubt your classification?" she asked while drumming her long, latex Chinese-style nails, redolent with tiny sparkly images of her favorite EASYs.

"No, I don't," he answered without hesitation.

"Hmmm....Are you sure? "

She snapped open her Palm Pad screen to show it to him adding, "Your profile indicates that in your Learning Center Senior year, you were directed to the head of the Human Capital unit. You were dissatisfied with your classification. You believed it to be an error, correct?"

"Ah, ah, well, you see I…"

She held up her hand to stop his stuttering, snarling asking, "Then what are you doing in my office you stupid little shit? Do you think SBU needs your tuition? Do you think we need to waste resources on you? Yes, WASTE. It will WASTE an important university professor's time. It will DISPLACE another student from the class. It will DISTRACT you from your goal, which is to be the best damn 3-D graphic designer you can be. Perhaps, I should flag you as a WASTER."

He flinched. He blanched. He swallowed hard. She had hurled a serious threat at him. If she actually made good on it he would have a hard, if not impossible time, getting a job. In fact, he might not get any employment at all which, as everyone knows, would quickly lead to reclassification as a TAKER. If that happened, he would be sent to a Project. Paul was terrified. It never occurred to him that what he saw as a simple request would toss him into the eye of a hurricane.

"Please, ma'am, it's all a misunderstanding. I mean I am not complaining; I didn't realize the implications of what I was asking. I do now," the almost pleading, next to tears Paul, offered in hopes of mollifying her.

"Oh, so now you are not complaining? Then what are you doing in my office wasting resources? Time is a commodity or were you at that fancy museum when your Learning Center downloaded that unit?

"Please, I promise never to ask for anything like this again. I am very happy with my career track and this center."

"Well, what do you recommend we do with this?" she asked as she picked up the form waving it in front of his nose, teeth bared, positively dripping saliva like a rabid animal going in for the kill.

"Rip it up," he squeaked like the timid little dormouse he had become.

"Yes, we can," she exclaimed triumphantly as she fed the form into the shredder reposing desk side, its maw open, ever ready to receive.

He sat there for a few moments stunned. As if he had received a blow to the head but then his sense of self-preservation kicked in and he asked himself: What in the world am I still doing in her office?

He rose from the chair and was about to turn and bolt out the door when it occurred to him this would all go into his file anyway so he might as well make one last appeal to her.

"This convo won't go into my file, will it? You're not going to flag me?"

"Mmmmm, well the conversation will, but I won't flag you. But tell you what. If you have no more incidents like this I will expunge the record of our little tete a tete before you graduate. How's that?" she asked positively glowing!

"Oh, how can I thank you? I see now I was completely wrong to ask for, or, even consider this. Of course, it's not for me. Truly, I am sorry to have wasted your time as well. Your guidance has enlightened me, made me understand, set me straight. Trust me I am back on the path to a successful and productive career."

"Fantastic! I'm glad you stopped by. I think you still had some lingering misconceptions left from that trip you took to the museum… Really it was not **all** your fault…bad programming."

She shook her head disapprovingly then brightened again, "So, our little counseling session was a success?"

He nodded his head up and down like a bobble- head doll.

"That's what I am here for. To keep you all on the straight and narrow! So, unless you suffer any relapses, I would say case closed."

She reiterated this by dramatically lifting her hand slamming shut her Palm Pad, a big grin plastered across her face. How plastique Paul thought, but quickly admonished himself for this errant pop up and with a final vigorous obsequious nod of the head, that came close to turning into a full body bow. Paul turned and fled.

Back on the Platform [GTE, 45]

Now, years later, as Paul stood sweating, waiting for his train, he winced at those memories and wondered if he was perspiring because he was still sick or from that recollection, the consequences of which still filled him with terror.

Ever since that brief flirtation with disaster he had been a model MAKER, an upstanding WE. He graduated #5 in his class and immediately snagged a six-month contract in New York City at Trendytrends, a top 3-D design firm. They loved him so much that after the six months were up, they signed him to a three-year contract that had already been renewed two times. He was now more than six years at the same firm. That, in itself, was a real accomplishment. His future looked bright. Most importantly, his Team Leader liked him and the boss, well you couldn't expect a busy JC to pay too much attention to him, but once, as the boss was striding down the corridors of dividers towards his big, lavishly appointed office, he glanced into Paul's space and said: "Hey fella, that was a great job you did on the 'Butterflies in the Garden' campaign. Viewership at the Botanic Garden popped! Your work was certainly instrumental in making that happen. Keep it up and renewal will sail through."

He beamed at Paul as he said that and Paul beamed back. In fact it was more like Paul had morphed into a shaggy dog groveling at his master's feet happy to receive whatever crumbs dropped.

"Thanks, sir," barked Paul as his master tossed him the bone.

The master patted him on his shoulder and continued down the corridor occasionally stopping to dispense his largess on the grateful WE.

"Well," Paul thought as he glanced at his watch, "if I don't get to my office on time all I'll be receiving is a letter of reprimand and have one foot out the door."

Paul understood he was only as good as his last success. In the CSA there was no good will in the bank, never mind sick or vacay days. Use them or lose them. In fact, sometimes you used them at your peril. When it came time for Paul's re-evaluation everything would be quantified and assessed. Had he used all his sick time? If so, maybe that indicated a chronic health problem looming in which case it might be best to release him before he became a liability. If the company felt really twitchy about an associate's health, it might require a full body scan [at the associate's expense, of course] to reassure itself it was not about to offer a contract to an unhealthy associate.

The ramifications of this extended beyond that particular employer's walls. A negative health finding became part of a WE's file, practically guaranteeing no future employment, anywhere.

There were so many unofficial rules for maintaining full employment that most WEs rarely planned anything, including vacations, more than a few weeks in advance. The only real quotidian experience was the job. It was everything. No one truly wanted to become a conscript in self-employment, hustling here and there for enough credits to keep the Project's gate at bay.

Paul again glanced at his fashionably thin watch. It would have to be quickly pawned to pay rent if he lost his position. "Oh, shit, I can't let that happen to me!"

Fashion, thin and thinner. It had been like that for more than one hundred years. It seemed what was thin a generation ago was now plump. Fat was equated with poverty, the Projects. No wonder the trend extended to accessories as well: watches, Palm Pads, glasses, and so on and so on. Take Paul's watch. It was so thin it seemed embedded in his wrist, but, of course, it was not. It was simply the style.

Paul began to sweat so profusely that his thin and thinner watch started to slide on his wrist, his sweat now more from fear than sickness because the train was running late. If it did not come soon he would be forced to sprint the three blocks from the station to his office and he was not sure he could muster that kind of energy.

Lateness would prompt the Team Leader to check the time the train pulled into the station. Even if, as Paul alleged, the train was late, he wasn't yet off the hook. His Team Leader would then calculate how fast he should have power walked to arrive on time and docked him the corresponding credits.

If this became a chronic problem, a complaint would be sent to the Metropolitan Transit Company and the situation would be investigated. Any number of factors could impact train times: passengers failed to board efficiently, or the engineer did not leave the station rapidly enough, or, perhaps, mechanical problems existed. Whatever the reason, the cause would be determined and rectified. Time was now fully commodified as Ben Franklin had intuited so many hundreds of years ago when he declared: "A stitch in time saves nine."

After what was almost a forever, the train, to Paul's great relief, pulled in and he got on. He glanced again at his watch. "Actually," he realized, "only twenty seconds off the mark. He'd still have to hustle, but power walking would not be required. He would arrive on time.

Chapter 10: History

Excerpt from an official history: *The Restored History of America from 1492 to the Great Transformation,* Chapter 65, Reclaiming God

The Third Great Awakening was a preview of religion's role in the soon-to-be revamped U.S.A. In the old world, in what used to be referred to as the "good ol "U.S.A.," there was a notion that the Constitution forbid an official religion because over the centuries the Supreme Court had erroneously interpreted the clause "Congress shall make no law respecting an establishment of religion, or prohibiting the free exercise thereof..." It was, of course, a ludicrous interpretation of the First Amendment, the result of an un-clarified Constitution.

As soon as he took office, President Pablo Cross declared that the Church of the Revealed Saints, the "CRS," to be the USA's official creed. He immediately called on the Supreme Court for a "clarification." The old Liberal elite immediately took to the streets demanding the President withdraw both his request and statement. "What was a clarification anyway?" No one had ever heard of such a thing.

But President Cross, undeterred by these hooligans, refused to back down. He knew the tide of history was in his favor.

The court quickly scheduled the arguments and within the month the Supreme Court issued its Clarification #1:

"This Court is ready to clarify the Constitution's First Amendment ... The Founders never meant to imply there could be no state religion simply that government could not prohibit the worship of other religions…. The First Amendment is so clarified and we direct the government to proceed in conformity with this." 5-4 U.S. Supreme Court Clarification, #1, [March 15, 2021].

Clarification #1 sent shockwaves across the nation. Most sensible Americans were ecstatic. At long last the Feds, backed by the Court, were bringing clarity and sense to the nation. Now, not only was the American president leading the nation back from the fiscal brink, but its spiritual slide was also at an end.

Not all Americans followed willingly. The Left, sensing its imminent demise, regrouped: the unions, the TAKERs and many misguided university students swooped down on Wall Street to shut it down. Immediately, President Cross took to the airways imploring the rabble to stand down reminding them, and a fearful nation, they were threatening hallowed ground. They refused.

Mayor Rosehill wasted no time putting New York's finest on the scene, but the NYPD, not wanting to kill civilians, were quickly overwhelmed, leaving President Cross no choice but to ask New York's Governor Lakeside to call in the National Guard to stop the sacrilege. No sooner did these brave Firsters confront the mob, fire a few shots, and lob some tear gas, then the sniveling whiners dispersed. They were not prepared to die for their so-called cause; resistance evaporated. They retreated back into their holes; and with few exceptions fell into line, got with the program, became productive MAKERs.

Clarification #1 forever changed the relationship between the Court, the Constitution and the elected branches of government. The Court, confident the Executive branch could and would protect them if they ruled courageously, began returning us to the Founders' original intent, Clarification by Clarification. In so doing, the Court breathed new life into a nation gasping for air.

Chapter 11: I.M. Coyne

Paving the Way [1980]

Clarification #1 paved the way for the rise of the Church of the Revealed Saints [CRS], which grew in the fertile soil nourished by the Third Great Awakening. Its success was not instantaneous, although it seemed so to many observers. Its antecedents dated back to 1980. It was a momentous year for many reasons. It was the year Ronald Reagan was elected as president marking the beginning of our steady march towards a new era, but, just as importantly, a young man by the name of Ira Manfreddo Coyne was "awakened."

I.M., as he was called [pronounced "I Am"], was sixteen years old and living in the heart of the South's old "Blackbelt." His daddy, born in Clarksdale, Mississippi on April Fools' Day 1940, was a sharecropper like his father and grandfather. His great-grandfather was born a slave, but died a sharecropper. All the Coynes, for as long as anyone could remember, lived and died right there in the Clarksdale environs. The Coyne family was, you might say, as deeply rooted in the rich soil as the cotton it produced. And it bound them, generation after generation, to the land as tightly as had slavery. Young I.M. never questioned his destiny. He knew he would follow in the footsteps of his forbearers, living out his life in one of those wood and tin shacks, and from where he would one day, after a perfectly proper courtship, make a home with some young local girl producing, in their turn, the next generation of Coyne sharecroppers.

But something happened on his journey to the inevitable. Not the typical American rags to riches story, mind you. No one arrived in a fancy Thunderbird or Mustang or Cadillac to whisk young I.M. away from Clarksdale to some swanky boarding school, or recognized in him a remarkable talent; no, it was nothing like that. But it was something just as American: a dream. Indeed you might say that until the Great Transformation, dreams were as integral to the American psyche as mom and apple pie.

Back in the day there was the dream of a better life that inspired millions of immigrants to traverse oceans in pursuit of opportunities. It was the dream of a more perfect America that led the original Founders to throw off colonialism's yoke to create a nation where "men are created equal..." and could pursue "... Life, Liberty and ...Happiness."

It was voiced in Martin Luther King's "I have a Dream" speech that motivated tens of thousands of Americans, black and white, to take to the streets to challenge the orthodoxy of segregation.

Dreams were the deep reservoir from which all Americans had always drunk. On that steaming August 1980 night, a teenager by the name of I.M. Coyne, like millions before him, was about to drink from that well.

Selection from: *The Book of Darwin*, in which I.M. Coyne relates his Encounter with the Angel H.M.S. Beagalian:

It was late at night on the fifteenth day of August 30, 1980. I could hear the old tube TV with the rabbit ears still on in the little room that served as my family's living room, dining room, and kitchen. There were but two other bedrooms in our little wood, tar and tin shack. In one slept my Mama and Daddy, as we called them, and in the other, lined up like bodies in a morgue, slept me and my six brothers and sisters. The boys on one side, the girls on the other; both on separate straw filled mattresses, suspended slightly off the floor on hand-made hewn wooden platforms. A few makeshift shelves lined the walls where we stored our meager belongings. There was no indoor plumbing and we brought our water into the house from the well and daily filled the "water tank" next to the sink- a big iron barrel my Daddy had managed to scrounge from a nearby storage facility. It made Mama's life a bit easier. "Our" electricity came from an electric wire our Daddy had rigged up, that ran from a road light into the house, so each room was lit by a bare bulb. It permitted a bit of the outside world to come in through that old black & white.

*The outhouse was, well, out back. This was the most basic of living quarters but it was **our** home and we were content.*

My journey to God happened during one of those August hot spells they used to quaintly refer to as, "the dog days of summer." It was the kind of heat that made the tar holding those shacks together bubble into web-like strings threatening to bring them down. The kind of heat that made even those died in the wool Clarksdalians moan and curse the brilliant star that beat down on them as they toiled in the fields, persecuting them even after sunset, into those long sticky nights.

That heat. That heat, rose up from the soil enveloping them in its stifling grip from the moment they opened their eyes until, too exhausted from it and their labors, they finally fell into fitful slumber. So, it was no surprise that as soon as my head touched the pillow, I fell straight away into what I initially thought was simply a disturbing dream...

I heard a tap, tap, tap on the window frame. In what I supposed was a dream, I peered out the window and saw a firefly, brilliant, moving in circles. As I gazed, it stopped, appearing to look back at me, growing in brightness and size, morphing into a tantalizing angel, neither male nor female. I was astonished but unable to cry out. The angel, or so I assumed it was, appeared delicate in shape and form and, if you can rightly understand this, did not feel evil. It had no hint either in form or manner of the devil. Our minister weekly cautioned us against trafficking with Satan and often described his countenance. So, I was not scared when, upon assuming its final form, it leaned in towards me and stared. It was bejeweled and blazing and after carefully examining me for what seemed like a long time, lifted and extended its index finger touching my lips as if to caution quiet. Not knowing why, I obeyed. The creature then backed away still facing me, beckoning me with a flashing of its finger to follow.

I pulled on my field britches that lay in a huddle on the bedroom floor and stealthily went into that steaming August night to meet the creature I soon learned was the Angel H.M.S Beagalian. Beagalian immediately launched into what became twenty-one nights of sermons so intense, that by the time s/he physically put the GOLDEN TABLET into my hand, that which became known as the

*BOOK of DARWIN, the bedrock of the Church of the Reveled Saints-
I was, indeed, transformed....*

*On Beagalian's final night of instruction I was directed to hide
the Golden Tablet well, until s/he returned to command its
UNMASKING – on that day I would retrieve the Tablet to transcribe
its contents so as to begin to spread its Good News to all Americans.
It would, Beagalian instructed me, help usher in a new Golden Age
for an America in decline. When that might be Beagalian did not say
and I dared not inquire. However, I full well understood the
momentous implication of that revealed truth. It would, one day,
shake America and change our collective future forever...*

The Unmasking [2001]

As soon as Beagalian's nightly teachings were completed, I.M.
hid the **Golden Tablet**, as directed, in the hollow of an old tree that
stood stooped but firm next to the shack. It always reminded him of
the photos of those fancy British officers that guarded the Queen of
England's palace. How fitting to safeguard the word of God in that
hollow.

Though things changed in Clarksdale from that night until the
day he retrieved the **Golden Tablet** decades later, that old tree
miraculously remained untouched, even while the old shack was
removed and other houses were constructed in the area. It was not
until after the momentous events of 9/11 that changed America in
ways heretofore unimagined, that the **Golden Tablet** was retrieved.
It was during the aftermath of that nation shattering tragedy that the
Angel Beagalian returned. It was dusk in Clarksdale where I.M.
Coyne worked as a field foreclosure inspector.

Not very gratifying work for a man who grew up with his feet in
the earth and knew almost every family in town. But there you had
it, Clarksdale, like everywhere else, was changing. The need for
sharecroppers had steadily diminished as the cotton belt turned to
mechanization to reap those little round balls that had triggered so
much bloodshed more than a hundred years before. The result was
that many sharecroppers and their children, poorly prepared for
anything but agriculture, slowly drifted away, sank, if it could be
believed, into even deeper poverty.

All in all, time and circumstances had not been kind to Clarksdale and the Great Downturn that would envelope the entire nation in 2008 had actually begun earlier in certain pockets of the country, like Clarksdale, where family farms were dying.

In Clarksdale, this also meant the death of numerous businesses reliant on cotton and trade from the sharecroppers. Men, such as I.M., working for this or that bank or financial institution, stayed busy and employed by walking the ruins of what were once fields watered by blood and dreams.

Each time I.M. had to enter a home or walk a field that was in foreclosure, camera at the ready, notebook in hand, it put another nick in his soul. Tears flowed from mothers who gathered their children round as if he would snatch them away too.

His routine was always the same as he entered those grief stricken homes: he quietly tipped his hat to her to show his respect, then seamlessly and as quiet as a cat, moved through the home taking pictures for the bank. With a farm the routine was pretty much the same, except here he usually stuck his hand out to the farmer who inevitably clenched a shotgun. "Sorry, sir," he'd gently say, "It's a great shame. Please accept my apologies for having to intrude in this way."

Usually the farmer would just shake his sorrowful head and motion to him to do his job. Of course, on occasion, the shotgun would be leveled at him or he was greeted with a barrage of curses. But he knew his community and how to assuage the injured party, so no harm done.

"Jake," he once warned, "Don't you go makin' it worse for you and yours. You gotta' pretty lady inside and the cutest bunch of kids I've seen in a long time. They need you. Don't do something stupid."

"Yeah, well that's real easy for you to say workin' for the blood suckin' bank. Just as we rose from shacks and bein' tied to this or that cotton farmer. Just as we got our own fields and a decent little home with running water and electricity they take it from us. It's not fair."

"You're so right, Jake," I.M consoled the victim. "Remember when we was young and worked the fields after school how when we'd finished up we'd run down to the pond? Yeah, you remember. We'd be good and sweaty so we'd strip down and jump into that cool water. It felt good didn't it? Remember, we'd talk about doin' something different with our lives? Anything but pickin' that ol' cotton! And as hard as it be, maybe it's the Lord's way of fulfillin' that long ago dream. What do you think Jake? You're still young. You can start again. Go down to Cohahoma Community College. They'll get you fixed up in a new career. That's what I did."

"No good," Jake shook his head, "Never was much for school. You remember. Ya'al studyin' and me just wishin' to be anywhere else. Naw, I'm not college material. Can't see myself sittin' in class. Not at my age."

"You got it all wrong. They call it a college, but you don't need to do all that academic stuff like literature and history. No, no way. You just pick a career, like auto mechanics or welding or whatever strikes your fancy. They just call it a college to fool us poor folk into thinkin' they be givin' us the same opportunities as the rich folk, but that's not happenin'- never was and never goin' to. It's just a training center. But it helps the likes of us."

At this point he'd hooked Jake who placed the shotgun barrel side down into the earth, and with a faint trace of hope lacing his voice asked, "Do you think so?"

"I know so." I.M. tipped his hat and walked off into the empty fields so he could do what was required to make his report for the bank. He had, after all, a job to keep.

Don't be fooled. It was a misery to him and sometimes he felt as if the weight of all those peoples' distress and failures hung in his belly as if he were ingesting the rocks and stones on which he daily trod. Sometimes, seeing him so consumed by the misery of others, Mary, his wife, would try to console him, "Well, you got us out of the shacks and into a real house with running water, electricity, and the hopes of doing better. Remember, they'd lose their home no matter you were there or not."

Mary insisted he was actually helping the remaining sharecroppers and those still attached to the dying farming sector get out of that dead end rut by forcing them to truly live in the twenty-first century. Didn't Jake, she'd remind him, go to that community college and become an auto mechanic? Yes, he remembered. And didn't he get a good, secure job [well, as secure as anything was these day!] at the local Fixer-up-er? Yes, he'd admit, that happened. And wasn't he and the kids and Annie doin' just fine? Yes, just fine he'd parrot. Well, she'd conclude triumphantly, what you are doing is good work, valuable... worthwhile.

Yes, yes he'd concede... [And he would never say this to Mary] but what about the people who left never to return? Or what about the men who, despairing, abandoned their families? Or those who ended their lives? In a corner of his heart he couldn't help but feel like a traitor to his own kind. These were the thoughts running through his brain as he stepped into a field that was once the site of his family home at dusk on October 1, 2001.

"Hello," a voiced called to him.

He turned round but saw no one.

"I am here." He turned round again but saw no one.

"I.M. Coyne, look up in the tree."

He lifted his chin skywards and in the tree sat a glowing figure, familiar but different."

"Yes," the figure called down to him, "I am back as I promised you so many decades ago."

S/he cocked its head observing, "My, you have grown." Then, as if remembering this was no social visit or reunion of old friends asked more sternly, "Have you forgotten me and your promise to the Lord?"

"No, no of course not," he stammered.

He could barely believe what he was seeing. Over the years he'd returned from time to time to that old tree. He'd peer inside but never saw or touched the **Golden Tablet**. On more than one occasion he reached his hand into that knotty hollow only to pull out a handful of damp leaves, webworms, and beetles, nothing else. On another occasion he brought a flashlight with him and a stiff but slender length of cable, rooting it around in that tree's innards, but again, nothing.

As the years passed, it all simply felt like a dream caused by that endless summer heat. He'd just about come to accept it as no more than that. But now, here he was a grown man, with a wife and a responsible job and he was seeing a shining being, neither male nor female, sitting high up in a tree.

The being tossed him an apple laughing, calling out, "Just like the serpent you might be thinking, but knowledge now is power. Innocence was vanquished when man took his first bite, so you needn't be scared of that apple- BTW, it's from the Piggly Wiggly down the street." With that said s/he left the perch and fell softly into the field standing before him.

"I am indeed, H.M.S Beaglian returned to hold you to your promise. Do not fear, belief in the Lord will sustain you," s/he intoned sternly. "The time has come to retrieve the **Golden Tablet** and begin the hard work of disseminating the **Word** as clarified in the ***Book of Darwin....***"

The Unmasking is often referred to as the "Mississippi Miracle." How, many wondered, could the son of a sharecropper and a humble field inspector, accomplish so much in such a short time? The answer, of course, resides in the *Book of Darwin.* Coyne was clearly one of God's Elect, a Revealed Saint; his success encoded in his God-given genes. How else could he have ushered in the Mississippi Miracle?

Once he realized what he had, accepted it was indeed real, he set forth on the mission God had elected for him. The only dilemma was: how to transcribe the Golden Tablet so he could spread the Unmasked Word? Coyne's first step was to approach the IT guy at the bank, Jim Johnston. He explained to Johnston he had a large amount of material to put into a word document but didn't know how to affect a computer-to-computer transfer.

"Geez, I'd love to help ya' out but it sounds like a big job and ya' know..."

"Hold on Jim," I.M. said laying a hand on his upper arm, "don't say 'no' til you hear what the **Tablet** says."

"Tablet? Says? What kinda' tablet? I thought you said it was a computer?"

"Well, it looks sorta' like a laptop but its thinner - a bit like a small, flat chalkboard but it seems to function like a computer."

Johnston shot him a look of disbelief. "Well, why dontcha' bring that tablet, or whatever it is, over to my apartment some time and I'll take a gander at it?" Johnston queried in his long Mississippi drawl.

"I can't remove it from the house. It's not safe. Not permissible. Come on over this Sunday and my wife will fix you a nice supper. How about it?"

"Well, ok. Yeah, I'd really enjoy that. I don't get many home cooked meals since Jesse up and left me last year."

Poor Johnston, ten years before he had married a pert and pretty blond girl. She was a sunny twenty-one year old who quickly, after popping out three lusty tow-headed babies in rapid succession, turned sour. Then, one day, with not even a good-bye note, she snatched their three kids and vanished.

"Great!" Coyne exclaimed. "A good meal, a little company and then we will look at the Tablet. I think when you see it you won't be able to refuse to assist."

Jim sauntered over the next Sunday and after a great meal of fried catfish, greens long simmered with smoked hocks, a delish mac n' cheese finished off with a buttermilk strawberry cake Johnston tipped back in his chair content and sated for, perhaps, the first time in over a year.

"Ok, ok," he groaned, "you earned my help with that meal. But I warn ya', if it's a big project I might require another Sunday supper."

"I'm counting on it."

Johnston was astonished by what he saw. "I don't know what to say. I've never seen the likes of this machine or whatever it is. Where did you buy this?"

"Didn't buy it. The Angel Beagalian left it with me."

"The what?"

I.M. proceeded to tell Johnston about his first and second encounters with the angel and, as he spoke, Johnston's incredulity grew.

"Well," Johnston exclaimed once I.M. had finished, "You don't need me, you need a priest."

He stood up preparing to leave but I.M. implored him, "Don't go yet. Listen to the **Tablet** and if you are still unconvinced, then I won't hold you any longer," and added with a grin, "You can still come and take Sunday supper with us anytime."

As soon as I.M. lifted his palm the tablet awoke and began to recite the *Book of Darwin* beginning with I.M.'s role in receiving, hiding, and then retrieving the **Golden Tablet**. Johnston sat spell bound listening with an intensity that even he was amazed by. After listening for several hours to the new **Good News,** he leaned forward and asked I.M to stop the computer.

"I don't know what to say. Is this a joke or a miracle?" But he said it softly, almost to himself.

"A miracle, or at least that's what I believe. "

Then, as if anticipating Johnston's next question, he added," I don't know why **HE** chose me to deliver the **Word**. Who am I after all? A simple man, son of a sharecropper, the descendant of slaves…

I have asked myself this same question and concluded we simply cannot judge or understand the Lord's reasons. It is simply for us to obey and so I ask you Jim Johnston will you assist me?"

It was more a command than a question and as Johnston gazed into the eyes of this son of Mississippi, I.M. seemed to grow in stature.

"What choice do I have? I believe the decision was made for you and now for me. Count me in. I promise to assist you now and always." As Johnston spoke this pledge I.M.'s countenance softened and he seemed to return to his old self.

I.M. grasped Johnston's hand in his pumping it up and down exclaiming, "Now let's begin. It starts with us!"

Johnston, skilled though he was, was unable to directly transfer the **Word** to his computer, but he came over every night and a ritual began. Johnston would sit down for dinner with the Coyne family and afterwards Coyne and Johnston would retreat to the little office they'd set up in a corner of the kitchen working into the night. Sometimes the night was so far gone when they called it quits Johnston simply got a few hours sleep on the living room sofa before heading out to his day job at the bank.

All in all, it took forty days to transcribe the *Book of Darwin* into a word document. But don't think I.M. and Johnston were wholly focused on the Book's transcription. No indeed. He and Johnston were busy gathering together a core group of followers. In quick order they gathered together a handful of volunteers who, along with Johnston, formed the Faithful Ten.

The Chin [1860-GTE, 45]

One of these early supporters was Betty Chin, a sporty, young woman who plunged into what became the Church of the Revealed Saints- the CRS- with unparalleled enthusiasm.

She was a prominent member of the small but well-heeled Chinese American community brought to Mississippi during Reconstruction by white plantation owners, meant to supplant the recently freed slaves in their cotton fields.

Her paternal ancestor, Bao Chin, had crossed the Pacific in the aftermath of the destructive Opium Wars, which came to a close in 1860. Like so many Chinese, the Chins found themselves impoverished by the confiscatory taxes required to pay off the British combined with the impact of several years of crop failure. They were barely holding onto a few mou of land from which they just eked out sufficient rice with which to feed the family and pay their taxes.

Seeking relief from an unsustainable situation, the Chins cast about for a solution. Like many Chinese they were aware of possibilities in America. Since 1849 the California Gold Rush had attracted the Chinese, mostly men, to America's west coast seeking quick riches. In 1860 word of a new gold strike reached Guangdong Province providing the Chins with the impetus to send their youngest son off to California. Gathering up their meager savings and borrowing the balance from a ticket agent, they secured his passage to America. Hopes were high as he set off.

"You will come back in three years laden with gold," second brother told him.

"You will build a new home for mother and father," predicted eldest son.

"We will never want again," his young wife told him, bowing low holding their infant son in her arms.

"I promise to come home and raise up this family," he vowed solemnly as the ticket agent impatiently motioned him into the waiting cart holding a half a dozen other young men all dreaming the same dream.

Young Chin arrived in California eager to find his fortune and return to China and his family with the hoped for gold. He imagined how proud his family would be. Surely he would assume the status of elder son and ultimately family patriarch simply by virtue of the good fortune he provided. Birth order would be no impediment when riches paved his path. He'd knock down that dilapidated house, maybe even return with a few western style pieces of furniture, buy up land from failing farmers to whom he would re-rent that same land, establishing the Chins as wealthy landowners. His son would study for the Imperial exams, pass with high honors to become a prominent official in Guangdong province. How the Chin family would rise!

It never panned out that way.

"Hey," he asked one of the Chinese sailors as he was disembarking in California, "How far to the Gold Rush?"

"Too far for you to walk," chortled the sailor.

"What do you mean? My family paid good money to get me to that gold."

"Well then, they should have put you on a boat to Los Angeles. This is San Francisco. You are hundreds of miles from the gold fields of Halcomb Valley."

"I simply don't understand. The ticket agent told my family I would be taken to the gold."

"Hah, the ticket agent put you on the first available boat. Bad luck for you it was San Francisco bound."

Stunned, poor young Chin was at a loss. He sat down on the dock holding his meager possessions contained in the blue cloth bag his mother had thrust into his hands as he departed. He simply didn't know what to do. Lucky for him, one of the disembarking seamen, a seasoned Chinese sailor, took pity on him.

"Come on young fellow. Get up. Follow me. I know a local who might need you."

Chin meekly obeyed, following the sailor through the mud-laden streets until they arrived at what looked like a plain wooden shack. Inside were a few long wooden tables and a counter behind which was a wood burning stove with three burners, pots and pans everywhere, some barrels filled with vegetables, salt pork, fresh fish and a small table on which sat a variety of condiments.

Out through the back door was a small fenced in area where three young Chinese boys, no older than ten years, were hunched on the ground peeling and chopping vegetables, throwing each by kind into their own small barrels.

A middle-aged man, clearly the owner asked him, "Can you cook?"

Chin looked at him puzzled.

"Of course you can't cooked," laughed the good-natured Mr. Ai Bolin. "What Chinese man living in China can? But here you will learn to cook," he said clapping his hands on the young man's shoulders directing him back to the kitchen.

"I will pay you five cents a week and all the chop suey you can stomach. You can sleep on a mattress in that corner," he added motioning to a rolled up greasy pad. "Do you accept?"

Chin bowed low to indicate his acceptance.

"Good, now grab that apron over there along with that long spoon and get to work."

Chin worked in Ai Bolin's chop suey shack for five years. He sent most of his meager salary back to his family in China. He learned quickly and found that Ai Bolin, Loving Gentle Rain, was true to his name. A kind master who, perhaps because he was alone, eventually let young Chin move into his modest apartment at no cost. Like many older Chinese men who arrived in California right after the 1849 Gold Rush, Ai Bolin never married in America. He had, of course, a wife and two sons in China he had not seen in over ten years. He was forty when he arrived hoping to strike it rich quick and return. That never happened and a decade later, at fifty years of age, here he was still stuck in California.

Poor Bolin, five years after Chin's arrival a runaway horse and cart ran him over as he was crossing the street. He died instantly. Chin buried him in proper form and sent word back to his family in China along with the savings he guarded in a tin can he kept under his bed. His obligations discharged, Chin assumed ownership of the chop suey shack. Who was there to say no?

Chin had a head for business and within a short time moved the business out of that shack and established a real sit-down restaurant on the main drag of Chinatown serving not only chop suey, but also local American fare. He hired a black man to cook and soon platters of fried chicken, grits, steaks with fried onions and plates of mile high apple pie were flying out of his kitchen feeding the local and better off transient San Francisco community. He dutifully continued to remit money to his Chinese family but soon realized while he might do "well," he would never return laden with gold to his family. He dutifully resigned himself to live out his life in this strange and barbaric land.

And so he might have, but for the anti-Chinese riot of 1877, for two days white men looted and burned to the ground every Chinese establishment, including Chin's.

"Mr. Gund, where are you gonna' eat?" Chin appealed to the half-crazed man who appeared at his door carrying a lit firebrand. Gund simply stared at him tossing the burning stick into the kitchen, igniting a barrel of cooking oil. It was all over in less than twenty minutes. At the age of thirty-seven, Chin realized he would have to start over. How or with what energy he couldn't fathom.

A few weeks later, still dazed from those events, he saw an ad offering to pay train fare and put $5.00 in the pocket of any Chinese willing to relocate to Mississippi and pick cotton for five years. He boarded that train and left California behind forever.

He arrived at the Hopson cotton plantation near Clarksdale, Mississippi along with a small group of other Chinese who were immediately put to work. After five years of brutal labor, ticket debt paid off, he left that plantation to start a small grocery catering to the black folk he had worked side by side with in those fields. He prospered. At fifty years of age he married a relatively young Chinese girl, Daiyu, he met while working in the fields. Yes, he was a bit old, but Daiyu never regretted her choice. Her life in China had not been easy. So when Daiyu's father, deeply in debt, decided to sell her to a labor agent looking for workers for a cotton plantation in the American South, she was, relieved, even though she understood that in this life she would never again see her family or country. She bowed to what she strongly believed was her destiny.

In America fortune will surely find its way to me.

For that reason when Chin, a well-situated older Chinese man, asked her to marry him, she immediately bowed low telling him she would be honored to be his wife. She was content; good fortune had, at last, found her. Two sons healthy, sound sons quickly followed: Arthur and Roland. They were dutiful sons; good, devoted boys who took over the family business when father Chin died at age eighty.

His descendants stayed on, expanded the business, and occasionally intermarried with some of the local African Americans. Along the way the family added the Baptist Church, grits, fried chicken, and collard greens to their traditional repertoire of ancestor alters, Sunday pot stickers, and Lunar New Year's celebrations.

Betty Chin was the result of this heritage. It was writ large on her face and in the ease with which she moved between communities. By the launch of the *Book of Darwin,* she had the fledgling CRS on sound financial footing, had interested the local media in this new religious movement, and recruited two of the Faithful Ten.

No surprise, she became one of I.M.'s most valued confidants. It was said that I.M Coyne never made a single strategic decision without consulting with the Chin.

Chapter 12: Isaac

Savannah, Georgia [GTE 45]

The Reverend Isaac or "Ice" Freeman was enjoying himself immensely. He was proud. And why shouldn't he be? He had been at the helm of the Church of Revealed Saints for close to six years, since he was thirty-two years old, and his star was still ascendant. An African American, as dark as the Mississippi earth his ancestors were once forced to till, he was a most engaging man. Born shortly after the Great Transformation, he had the advantage of being raised during the earliest years of this new phase in the American experiment.

His father, the Reverend Abraham Freeman, one of the Faithful Ten, and later the First Keeper of the *Book of Darwin*, initial "come to God moment," was something of a fluke. Abe Freeman began his working life as a long distance truck driver. Back and forth he went between Clarksdale and multiple towns and cities in the Southeast hauling cotton, tobacco, and anything else that would fit into his hefty eight-wheeler. No one would have ever predicted he would emerge as a leading disciple of a religious movement. Yet, there were some indicators he was not unfit for that role either. Ever full of fire and brimstone, even at the breakfast table, his dissatisfaction with the federal government and a growing secular society, fueled by a steady diet of conservative Christian talk radio, exploded forth like an armed Athena springing full grown from Zeus' head, on hearing that a federal court required the removal of the Ten Commandments from a Montgomery, Alabama courthouse. At that moment Abe Freeman laid down his key, determined to dedicate his life to God. He sold his truck, invested the proceeds into converting an old barn on the family property into a church and set up shop as a Baptist preacher, offering salvation to all who would dedicate their lives to Jesus Christ.

"Praise be," the now Reverend Isaac "Ice" Freeman shouted out loud. "If the LORD hadn't moved my father to make that move to HIM, where would I be today?"

The thought discomfited him. He knew the answer: living as a WE and, most likely, working down the road at the local Chrysler factory.

"Well," he told himself shaking off that most disturbing idea, "the LORD moves as he sees fit and just! It is truly as Darwin proclaimed, all part of the Lord's blueprint."

The Baptist church built by the Reverend Daddy Freeman didn't remain part of that fold for long. On a chilly late November day in 2001, Abe Freeman stopped into one of the Chin markets to pick up some milk for his wife. There, sitting at the register was Betty Chin, the owner's young attractive daughter. When he approached the counter, milk in hand, he had to call her name three times to get her attention.

"Betty," he asked, "What are you doing here? I've never seen you at the register."

She barely glanced up at Abe murmuring, "Ummmm…Joe was sick and Dad couldn't find a replacement, so I'm helping out." She seemed in no rush to ring him up.

"What are you reading?" he persisted now curious as to what could possibly be so absorbing, "Some new harlequin novel?"

Ever serious, she looked up at Freeman a bit sternly but then softened saying, "Why no, no, nothing like that. It's the *Book of Darwin.*"

"The what?" he queried.

"It's the *Book of Darwin,*" and Betty Chin proceeded to tell him the story of the **Unmasking** that had occurred right there in Clarksdale, along with the basic precepts of the revealed **Word** according to Darwin. The story, the **Word,** the truth of it all, captivated his soul. From that moment forward, he gave up his life, and later his first-born son, to the Church of the Revealed Saints and its *Book of Darwin.* In short order he became one of the Faithful Ten, that is, one of the original ten disciples of the Church of the Revealed Saints.

His little barn of a church hosted that fledgling church's first in-the-being congregation. It quickly attracted a live congregation of about one hundred souls who each and every Sunday came to hear the Prophet I.M. Coyne preach the gospel according to Darwin. Soon it was standing room only at Sunday services, while the overflow stood in the nearby field listening to the Prophet's exhortations from a loudspeaker system.

A few years later, Freeman arranged for the Sunday services to be streamed and, as they say, "the rest is history." No one was surprised when Coyne got his own spot on a regional cable network that did very well indeed. Coyne, always an open-handed man, shared his prosperity with his disciples. For Freeman, this meant that a life once lived more bumping along the road than in his tiny 650 square foot home was now spent in a palatial 5600 square foot estate.

Only one thing was missing from Abe Freeman's life: a son. It seemed his wife Sarah, like her namesake in the Old Testament, was barren. Of course, her repeated pleas to consult a fertility specialist fell on deaf ears. No man should interfere with the Divine plan and his faith was born out when at the age of sixty in year 7, Great Transformation Era, God blessed him with his only son, appropriately christened, Isaac. No surprise, the Reverend Abe Freeman liked to compare himself and Isaac's mother to Abraham and Sarah. And, as the father constantly reminded the son, unlike most infertile couples whose little miracles were the product of a fertility clinic, his boy, his pride and joy, was truly God's gift.

Sanctuary [GTE, 45]

Isaac "Ice" Freeman opened an ornate wooden door, which stood in stark contrast to the sleek modern house. No one ever saw this door. It was tucked away behind a rack of clothing in the deep recess of his bedroom suite's closet. It was, he often smiled to himself, a secret room much like those the early Masons must have used when conducting their private rites and rituals back in the 18th and 19th centuries. This was his prayer room, his meditation room, his library and the repository of the holy *Book of Darwin*. It was, of course, the original.

Retractable lights were automatically activated as soon as Ice opened the door. He glanced from the large desk positioned in the middle of the room to the enormous old–style black and green veined marble fireplace that instantly ignited as soon as he stepped into the room. The mahogany paneled walls held inset bookshelves lined with thousands of in-the-being books, some centuries old written in the multitude of languages that used to confound humanity. A veritable literary Tower of Babel that seemed appropriate for this man of God.

He had either read or perused many, but certainly not all of them. The contained: words of wisdom, words of fools, words of false prophets; the false starts and empty promises men throughout the ages cleaved to were contained and documented in these many volumes. It was, he thought, the sad but true story of humanity. Yes, he reassured himself as he glanced over to the wood and glass case standing to the right of the desk which housed the book of honor in this mausoleum of long unread and forgotten books, those forlorn days were now over.

Next to the shelves was a small reading table and plush chair. On the mahogany table decorated with small intricate inlays of ivory, rosewood, ebony and mother -of -pearl, was a genuine tiffany reading lamp. From a by-gone era, it still used an incandescent electric bulb. Of course, he could have had that changed, but there was something about this anachronistic technology he enjoyed. He switched on the lamp and settled into the wingback, blood-red chair, reminiscent of the kind that adorned the Gilded Age mansions that once lined the upper reaches of Fifth Avenue in Manhattan. Most of those fantastic shrines to the spirit of the JCs had either been bulldozed [oh, so long ago] or housed in, in-the-being museums. But here, in this little warren, hidden behind a bedroom closet door, was a living homage to the past, a small re-creation utilized, as it would have been, during the time of those pioneers of capitalism.

Once comfortably seated, he traced the table's inlays with one of his long slender fingers. He appreciated each divot and imperfection. He appreciated its uniqueness and value. His was a world of not simply the mass produced, but of commodification so intense that almost everyone's time was carefully accounted for, where screen time was so ubiquitous that for many it comprised the majority of their 24/7.

In this, his reality, in-the-being experiences were increasingly unique and costly. The formerly simple act of sitting and picking up an actual bound book to read, alone, with no Time Keeper digesting one's activity for analysis, was an indulgence available only to the most privileged.

Ice reached for the book that was always the table's companion: the *Book of Darwin*. It was not the original. That was also housed in this room but kept, fittingly and securely, under a glass-covered table. What he held in his hands was almost as valuable. It was one of the few remaining hard copies of the *Book of Darwin*. It had belonged to his father; personally given to him by the Prophet I.M. Coyne. When Ice was about twelve his father told him how it came into his possession:

"Son, now listen up and listen well," he commanded while lovingly picking up the BOOK, cradling it in his arms like a baby.

"When I.M. Coyne, our beloved prophet, lay dying in his own home after being brutally attacked by a mob of atheistic liberals, his final action was to secure the BOOK along with the one I hold in my hand."

As always, he recounted those final, tragic moments that deprived the CRS of its revered prophet:

"Abe, Abe,'" he gasped holding my hand in his bloody one, "Get the BOOK. Secure the BOOK. "

"No, no," I said, "I need to get you some help first."

"Don't waste any time! Just safeguard the BOOK and take with you the one I always carry in public. It is yours to keep, yours to display in public, yours to pass on to anyone in your line that keeps faith with its teachings. It is my gift to you and your posterity."

"Here I interrupted the Prophet. I had no children and my wife, your dearest mother, was already nearing forty years of age. We had rejected the idea of defying God's plan for us by going in for IVF. As painful as it was, we had resigned ourselves to remaining childless. Yet, dying though he was and in the midst of dire circumstances, my human failing manifested as I pointed out my condition to him.

"Sainted be the Coyne, he smiled as if he knew a wondrous secret and simply murmured, "Trust in the Lord, there will be a child, but now do as I ask. Go. Retrieve the BOOK. Remember the mission and me whenever you take it in your hands. When you open its blessed pages remember the oath you are about to take. The BOOK

– the Golden Text is behind that wall of books. You have seen me open it countless times. Do it...it's under the glass you simply need to trace the code on the glass using your index finger. It's..."

Abe stopped short of imparting the code to his twelve-year-old son, despite his confidence in young Isaac's destiny. Regardless, that code was his and only his until it was time to pass it on.

"I went to the bookcase and repeating what I had seen him do on numerous occasions quickly obtained entry to the hidden room, traced the code, accessed the BOOK and swiftly returned to place it in I.M.'s hands.

"No, no," he said to me, "It is yours now. Yours to guard, yours to cherish. Now, as First Keeper of the Book, repeat the oath:

I swear upon all that is holy I will preserve, protect and defend the *Book of Darwin* and spread its Good News across this mighty land, from sea to shining sea, by the powers vested in me by our Lord and his Prophet Charles Darwin. Amen."

"Of course," Abe Freeman recalled, "I obediently repeated the oath and received the BOOK and not a moment too soon. I could hear the mob returning. To this day their howls still ring in my ears. With not more than minutes to spare I wrapped the BOOK and the display copy in spare vestments I.M. kept in his study and fled the house. I was fortunate to be able to get to my car and take the private road that led off the property. Once I was a good distance away I stopped the car and, like Lot's wife, turned to look at the wreckage. I was spared that biblical wife's fate, since I turned, not with desire, but to lament mankind's folly and bid our Prophet goodbye.

The home was ablaze and while I mourned Prophet Coyne's death I confess that at that moment I understood saving the *Book of Darwin* was paramount. Surely the mob would go wild once they realized they had killed the messenger but failed to destroy the message."

Isaac paused his review of those conversations with his father. After all, he knew by heart all that transpired after I.M. Coyne's death on April 15, 2010. His death rallied and augmented the church's followers. In the wake of his martyrdom, hundreds of thousands flocked to the CRS. Rumors spread, like wildfire across the web, that Coyne was more than a martyr, that he was a true American prophet. Some believed he heralded the "Second Coming" of the USA- that Coyne had died for the nation's sins so it might prosper again.

With Coyne gone, all looked to Abe Freeman to lead them, to continue the ministry, to realize the rebirth. After all, he was with the Prophet when he died and entrusted with the sacred texts. It was clear: Freeman was the anointed successor. He became the First Keeper of the Book.

Shortly after the Prophet's death the Faithful Ten decided it was time to move out of Clarksdale. They chose Savannah as the CRS's permanent headquarters. It was there, young Isaac was raised and observed the power of the CRS and his father, daily demonstrated by the endless parade of dignitaries who came to meet with Reverend Freeman. The CEO himself visited Savannah. Yes, he came, in- the-being!

Ice smiled, recalling his father always ended these stories with a summary of what was expected of him:

"My boy, the BOOK is your inheritance. More than this house, its contents, credits, cars, or anything else I might leave you. Our future and that of our posterity is written in this BOOK. Guard it well, cherish it, serve it, and worship it. Never forget the Lord ordained our role. I took an oath to serve, as one day you will. Cleave to it and your future, your son's future and those you will never meet, will be secure."

On saying this he strode from the room, the BOOK enveloped in his still muscular arms booming, "AMEN....A...MEN!" as if the matter were settled. And, indeed, it was. Isaac understood his destiny and never, not even for a brief moment, questioned or considered deviating from it.

Now, as Isaac thought about his father's remonstrance, he picked up the BOOK given to him by his father and re-read, for perhaps the millionth time, the introduction to the *Book of Darwin* written by the Prophet Coyne himself. It was the only selection within the *Book of Darwin* written by man. Once, during an interview, Coyne was asked by a reporter why he felt it necessary to add to the *Book of Darwin* his own personal history.

"Why not," asked the reporter, "just let the BOOK speak for itself?"

In his typically earnest but forbearing manner, he grabbed the reporter's hand exclaiming, "Pray on that thought with me for a moment. True, the hand that put those words on paper was mine, but the Lord directed all that occurred. So how could I leave out what His Majesty on High directed?"

"I see what you mean," the reporter responded in a rapt tone.

"So… how about we say a big Amen together?

Chapter 13: History

Excerpt from an official history: *The Restored History of America from 1492 to the Great Transformation,* Chapter 70, Pay As You Go

As inexplicable as it was, there were some who didn't quite get it; couldn't adjust to the new reality. It took a few burnt down homes and individuals dying on hospital steps for people to grasp that the new CSA didn't tolerate free riders. Those bad old days were GONE. The new minimalist government existed to oversee national defense and act as a clearinghouse for contracts for the private companies providing health, welfare and safety services. The government wholly washed its hands of delivering infrastructure or even regulating food, drug, water, or workplace safety. It relinquished its role as the nation's employer of choice.

The CSA excised that cancer. The national debt, which had skyrocketed by the early twenty-first century to dangerous levels, was no more. The legions of Americans who had succumbed to generational dependency, terminated. Americans, at long last, utterly rejected Roosevelt's New Deal enslavement screaming in unison: "No Rosey way." They cheered, yes, cheered when the highways, airports, mass transit, sewer and water systems were all privatized.

For the first time in our nation's history 100% employment was at hand, along with the promise that each and every MAKER would keep a fair share of his earnings. Uncle Sam would no longer act as the national pickpocket on April 15th.

Instrumental to ushering in this new Golden Age was the landmark MAKERs' Relief Act. This landmark legislation formalized the two major classifications: MAKER and WELLFARE RECIPIENT. MAKERS were further divided into: PROFESSIONALS, AND WAGE EARNERS. PROFESSIONALS were then further subdivided into JCs, GODSTERs, EASYs, PROFFS, PROFFIES, POLS, MINUTEMEN, and others. WAGE EARNERS were made up of thousands of sub-categories such as Fabricators, Firsters, Content Facilitators, 3-D Graphic artists and the like.

The act also provided for the construction of the segregated, gated Welfare communities commonly referred to as "the Projects." A collective consensus was reached: to live amongst the general population, to be part of the commonality, everyone had to be a "MAKER" not a "TAKER." It gave political legs to Darwin's notion that not only should the fit thrive, but be rewarded. The MAKERs' Relief Act was the implementation of a Darwinian inspired blueprint, which gave the nation the moral permission to resolve its perennial problem: what to do about the TAKERs?

This change permitted the government to significantly lower taxes, nearly eliminating all mandatory levies by putting the new CSA on a pay-as-you-go footing. You want to eat? You pay. You want a roof over your head? You pay. You want clothes on your back? You pay. You want the hospital to patch you up? You pay. You want your kids to attend school, at any level? You pay. You want to cross a bridge? You pay. You want to use the roads? You pay. This requires 100% employment. No more food stamps, welfare, or Section 8 housing, minimum wage, hospitals obligated to treat everyone, or free public schools for people to misuse and abuse. As President Cross proudly proclaimed, "taxes are now customized."

The Patriots' Duty is the only tax everyone pays. It funds the military contractors, the Pols, as well as the Projects. Sure the TAKERs are all required to perform daily assigned tasks to underwrite their upkeep, but the Projects' costs far surpasses its inhabitants' pathetic contributions. Yet, no one complains. As the Pols pointed out, the Project population was a small fraction of what the prison population had been in the waning days of the USA when it had soared to approximately 2.3 million.

Nowadays, no more than 250,000 people, at any given moment, were resident in ten sites equitably distributed throughout the country. And fantastic news! That number is projected to sharply decrease as the children exit the Projects. Mental health professionals and geneticist have predicted that by GTE 60 the Project population will fall by fifty percent permitting the closing of about half of these facilities resulting in further savings to the MAKER. The CSA triumphs again!

Excerpt from an unauthorized history: *What Really Happened to America from 1492 to the Great Transformation* [accessed by a special password only]

A few years after the implementation of the MAKER Relief Act, CEO Bill Golightly was asked by Krafty Network's news personality Chrystal Wallet about its implications:

"Ok," she acceded, "I understand and I think most Americans would agree that putting tolls on all roads, eliminating food stamps and Section 8 housing is a great idea. But fire departments? All public schools? Come on, even you must admit this seems a bit too drastic. Do we really want houses to burn down and children to go unschooled?"

"Not at all, not at all," Bill Golightly responded as he adjusted his wire-rimmed glasses while shifting his body in the interview chair. "In fact, let me say that the Bill and Leeza Golightly Foundation just published a study which found that the vast majority of MAKERs will gladly pay for these services when they need them, and," he emphasized the **and** as he leaned in toward Ms. Wallet, "people who pay directly make the type of wise consumer-based decisions needed to maximize their benefits. It's all about customization."

"How so? If you don't mind my asking, Mr. Golightly."

"Well, let's take the tax or, if you will, annual fee for fire department protection. It's structured so that each year, if the consumer makes no demand on that service, the fee either stays flat or the end user receives a 'careful warden' bonus for not utilizing the service. On the other hand, service users will see their premiums go up per incident; the precise increment depending on the severity of the fire, the loss suffered and, of course, fault. So, for example, if an unattended pot on the stove causes a fire and the house burns down, well, the heavy loss and the owner's negligence will cause the premium to rise. After all, why should innocent neighbors shoulder the burden created by a careless individual? Seems only fair, right?"

"I see," Wallet intoned pushing a burnished curl away from her cheek, "It does seem to make sense."

"Of course it does."

"But what about the schools?" she suddenly persisted as the fog of worrying about her hair dissipated. "How can we be assured children won't go without training? Doesn't business demand a trained workforce? Doesn't society, the nation even, depend on it?"

"Yes, Chrystal, indeed it does, but just remember what a disaster our public schools were until GTE, 5 when they were all sold off to the Scholastic, Training & Development, Corp. The STD immediately partnered with the Corpus to build an educational pipeline through which a continual stream of human product could be delivered to the Corpus. And the reward for the fully trained MAKER armed with relevant skills and prepared to compete for employment? Full employment! The MAKER is now fully empowered to succeed! How great is that, Chrystal?"

"But," she persisted, "shouldn't everyone contribute to the cost of training the MAKER?"

"Listen, he continued as he leaned in, gently taking her hand, "do you really think the childless couple should pay? Or what about Grandma trying to get by on her Senior Savings Plan? Do you really want to force granny in her golden years, after putting her own brood through school, to pay taxes to support others people's children?"

He released her hand, his voice becoming shrill, rising as if exasperated he even had to explain this [yet again] to another inferior being.

"I mean where and when does it end? When do we give our seniors a break?"

"I see," Chrystal intoned passively, but before the interviewer could continue Golightly cut in.

"Don't you see, Chrystal, don't you understand? The public schools have been failing us all for decades. Bleeding the MAKER dry, what with those unions with their excessive demands. And parents! What about all those parents who take no responsibility for their kids' education because it's free? So what kind of educational system have we had? What has our society reaped?"

He rested for a moment giving her a look that conveyed: *Keep your mouth shut you vapid bitch. This is my platform and I'll ask and answer my own questions.*

And, indeed, Ms. Wallet's mouth filled with perfectly pearly whites quickly clamped shut as our Mr. Golightly responded:

"The harvest: an unprepared workforce and a bloated educational bureaucracy. That's why thirty years ago, hoping and praying a new day would dawn for this nation, we began to pave the path for a new educational system. Our *Shine the Light Foundation* provided some of the first grants to fund private charter schools and other cradle to work engagement approaches to educate our future MAKERs. We have labored to construct an educational pipeline that could successfully funnel the individual into the workforce. To realize this goal- and thirty years ago it was nothing more than a dream - we funded giant open online learning modules, even building the platforms needed to permit tens of thousands of students to take the same course simultaneously, thus eliminating pedagogic inconsistency, the dissemination of extraneous and erroneous information and, as an added bonus, this mass distribution of knowledge permitted publicly funded colleges and universities to cut back on expensive instructional personnel."

He finally paused for a breath. Then, as if he had gotten a second wind, his arm shot into the air while twisting his wrist in that way magicians have when asking the audience to applaud a trick, "It has all paid off. All that time and effort, going up against the nay sayers and accursed teachers' unions made this day possible."

Looking straight into the camera as if the interviewer didn't exist at all – and in fact in the mind of Mr. Golightly it was just him and his unseen audience - he finished with this convincing summation:

"So, where are we now? Where we should have been all along. Living in the greatest nation on earth because at long last we pay as we go, turning everyone into a stakeholder, a shareholder if you will. As a shareholder you want to invest your money carefully, wisely. So, invest your hard earned credits in the education tax fund and you will damn well make sure little Johnny learns. Trust me, the educational corporation will see to it he's properly assessed and assigned an appropriate instructional regime. No waste. And if little Johnny refuses? If he's a bad seed, as Darwin, sainted be his name, understood some of us simply are, well you are no longer obligated to throw good money after bad. The system guarantees that even a Johnny Rotten Core will find his level, even if it is as a TAKER."

He stopped to wipe the spit from his mouth before continuing, "And now, pay –as -you –go, extends into almost every aspect of our quotidian existence. Want to regularly drive your car on a road, a highway, or cross a bridge? Then pay the yearly fee. Only use it occasionally? Pay a one-shot use charge. It's fair. It works. Everyone gets what he pays for - nothing more, nothing less. It's as simple as that."

As he finished these last exultations he sunk back into his chair like a boxer who had just finished his round resting in his corner so he could come out swinging again.

Realizing she had totally lost control of the interview, the stunned Ms. Wallet finally dared to speak up. Managing to smile brightly [it was her trademark after all] to interject, "So, what will happen to those who can't pay? Say, for example, you have cancer but no health insurance. What then?"

"As I said, you don't pay, you don't get. In the new CSA there's no free lunch"

Chapter 14: Layla

GTE, 44

When Layla exited her single occupancy room she never looked back as people often do. Have you ever thought about that? Just as you are about to close the door you hesitate; you turn and run back in to make sure the lights are out, or the stove is off or, maybe to simply glance behind you as if to say, "Dear home, I will return. Please be here." Layla never did this. Like all single TAKERs she lived in a space so small she could barely turn around. It consisted of a single, narrow bed- more cot than bed really- a narrow closet, dresser, counter with a hot plate and mini-fridge. A single light bulb illuminated the room. She shared a communal bathroom down the hall with fifteen other residents along with the large communal kitchen. No cherished memories were embedded within its walls or in the creak of a floorboard. These were nothing more than holding pens and everyone knew it.

The sky was barely light, streaked only by amber highlights, but already Layla was making her way to her grandmother's place to feed her breakfast, assist with her toilet and leave her a little lunch. She wouldn't be back until late when they shared a small dinner, after which Layla put her granny to bed, switched off the lights and collapsed into her own bed until she woke to replay this routine.

The elderly lady, now seventy-two years old, had raised Layla since her parents "passed away" during the Last Uprising. Layla was two. Until she was eighteen they had lived in a cramped two-room "pen" as the residents called these. On Layla's eighteenth birthday they were evicted.

"Please," she had begged her living unit's supervisor, "I am all my granny has and she's all I have. What harm can it do for us to stay together?"

"Rule is rule," retorted the puffy blonde woman, fat from nights swigging beer and eating fried "C" patties shaped to look like old-fashioned burgers.

"Pack your stuff. You got twelve hours to vacate or the cops will come and do it for you."

"How about you just let granny move into a single pen next to mine? That way I could still care for her. She's not well. She pointed to the crumpled grey figure in the sole chair set next to the four by four window looking out into an equally dreary courtyard where TAKER children played on a cement patio.

"No can do," Superintendent Puff-face stated with finality while picking at her yellowed teeth with a toothpick. "In fact, she's gonna' be moved down to the second floor to her own single occupancy pen today. Can't have an old rag taking up so much space, can we? Not an efficient use of resources."

"No, no of course not," Layla agreed switching tactics. "But wouldn't it be more efficient if we each had our own pen in the same building? After all, she needs care; you can see that, can't you? Who's going to care for her if I don't?"

"That's your problem, honey. No concern of mine if you do or you don't. I'm just a rule enforcer. That's my job and I'm sticking to it. No deviating." She cocked her head at Layla as if to say: "Isn't this conversation over?" But Layla persisted.

"Well, of course you must enforce the rules and Darwin, sainted be his name, certainly advocates we accept the world order as it has been revealed, right? But didn't Darwin [sainted be his name she quickly intoned, yet again] tell us to use time efficiently? 'A Stitch in time saves nine,' after all. I am simply suggesting I could be far more productive if granny were close by. You can see that can't you?"

"I am not in charge of time management. It's up to you to make sure you use your time efficiently. If you decide it's a good use of your time to care for a used up TAKER, well, that's on you. I don't care what you do."

The Superintendent made her move to leave, turning her back to Layla while clasping the doorknob with her greasy fingers. She paused, rotated her head to give Layla one last bit of advice, "I know what I would do. Kiss the old thing goodbye and let her slip into oblivion. Sure she can't go to heaven- if she were one of the Elect she wouldn't be here, would she?"

A final chuckle rolled from her throat. "None of us would be here if we were one of the Elect, a Revealed Saint, now would we? Can't fight evolution. Only the fittest survive, prosper then reap their final reward in heaven and that ain't any of us- now is it honey?" She opened the door, lumbered out disappearing into the dingy hall.

Layla stood there. She had twelve hours to get out. Twelve hours to occupy her new Pen five blocks east and move her grandmother and her things to the second floor Pen in their current building. It could be worse, she considered. They might have made them both change buildings. Well, there was nothing more for her to consider except how to get it done.

When she reflected on it, there was little for her to gather up and take for either of them. Just a few clothes, some personal items of no real value to anyone but her: birthday cards from her grandmother, a little copper bracelet left behind by her mother, and a few other small items. Efficiently situating her Granny in her new pen wasn't going to be the problem, it was figuring out how to go back and forth between the two residences and get to her classes on time. It would be tricky, but she knew with organization and proper time management it was manageable. Layla, if nothing else, was a master of time management. A regular time hacker!

That was how Layla lived for four years while she went to the Consolidated City University-CCU. Like all TAKER children she had the opportunity to advance, to leave the Projects. For most that meant reclassification to a WE. The JCs proudly touted this as fulfillment of the CSA's promise: the guarantee of true equal opportunity. Like all children, Layla had been assessed and tracked since childhood. And, as it turned out, she was to become assessment's poster child. The very fulfillment of the CSA's promise that under its regime, its tender policies, America could and would be, at long last, a true meritocracy.

Chapter 15: History

Excerpt from: *The Restored History of America from 1492 to the Great Transformation,* Chapter 71, Higher Education

New York City's public higher educational system, founded in 1847, was the behemoth known as CUNY- the City University of New York. Over scores of years and through numerous incarnations it had morphed into a purveyor of an ineffective, undifferentiated educational product and was ripe for the taking. While the public K-12 system had been privatized in GTE 5, it took another nine years to do the same to public higher education. Accordingly, in GTE 14, the Scholastic, Training & Development, Corp., "STD," snapped it up, promptly shuttering its twenty-four campuses, merging them into two locations, one academic and the other focused on workforce development, both administered through a single command center. The academic and research campus was cited in Wall Street, while the career center was uptown. It was rechristened Consolidated City University, "CCU," and the Wall Street campus blossomed into one of the most prestigious institutions for higher education in the CSA PROFESSIONALS of all types- POLS, performance EASYS, JCs, PROFFIES, and all manner of aspirants from every corner of this great land sought admission. Some claimed it was the rarified air of Wall Street, home of the Corpus, which lent it such cache. Whatever the reason, CCU quickly leapt over the competition, outshining them all.

Once acquired, the STD declared the faculty unions no more, promptly fired all CUNY professors rehiring many as contingent faculty. These individuals were classified as WEs and given yearly renewable contracts to work at its uptown career center. The luckiest, those destined for the academic oriented Wall Street campus, received long-term contracts and were classified as PROFESSORS (part of the Professional category) and affectionately referred to as "PROFFIES."

Gone was that invidious system, tenure, summers off and long inter-session breaks. Educators, at every level, were all required to pay their own way.

The Corpus demanded true value from every sector of the labor force, no exceptions, and no more slackers. In the CSA there were no more TAKERs only MAKERs. As that now popular saying goes: *There's no free lunch, there's no free lunch, there's no free lunch...*

Chapter 16: Layla

Scatter Day [GTE 27]

Layla was, in a word, brilliant. There was simply no denying it. Her SAT scores were off the charts belying the Assessors' reluctance to provisionally reclassify her as a PROFFESSIONAL. The hesitation: her parents had taken part of the Last Uprising. They remained defiant until the end. What if she were prone to the same proclivities? No evidence yet existed to link rebellion or nonconformity to a gene, however psycho-geneticists hoped the mass release of these TAKER children to the outside over the upcoming decades would begin to provide the concrete evidence needed to answer this hotly debated question. This was, for certain, uncharted territory. On the other hand, all her evaluations indicated she was an engaging girl who followed instructions, worked hard, and was a true time hacker. After much agonizing, they reclassified her, but flagged her for special monitoring once on the outside.

So imagine the Project dwellers' astonishment when Layla was not only plucked from their midst but assigned to CCU.

"Unbelievable!"

"Unprecedented"

"This will provide convo for years to come!"

Director Jad Koningu announced the results at Layla's Learning Center graduation:

"Trainees, Trainees, silence please! I have an important posting. One of our own has been elevated! Yes, yes, our very own Layla Saenz has been provisionally reclassified as a PROFFESSIONAL," exclaimed the Director as he turned in Layla's direction motioning her, exhorting her, to stand up. Reluctantly, face flushed, she popped out of her seat and immediately sat down again.

"Layla, Layla," he persisted, "stand up again! Let your classmates focus on the face of success, Darwin's promise made and kept, the fruit of the CSA's meritocracy."

Layla, not only mortified at being singled out, instantly began to assess both the short and long-term ramifications of this public announcement. Would she be kidnapped? Would acid be thrown in her face as a warning to others not to get uppity and out ideas? More practically, how would she pay the tuition?

Yes, it was understood [hoped] that many if not most of these TAKER children would exit as WEs, never to return. It was almost expected. But to be sent out as some rarified provisional PROFFESSIONAL? That walked up to the line of repudiating the group, as well as giving legs to the CSA's mantra: "We are a true meritocracy." Layla being plucked from their midst as a PROFFESSIONAL was the proof of the CSA's pudding.

TAKER life, as chaotic as it might have appeared to outsiders, was governed by a strict code. A kind of misery loves company solidarity. No matter the offense, no snitching or squealing was acceptable. And no airs. Absolutely none; no matter your classification on the Outside. Because truly, none of them gave a good god damn if one's TAKER status resulted from criminality or rebellion, a fall from grace, or due to mental infirmity. Once inside, all that was erased and forgotten. TAKER is TAKER, now there's true social equality! All shared equally in the economic and daily hardship that was the true coin of the Project's realm. So, no doubt, Layla's [provisional] reclassification was bound to shake and bake the Project's inhabitants- at least a bit.

Maybe all this anxiety was inevitable. These graduates were, after all, part of the first wave wholly raised in the Projects. What would become of them was really anyone's guess. Were they capable of being life-long Contributors? Would some, or even most, eventually be returned to the Projects? Would they replicate their parents' proclivities for violence, criminality, or, in some cases, rebellion? Much convo and speculation both on the Outside and Inside was woofed, posted, and bandied about.

Of course, expectations for these TAKER children were not high. Most, all concurred, would never rise above the lowest rungs of WE grade occupations. This gathering consensus was reflected in the language used at their Learning Centers. At the Outside Learning Centers directors typically addressed the attendees as "students," but at TAKER Learning Centers these children were increasingly referred to as "trainees."

This tag was not mandated but had crept into these directors' lexicon as if via osmosis, inculcating in their young charges assumed limitations. True, these children, like those on the Outside, had been tracked and assessed, but any objective observer could see that the resources put at their disposal were far inferior from those at the Learning Centers attended by the JCs' and even the less resourced WEs' children.

In the new and improved America, a tiered educational system was now effectively, uncontrovertibly in place. Education, like everything else, was a private affair paid for directly by the end user. This was as true at what was formerly K through 12 as in the post-secondary colleges, universities and the new career centers. It was accepted that the child of a JC was going to have a better-resourced educational environment than that of a WE child or certainly a child of the Projects. Why shouldn't the JC's child, if she could afford it, attend a better-resourced Learning Center? It was, they all agreed, as it should be: "each according to his owns means." *Book of Darwin,* Ch. 5, verse 6, line 12 [**AMEN**].

Not surprisingly, under such conditions, [rumors to the contrary] mobility was rare and no TAKER child had ever placed out above a WE. Layla was the first to assume this distinction and, unbeknownst to her, about to become a quasi-celeb. She personified the perfected Darwinian society. She corroborated that old adage: *cream must rise to the top,* no matter where or how it was stored. It verified the consensus: *If you were meant to excel you would no matter the circumstances of your youth.*

Lots of woofing and cheering [and jeering] followed the announcement as Layla stood wishing the floor would open up and swallow her. As she looked around she realized that a few of her classmates were destined to remain forever behind the Project gates, TAKERs for life, but the majority would exit as WEs. Most would Scatter across the country to occupational finishing centers far from their home Project destined for one, two years of training max, then off to become fabricators, flippers, runners, fodder for military contractors, and all manner of cognitively undemanding occupations. Others, the more fortunate ones, were assigned to two-year skilled career centers. As a group they appeared satisfied with their placements; relieved, if somewhat anxious, to be leaving these confining walls; they knew no other life.

Like her classmates, Layla now faced a life not only different from what she had known but, in her case, far different from what she had anticipated. She had simply assumed she would be assigned a career track requiring one maybe two years of training, then slotted into some low-level job. Now, however, it seemed her path would diverge from the others and, truth be told, she was frightened. She knew little of the Outside as the TAKER's referred to the world beyond the gates. TAKER children never traveled unaccompanied outside the confines of the Projects. The only things they knew about the Outside were gleaned from their quarterly visits, which was meant to give them a taste of what they were missing. Like the ol' "carrot and stick."

Seated again, tuning out Director Koningu, Layla revisited those trips. One, in particular, came to mind. She was fourteen years old. A Content Facilitator ushered them all onto the bus. On the outer side of the bus in bright lime-green letters was plastered: "Project Bus." It might as well have read "Caution: Wild Animals," because that's how the Outsiders regarded them. That sign alone made them the subject of curiosity and not an insignificant amount of derision. Certainly, their bright orange jumpsuits conspicuously labeled with the word "Project" on the front and their individual ID number on the backside added to the impression they were different from normal children, more reminiscent of criminals from prisons of days past, but without the manacles or chains. Jeers and shouts greeted them as the bus rolled along or when they dismounted. The Outsiders called out to them:

"Lazy Fucks!"

"Get a job"

"Freeloaders"

For that alone TAKER children dreaded those quarterly trips.

Each trip also brought with it the standard "lecture." As they pushed through the Project gates their chaperones read them the canned "riot act."

"Trainees, today we tour the 'Outside' as you all call it. Remember, this is NOT the 'Outside,' but the reality you all aspire to. Those people you see on the streets, in the stores, are productive **CSA MAKERs-** this is the norm. It's how life is **supposed** to look, feel, and function- MAKERs going about their daily business **contributing**."

The Content Facilitator looked over his charges, wondering if any of these children truly had the capacity to move beyond these gates. He knew that it was his job to try to get them to realize whatever God given potential each might contain. He continued with the canned lecture:

"God ordained it and Darwin [all crossed themselves intoning, Sainted be his name] revealed it. This is the life you must look to as **your** model regardless of your parents' mistakes or proclivities. We all hope and pray that whatever genetic limitations or inclinations each of you may harbor, the nurture and excellent care the good and decent CSA MAKERs have provided will inspire you to overcome. As the Ol' Negro spiritualist, the sainted Martin Luther King proclaimed, "We shall overcome!"

At that, the students linked arms and began to sing: "We shall overcome, we shall overcome, we shall overcome some dayayyyy....Oh, Oh, Oh, deep in my ha-a-art, I do believe, that we shall overcome some day..."

At first blush, Darwinist society appears straightforward but, in reality, it is complicated to navigate. On the one hand, they profoundly believe we are all genetically prescribed by God; meaning there are things each individual is either capable of achieving or not, hence the need for constant assessments. It simply makes no sense for society to waste its limited resources trying to force square pegs into round holes. At the same time, the Darwinists teach that even though not every individual can become an Einstein or a Michelangelo, or even rise to the highest echelons, except in all but the absolute worst cases, each of us can, with proper assessment and training, "overcome." Now how wonderful is that?

Hand in glove with this belief is also the conviction that if an individual is pushed beyond his or her natural limits, the vessel will "break." Hence the high rates of ADD, ADHD, socio-paths and all forms of mental illnesses as seen under the old regime where everyone, regardless of personal limitations, were expected to become, "well-rounded," "well-educated." The pressure of it all simply shattered many fragile receptacles. *Well*, the Darwinists gleefully point out, *we now know better*.

As soon as the trainees finished singing, the Content Facilitator picked up from where he left off:

"It is true that you live in the Projects through no particular personal fault. You are here because of your parents' failings. They were either unable or unwilling to contribute. They rejected the Darwinian ideal of *doing good, by doing well*. They opted to be dropouts, perverts, deviants, or criminals. For some, your genetic inheritance will prove too great to overcome. If this is found to be the case, your TAKER classification will be made permanent and you will live and die behind these Project's gates. But many, indeed we believe the vast majority of you, can and should be able to overcome your unfortunate inheritance- so that you may walk through those gates to become full CSA Contributors..."

The canned lecture completed, the seated trainees sallied forth for their in-the -being "tour" of the outside world they surely aimed to join one day. Like children with noses pressed up against a candy store window they "oohed" and "ahhhed" at the beautiful sights: the clean streets, the 3-D images jumping out in vibrant tones hawking goods rarely seen in- the- being on the Inside, the restaurants, the multitude of thin and thinner MAKERs all equipped with a variety of appliances attached to wrists, head, ears, feet moving in a kind of elevated, atomistic rhythm that somehow collectively created a composed composition.

The highlight was a visit to a McJoy, serving cheap but **real** beef burgers, **real** fries and **real** milkshakes- none of that composite shit they all consumed daily. Have you noticed the CSA loves acronyms? It makes everything seem so cozy, so home grown, so user friendly. Yes it does. So we all preface our composite selections with a "C" as in C- chicken, C- meatloaf, and C- biscuit. It not only avoids confusion with the real thing, but also erects another intangible barrier between the MAKER classes much like fancy buttons did in seventeenth century England. Regular **Real Eaters** are currently only found amongst the highest of the high.

But what these TAKER children didn't realize, as they eagerly hopped off the bus for the only enjoyable leg of this outing, was that even on the Outside most WEs only occasionally treated themselves to "real" food. Composites also comprised the bulk of their daily sustenance. Only the JCs, along with the most successful, EASYs, POLS, GODSTERS and the like, never consumed that C-dreck. But to these TAKER children, their quarterly taste of the genuine article seemed an incomparable luxury.

Most excited by these visits was a trainee they all referred to as "Fat Boy." He was a grossly overweight sixteen-year-old who bore a striking resemblance to the old "Pillsbury Dough Boy" featured on that company's TV ads during the mid-twentieth century. Fortunately for him, his contemporaries had no knowledge of that old mascot hawking a quick and easy way to provide a family with fresh dinner rolls for the table or surely they would have christened him Pillsbury Dough Boy, rather than Fat Boy.

Every evening his pudgy, doughy fingers deftly stuffed into his mouth as many C-rations as his mom had been able to secure and fry up for him. She absolutely delighted in presenting him with this nightly heaping platter.

"Eat up my little Johnnie cakes, wouldn't want ya' ta' go ta' bed hungry. See, what your Ma can provide? Not too bad, huh?"

"Yeah Ma, ya' got it all goin' on!" he mumbled which caused him to spit out a few masticated bits.

Every last bite was washed down by gallons of high fructose sweetened, artificially flavored sodas. Even by the typical unhealthy eating patterns of most TAKERs, his habits were beyond the acceptable. Amongst a cohort with the highest rates of diabetes, hypertension, obesity and every other poor nutritionally linked disease you can think of, the extent of his food abuse was exceptional. Yet, Fat Boy, and his mother, relished it, wallowed in it, took absolute pride in this, his only claim to exceptionalism. And why not? The CSA hawked the theory of American exceptionalism morning, noon, and night, from cradle to grave. Better to excel at something, even if it killed you, than at nothing.

As the bus approached the McJoy, Fat Boy's salivary glands worked overtime. It started as a trickle of drool running down his labial crease, settling between two great mounds of fat, then turned into a torrent like a great river bursting from its banks, flooding all in its path. When the bus finally came to a halt, he bounded from the bus dashing into McJoy's [no one could hold him back so great was his exuberance] exclaiming, "What heaven ta' eat like this every day!"

As the trip's Content Facilitator gazed at Fat Boy's corpulent body, he reflected on the fact that the only time Fat Boy's usual dull gaze brightened, was when eating or contemplating food. It occurred to him that in a few years he might very well see Fat Boy again, right here at this very McCoy's, standing behind the counter flipping burgers. "If this boy's not destined to be a flipper then I have no right to be in the training business!"

Suddenly, Layla shook off this memory as her attention was drawn, once again, to Director Koningu at the podium:

"Go forth from these Project's walls confident in your future. Go forth resolved to become productive MAKERs. Go forth committed to never return to this Project except to attend to the disposal of a parent or relative. Now there's an aspirational goal!"

Layla glanced around. As the Director's speech wound down and the woofs and cheers subsided, she became aware of her fellow trainees shouting out their postings. None, however, was more joyous than Fat Boy. Jumping up and down in place, the rolls of fat undulating under his shirt like continuous waves of ocean water lapping onto a shoreline he cried out: "I'm ta' go to Zone 2! I'm going ta' be a flipper! If I work hard, bet I wind up with a contract at a McJoy. No one's goin' ta' work harder than me. No one. One day I'll be a head flipper – u'll see, just ya' all wait n' see. U'll walk inta' the baddest McJoy anywhere and there I'll be- the head flipper! Who knew I could go ta' heaven in this world!??!!!"

Pay It Forward

With few exceptions, Layla's fellow students at CCU were culled from the ranks of the children of the JCs and other economic toppers. Typically, these families set educational trusts to pay set the exorbitant cost of higher education. This permitted their children to commence their lives as Contributors with little or no debt. The average MAKER, however, didn't have the ability to shift their economic resources into such trusts. Instead WEs paid for their finishing with the "Pay it Forward" plan. All considered this a huge step forward in educational financing.

Learners attended their Finishing or Career Centers with not one red credit of upfront costs. After finishing, these newly minted MAKERs contributed a percentage of his/her income for a predetermined term of years.

After that, it was home free. Payments went back into the Educational Finance Trust Fund, a for-profit corporation whose shareholders reaped enormous profits. All agreed this system was just and fitting. It resolved the former financing problems, the burden of which, in the good Ol' USA, had fallen heavily on the public - even on those who had no children in college [where was the justice in that?]. The upshot had been that many students were priced out of the educational market or bogged down with student debt, even if their education failed to yield actual employment. Many simply defaulted. Pay it Forward connected future repayment directly to the MAKER's true earning power. Since all education was connected to workforce development, with few exceptions, an individual's investment in his or her education was value guaranteed. No more unpaid debt. No more leaving the MAKER or the Corpus holding an empty sack forcing the innocent to carry the load for the slackers. Yet another CSA success story.

Unlike the other grads, Layla was not exactly leaving the Projects. She didn't have the credits to live on the Outside as her scholarship only covered her tuition up to 75%. The rest was up to her. She could have applied Outside living expenses to her Pay it Forward plan but Layla, ever practical, thought it foolhardy to take on extra debt. As it was, she'd be paying off her education for years. That, plus her granny, determined her to live in the Projects during her CCU years even if the commute killed her. As Trudy Evermore wisely pronounced, "More is more." Now those were words to live by.

NYC, The Platform [GTE 45]

Ten years later Layla, a newly minted history Ph.D., was still in the Projects. She had twenty minutes to get her granny fed and cleaned up if she was going to get through the checkpoint and fed into the MTC system that would take her to her job at CCU.

She couldn't believe her good fortune, snagging a coveted long-term contract as a Professor in its History department.

"Luck?" her best Outside friend Francesca exclaimed. "Really, Layla, there's no such thing! It's all merit. Don't be so modest. You **earned** this!"

Truly, Layla was the envy of her classmates. She was a phenom. She was a living, walking example of the tenets of the *Book of Darwin* and the promise of the CSA all rolled into one.

CCU obviously thought she had promise. Her assigned office had a stupendous view of the Freedom Tower. Her classification as PROFFIE now permanent. Yet, despite her original resolve to leave the Projects on graduation, she remained. She simply couldn't leave her grandmother. She explored the possibility of moving her granny to the Outside. Told them she'd live with her. Promised to accept full financial responsibility. Sign any document required. The answer: "No." So she remained in her Pen in the Projects still rushing to change and feed her granny in the morning before dashing out to CCU.

Her acquaintances and friends alike chided her for expending her resources on the "old" rag. Layla's dearest Outside friend, Francesca, also a rising PROFFESSIONAL, a lawyer at a prestigious law firm, constantly questioned this bizarre living arrangement.

"But Layla," she'd say using that nasal whining voice so popular with her class, "Why, I mean, why in the globe do you stay there??"

"I have told you a million credits worth of time. It's for my granny. She raised me and I can't just abandon her."

"Well, no one would think of it as abandonment," her whine more pronounced. "You are the poster child- I mean the friggin' outstanding example of the CSA's beauty, our meritocracy. You shouldn't be living in the Projects. It's unseemly. Really Layla, it is. Leave her be and the old thing will simply fade off to the next step, just as Darwin [crossing herself] says we all must do."

"When that time comes," Layla replied patiently," it will happen and I will move out but until then…it's hard to explain, but I hear you…just don't pressure me about it anymore. Ok?"

"Oh you poor thing," crooned Francesca stroking her friend's arm much like you would a cat, "it must be so hard for you. Well, we won't talk about it anymore. Ok?"

"And stop woofing me about it too," Layla warned, "or I won't answer you. I am truly sick of this discussion. We are powering this convo down for good, agreed?"

"Promise. All deleted."

And so it went, Layla mused as she pressed the elevator's button to go up the two flights to her grandmother's Pen. She could have taken the stairs, but she wasn't in the mood for surprises. She would, she acknowledged to herself, live amongst the Outsiders one day, but she'd never be of them. *No way. It wasn't possible. I'll always be a Project case, a TAKER. It's in my bones, sunk into my very marrow and nothing can ever extract it. It's why none of these Outsiders understand my attachment to the "old rag."*

The elevator came to an abrupt halt. *Damn, stuck again.* She jumped up and down landing hard to jolt the troubled contraption back into service. After a few tries it resumed its ascent for the few feet needed to reach the second floor. As usual, the door didn't open automatically but needed a bit of assistance, which Layla provided by wedging her fingers through the door's partition area forcing it open. She stepped out and walked down the bleak corridor, its walls decorated with graffiti. She fished through her bag for the key and opened the door.

Granny was seated in her chair facing the wall.

"Granny," Layla called out to her taking the short four steps needed to cross from the door to the tiny window where the elderly woman was seated in her chair.

No answer.

Layla laid a hand on her grandmother's shoulder and her she crumpled like, well, like an old rag. She was dead.

A few hours later a truck came to take Layla's grandmother to the Disposal Center. That's where all TAKERs, and increasingly more MAKERs, went once they died. Except for the most affluent, no one wanted to expend his or her precious credits on body disposal. Darwinism and the CRS deemphasized the need for the type of pomp and ceremony that marked pre-CSA passage. All agreed these things had to be done on one's **own** time, no more taking bereavement leave. Steadily the sendoff was simplified.

Typically, a minister, priest, rabbi, imam or whatever type of traditional expediter a family used, was called in to say a few prayers and words right before the disposal truck came to pick up the body.

Anything else was simply too expensive, a waste of credits. Large memorials were reserved for the upper tiers. Increasingly, the most important departings were screened [copyright pending]. But other than that, saying one's adios to the dearly departed was a strictly private, off-hours affair.

Consequently, when poor Layla discovered her rag tag of a granny practically mummified, though only a mere fourteen hours had passed between visits, all she could do was alert Superintendent Puff-Face who simply smiled, slapped her on the back saying, "Congrats honey, your liberation is at hand. Now you can get out of this shit-hole and begin living!" And with that she waddled away to call Disposal.

Within days, Layla had found an apartment close to CCU, packed up her meager belongings, passed through the checkpoint for what she hoped would be the last time, and stepped onto the transport platform to take her to the Outside.

Chapter 17: Paul

Time is of the Essence [GTE 45]

He would not arrive on time. As soon as he stepped out of the train onto the subway platform he collapsed. Passengers nimbly stepped over him like sheep rushing to return to the safety of the barn. Who could blame them? The train was late and that meant everyone on it had to hustle to get to work on time. Music hummed in the background as they exited exhorting them to be mindful of their time requirements:

A stitch in time saves nine, a stitch in time saves lives, a stitch in time drives time, a stitch in time builds the divine, with a stich in time we will thrive... It was set to a catchy beat they all bleated as they hoofed it up the moving stairs spilling out into the street, arms rhythmically pumping to propel them even faster to their destinations.

Paul must have lain there for a good ten minutes before a Metropolitan Transit Company worker bent over him nudging him gently with his foot. Paul stirred.

"Hey Dude, you can't lie here. Unless you're gonna' expire. Are you gonna' ta'?

Paul did not respond so the MTC worker pressed on, "Well if you're not gonna' expire let's get you up and out o' here. You know what they say: up and up or down and out!" That thought seemed to amuse him provoking the emission of a cawing, crow-like sound of "down and out, down and out" over and over.

Those words, that squawking, penetrated Paul's fog, slowly rousing him. He raised himself onto his elbows attempting to snap to, but he didn't have the strength.

"Need a bit o' help, boy?" chuckled the MTC worker repeating his offer to assist.

Paul nodded.

"Well just say so! That's the trouble will all of ya' these days. No one stops to help. No one even has time, as they used to say to, 'smell the roses.'"

Still thoroughly amused by his words, the older man held out his hand to Paul. Moments went by but Paul still did not reach out.

"Take a hand when it's extended to ya'! Jeezus, u'd think I was the serpent in that old garden. Well, I'm not. Just a fellow human being offering another a helping hand up."

Grasping that what he was trying to get through to Paul was either totally alien or incomprehensible, the MTC worker repeated the CSA mantra he had mouthed earlier to Paul: "Up and up or down and out, boy! Are you gonna' let me help ya' to your feet or are you ready for 'down and out'?"

At that all too familiar admonishment, Paul held out his hand to the MTC worker who pulled him to his still shaky feet. Eye to eye with his "rescuer" he noticed the MTC worker's uniform seemed old and shabby. He had what looked like a three-day stubble on his leathery brown cheeks, while locks of frizzy, matted gray hair escaped from under his frayed MTC cap giving him an altogether grizzled appearance. Standing face to face with the man Paul realized he looked way past the age for an underground worker.

Strange MTC workers always dress in crisp blue and white uniforms, shirt collars pointed to the sky even while their feet remain planted underground. This man could never, would never, pass his daily inspection.

The older man interrupted Paul's thoughts persisting, "Can ya' speak now, boy?"

"Thanks," Paul slowly mouthed, finally fully coming to, "I just don't know what happened. The doors opened, I looked at my watch and…" Paul looked down at his empty wrist.

"OMG! Where's my watch? Where's my watch?" he screamed as he frantically began to search the platform.

After watching Paul scour the platform for a while like a tiny hamster endlessly spinning in its wheel, the MTC worker sauntered over to him laying a weather-beaten hand on Paul's shoulder parroting, "Where's my watch? Where's my watch?" he chortled.

"Where's your watch you ask? Why on someone else's wrist of course. Ya' know what they say: 'you snooze, you lose.' "

Paul's mouth dropped open. He simply couldn't fathom what was happening to him. Who was this man anyway? No MTC worker, that was for sure. But before Paul could continue his mental meltdown the greying MTC worker gave him a wink, turned on his heels, and sauntered off heading for the darkened tunnel. Right as he disappeared around the bend he looked back at Paul to give him one last bit of advice, "Ya' better hop to it son. Your day's not over yet and you know what they say, bad things come in threes."

"Paul, Paul," his Team Leader, a middling aged, middling height, middling weight, and all around middling person- the perfect middling archetype- called out to him. "I need to see you now. That's n-a-ow"

Paul glanced at the wrist where his watch used to be then looked at his cubicle's wall where his Time Keeper clocked not only the time of day, but how many hours, minutes and seconds he worked on a given task, took for lunch, snack, a bathroom break, private phone calls, office business calls... It was truly a fully commodified life and it was about to bite him in the ass

"So, Paul," his Team Leader began while waving him onto the nearby stool. A stool was considered the appropriate-style seating to offer a subordinate in a Team Leader's office as it said many things to the worker:

Don't get too comfortable.
Don't think we are going to have a two-sided convo.
Stools are precarious perches and so is your position here.
Paul sat down on the proffered stool.
"We have a situation, don't we?"
Paul merely shrugged.
"You have used up all your away time. Something I hope you noticed this firm has generously overlooked up through today."
Paul nodded in agreement. His tongue remained paralyzed. He feared he might choke if he tried to speak.
"Well, you arrived forty-eight minutes late. Did you think you could just slide into place and not be noticed? We are **all** accountable, **all** responsible for every facet of our lives. Our every choice, decision, and action is a product of our free will only limited by our genetic predisposition. PERSONAL CHOICE. PERSONAL

RESPONSIBILITY. That's what it's all about! Are you telling me you are a slacker by nature?"

Paul realized that this was a real question that required an answer. Slowly he willed his tongue to work in conjunction with his mouth and vocal chords to barely croak out, "No, no I am not."

"Well then," his Team Leader answered more cheerfully, a full grin plastered on his face, slapping the desk for emphasis. "That makes our decision **much** easier! You admit your decision to arrive late was volitional. That's wonderful. That's what the Corpus likes to hear; owning one's faults, omissions, dereliction of duty. It makes you part of the ownership community; goes a long way to putting the brakes on the slide."

Pleased with that summation he stood up, came out from behind the desk, seized Paul's hand to pump it vigorously while proclaiming, "So you agree we have to delete you, right? No other choice. None at all."

"Delete me?" Horror crept into every word.

"Yes, delete you. But since you've been so forthright about the situation **and** because your work was always excellent up 'til now, we have another opportunity available to you. Just not here, you understand."

He paused here for a moment. Clearly he expected Paul to bobble his head in agreement but Paul's face remained a frozen mask of astonishment.

Not discouraged by the silence the Team Leader continued. "In fact, this is **your** lucky day. Normally you'd just have been deleted. Down and out with your standard sixty days WE relief benefits. In your case, however, we've made an exception. This a.m. we received a job network alert that CCU is searching for a 3-D graphic designer to help with its Social Media. Knowing we were on the road to deletion I took the liberty to upload your credentials to send in the event this little chat went well. So what do you say buddy, should I press, send?"

Paul nodded vigorously.

"Ok, let's give it a go and see what shows," he joked while pressing send. A few minutes went by. They sat in silence while his Team Leader idly surfed his net on his Palm Pad until the, "ping" broke into his miasma.

"Here we go. We have an answer. So, let's see what they sa-ay." How offensive Paul thought, he's using that stupid game show voice like this is some kind of joke. But Paul said nothing. Finally, he knew better.

His soon-to-be former Team Leader instantly sent the posting to Paul's Palm Pad along with a notification that CCU would be delighted to have Paul join TEAM CCU. Paul's Palm Pad instantly glowed indicating receipt of the forward.

"Lucky for you this went so well or I wouldn't have mentioned this to you. Can't be sending the unrepentant on to other contracts on our recommendation, now can we?

"Of course not." Paul's head bobbling in agreement.

His soon-to-be former Team Leader grinned broadly. "On the basis of our fab recommendation you have a conditional contract. Only six months mind you. You get that you have to prove your worth all over again. Fortunate for you, you handled this well, took the responsibility, made no excuses." He sighed. "I don't want to know why you have fallen down, but this is your chance to pick yourself up by your boot straps, get a fresh start. Redemption, rebirth is at hand! Never let it be said the Corpus lacks compassion." God but he was pleased with himself!

Paul looked down at the "invitation" blinking at him from his Palm Pad.

"Do you accept?" it queried. "Yes," he indicated without hesitation. After all, what choice did he have?

Chapter 18: Isaac

The Cathedral of Commerce [GTE: 10]

It was not until after the Prophet's death and the Corpus' admission to the CRS as one of the Elect, a Revealed Saint, that the Faithful Ten began to contemplate a move to Wall Street. Not surprisingly, it was the CRS' financial wizard, Betty Chin, who first broached the topic at one of the Faithful Ten's regular meetings. Quite uncharacteristically, the Chin took the floor to address the Ten and Keeper Freeman. As usual, her salt and pepper hair was pulled back in a bun so tight it stretched her eyes to its furthest corners as if to say, 'See, I really am Chinese?' Like most Clarksdalian Chinese she was not "pure" Chinese. She certainly was not ashamed of this bit of burnishing but, like most of her community, the foot she put forward was more firmly bound to distant memories from across the Pacific rather than the Atlantic Ocean.

Her great-grandmother was a local African American woman. A real beauty who tossed her glossy, straight black hair at Arthur Chin every time she sauntered into the Chin's store.

"My father says you got that hair from an Indian ancestor."

She laughed. "You Chinese, r'all sure obsessed with that ancestor stuff. And it's Choctaw mind you. Lots of Choctaw in my family.

"Hmmmm...I like that," he said coming out from around the counter to fondle her hair.

Arthur was sure drawn to that hair and, truth be told, to everything else about her. Maisy was her name and one day her irate father paid a little visit to Father Chin. Twenty minutes later Arthur found himself engaged to Maisy. It was an extraordinarily fortuitous union. Maisy was a hard worker, had a keen eye for consumer trends and softened the sometimes-brusque approach the Chins took with their customers. She was the "touch" they needed. With Maisy and Arthur at the store's helm, the business exploded.

An innately sensitive soul Maisy was respectful of her in-laws' traditions, learning to cook their customary foods, which she served up every Sunday next to local Clarksdalian specialties. Jesus and crosses were added to the walls, but the ancestral altars remained well tended, always front and center. She wove the Chins into the fabric of Clarksdale even while leaving their Chinese inheritance firmly in place. Her great-granddaughter surely owed as much of her business and cultural acumen to this ancestor as to any on her paternal side.

"I know," Betty began by flashing the assembled a slight self-deprecating smile, "that I am out of order. Certainly no one appreciates order more than I, so I do beg your forgiveness for speaking out of turn; for not putting what I am about to propose on the agenda."

She glanced round the room checking to see if anyone objected. Seeing no objection she boldly moved forward.

"Why are we stuck in Savannah when we need to be on the Corpus' doorstep? Breathing the air they breathe. Let's show the public the Corpus' success is linked to their belief in the **Unmasked Word**. That salvation in the next world as well as in this world depends on following the will of the Revealed Saints as spelled out in the *Book of Darwin*. We can't do that efficiently from here. We simply must come to grips with the fact that our mission can only be fully realized by headquartering on Wall Street."

Abe Freeman now held up his hand out to stop her. "If the Lord wanted us in the belly of the beast he would have chosen someone from, say, the Projects in New York City to deliver the **Word**."

Not daunted, the Chin only lifted her chin a bit higher. Freeman knew that look. It meant she was determined on this course of action and unless he and the others had a damn good reason to deny her, she would [and should] get her way.

This particular facet of Chin always amused Freeman as it had Coyne. She was, for the most part, quiet, even at these gatherings, reporting in her perfunctory way on the finances then sitting back in her chair content to let Freeman or one of the other Living Apostles discuss the momentous matters at hand averring to the majority's will.

So when she stood in this manner he understood, indeed deeply respected, that what she was about to propose was not only carefully thought out, but planned out to the smallest detail. So, if he were wise, he would only refuse her if so signaled by the Lord.

"Maybe yes and maybe no. I don't think the two are connected. Obviously the Lord has laid out a clear mission for the CRS, for us! And what is it? We serve as midwife to an American rebirth, its restoration. We supply the spiritual fuel. And who has been more helpful in that effort than the Corpus? Who donated time for 'Faith on Fridays,' if not the Corpus? We stand as the official church of the Corpus. Shouldn't our home church be near where our dearest parishioner essentially resides?"

She paused. The Keeper waited a few seconds to make sure she was finished. He always liked to let Betty conclude before commenting on her suggestions. It was a sign of his ultimate respect for her.

"By the Coyne, if Betty doesn't make a good point, as she always does! Damn, if I don't often ponder why I was selected by our Prophet as Keeper of the Book, to lead this church and not Betty," he said with a wink of an eye and a nod of the head in Betty's direction as much out of deference to her, as to indicate he was also amused by his own thought.

"Yes, I think Betty has persuaded me. I am loath to move our headquarters to New York City. You all know where my feet are rooted. But then again, this ain't about me now is it? It's not about any of us, but what's best for the Church and the nation." He turned to Betty for emphasis.

"Betty here has rightly, mind you, reminded us **all** of our duty, our obligations to the Lord. Of the oath I swore to the Prophet as he lay dying and placed the Book in my hands. So, yes, Betty you are correct, we need to make that move."

He looked round. They were waiting for more. Betty silently nodded her head in his direction and quietly slipped back into her chair. Time to conclude.

"Of course," Freeman emphasized, "we retain our Savannah compound as the personal residence and retreat for the Book's Keeper. And the Book remains there. There's no discussion now or ever about that. It is **never** to be moved. Our temporal feet must always remain firmly planted in the rich soil from whence we came. We take our spiritual nourishment from this earth, as will all those who inherit our positions when we're gone. They will, without a doubt, require that renewal even more. Never forget, this nation's religious heart rests in the South. Agreed?"

He scanned the group feeling reassured the Ten joined with him in this. Shifting tone from stern patriarch to practical businessman he returned to Betty's proposal. "Yet, I agree with Betty, we need to make this move; to physically join as one with our Corpus. Unifying body and soul. It makes sense."

Abe Freeman, who had been seated this whole time, rose for emphasis. "So, I take it we are all agreed. We embark on this venture."

The Ten nodded their assent. Betty looked down at her still closed hands intertwined in that "here's the church" fashion which she slowly, deliberately, disengaged each from the other to lay flat on the table releasing the tiny tension butterflies her clenched hands had been holding onto. Freeman glanced her way as those butterflies flew past him.

"It's decided. Get on it Betty. Crunch your numbers; perform your usual fund raising miracles and make it happen. But, let's always remember, as Betty has reminded us, Prophet Coyne's death was not the end, but the beginning. So too, with this edifice, it's not a victory symbol, but merely a site from where we will continue our march to salvation, to rebirth. From there, with the help of our blessed Corpus, we will finish guiding the nation back to the light, back to being what President Reagan called that 'shining city upon a hill whose beacon light guides freedom-loving people everywhere.' Thank the Lord for the Revealed Saint Ronald Reagan. Amen."

"Amen," the Faithful Ten intoned in unison.

The Road Through Clarksdale [GTE 45]

Now, years later, the mammoth glass and steel structure which spiraled upwards one hundred-fifteen stories making it the tallest building in New York City, was finally ready for its dedication. It was not only located in Wall Street but in the center of CCU's Wall Street campus. Much had changed since those initial plans were made. Without a doubt both Betty Chin and Abraham Freeman were sitting on either side of the Prophet Coyne at the Apostles' table even as their children stood in their stead. Ice as the Book's Second Keeper and titular head of the CRS, and Theo Chin Chin [yes, Betty married a man with the same last name] as its CFO.

TC Chin was tapped to occupy the Cathedral's official residence. After all, it was TC who oversaw the CRS's finances, made the daily rounds to schmooze the upper echelon JCs, kept the income toppers onboard the CRS ship that was moving steadily towards the Promise Land. TC was comfortable with Wall Street and who spoke the Corpus' lingo, so who better than TC Chin? All agreed it was a natural fit.

True to his word, the son who succeeded Abe Freeman maintained his personal headquarters in Savannah where the BOOK continued to reside. Indeed, from Abe Freeman, the first Keeper of the Book who passed to his heavenly reward before the Cathedral of Commerce's completion, to Ice Freeman the Book's Second Keeper, there was a clear preference for Savannah. Nonetheless, the Cathedral's planners provided for a private apartment for the Keeper separate and apart from the Cathedral's religious and office business areas, in that edifice's post- futuristic tallest, but most diminutive in square footage spire. Neither as mammoth nor formal as the official residence TC inhabited, it had its own crown jewel, its own grace, a wrap-around terrace with sweeping views of the Freedom Tower and the Hudson River.

Ice, entourage, security, baggage, vestments, and the display **Book** all arrived a few days prior to the Cathedral's dedication. This would be the first time he occupied his apartment in the completed edifice. Like many southerners, New York City was simply not his glass of sweet tea. It was ok for a quick visit, a fancy dinner, and maybe attending some gala, but he never really felt at home in New York.

There was something alien about it, so very not-CRS. Sure, a huge number of New Yorkers [not all he lamented] attended CRS services. Some even attended in-the-being services, but most screened them. He couldn't help but suspect many programmed their screens for the 10:00 am Sunday service and then went about their business, the screen droning to an empty chair. Even the top JCs struck him as, how to diplomatically put it, not observant, not fully committed, they were fool's gold if you will.

None of this made a dent in TC. He loved New York; his pulse was set to the rhythm of commerce, the beat of the multitudes pounding that pavement in search of a credit, their fortunes if they were so blessed. He'd say, "Smell that air! Ice, my man, I smell money! And just think, these are all our parishioners. When the plate is passed they dip their card for thousands of credits at a pop! It's a blessing I tell you Ice, a blessing, manna from heaven, God's little piggy bank."

Inevitably this little speech would cause the corner of Ice's mouth to pucker in distaste. "TC, so crass. What would the public, our parishioners think if they heard such words, such sentiments fall from the mouth of one of the Ten?"

"They'd think: 'Why there's a man who knows how to put a value on his parishioners as is right and proper.' Look Ice, I know what you truly think about the One Percenters. In your book they're apostates, using the CRS to advantage themselves. But Ice, Ice, my dear friend, re-read your *Book of Darwin*! Doesn't it tell us, *Ye shall know the Revealed Saints by their worldly raiment*? Don't we celebrate the accumulation that, more often than not, is the sign of the Reveled Saint? In this very gritty world, isn't it the mark of accumulation that lets us separate the wheat from the chaff, the sinner from the saint, and even gives us the ability to remove from our midst those who would destroy us? Isn't that how we justify the Projects?"

Standing on that swank, magnificent terrace looking out over his flock's domain, he realized the truth in TC's words and looked inward at his own prejudices, stereotypes if you will, which were preventing him from fully embracing the Corpus as a true Revealed Saint. He acknowledged he had taken for granted this gift from the Lord. He examined the facts supporting this conclusion. Neither his father nor anyone who graced their inner circle sought out the Corpus. After all, the Corpus reached out to the CRS early on.

TC loved to remind him about how fortunate it was his mom, Betty, was in the habit of sitting for hours on end in that tiny CRS office in Clarksdale, waiting for the phone to ring. They maintained that office even after the move to Savannah. She just couldn't let it go.

"Church of the Revealed Saints. May we add to your blessings today and in the world to come?" She always answered the phone that way. When Freeman asked her how she came up with that greeting she merely shrugged nonchalantly adding it had simply popped out of her mouth one day. It felt right, so she stuck with it.

"Clever woman," approved the Keeper adding as he frequently did, "I often think the Lord should have anointed you as Keeper and not me.

"But **He** did," rejoined Betty, "Never forget, each according to his or her our own abilities. We work to fulfill the potential HE endowed us with, nothing more and nothing less. So says the *Book of Darwin*. Or am I mistaken, Keeper?

"Betty, no wonder we all rely on you. Well, I am glad you set me straight."

Truth be told, Freeman, like the Prophet beforehand, loved Betty best of all the Faithful Ten. Of course, he never declared this, not then nor ever. Not even as he lay dying in her arms. Innocent enough. It was in the office. They were going over accounts when he simply keeled over. Heart attack. No two ways about it. There were, for sure, some vicious rumors, whispers of a long-standing sexual relationship. None of it true. Malicious gossip all.

"So, what did the Corpus want?" Freeman asked Betty.

"To join the true Church."

"The CRS?"

"Is there any other?" she chided him. "Their spokesman said that it was time for the Corpus to, at long last, avow a religion, express its convictions like any other American citizen. After much prayer and soul searching the Lord has led them to us, to the CRS. It wants to join the CRS as a Revealed Saint."

"And what did you say?"

"I directed him to the website and told him I would send out the printed materials as well. I suggested they carefully review the criteria and, if after due consideration, Corpus still wants admission as a Revealed Saint and not just as a routine member, we would schedule an appointment for the Corpus to come to Clarksdale to make its profession of faith.

"Clarksdale, why not Savannah?"

"I thought its humble setting more fitting, more impactful."

"Betty, you really are amazing."

"I also explained that because the Corpus was not a flesh and blood being someone would have to stand in for the Corpus as its designee to make its Profession of Faith; its belief in salvation and the **Unmasking** of the true **Word** of the Lord in front of the Keeper and the Faithful Ten. Demonstrate it was more likely than not that the Corpus was a Revealed Saint. Of course, I assured him that if the Keeper and the Ten rejected the Corpus as a Reveled Saint it could still join the CRS as a regular parishioner. Just not be fully baptized."

"You did what?"

"I assured him the Corpus could still be partially baptized and join the church, simply not as a Revealed Saint. Then, Darwin be blessed, Justin Berberi himself, head of the recently created Board of Twenty, got on the line-----oh my Lord what a charmin' man [her southern accent always became more pronounced when she lapsed into any kind of reverie]. He'll be making the Profession of Faith. Can you imagine? The CEO himself! He says he is looking forward to doin' so and has no doubt but that the Corpus is a Revealed Saint."

"Betty, you are unbelievable," was all Freeman could muster while digesting that the Corpus wanted to align itself with the CRS.

A few weeks later, Betty, ever practical, on top of all things, enticed media attention of the upcoming profession using a sophisticated social media campaign.

God's secrets revealed!

What does this CEO /Billionaire know that you don't?

And they came. Tens of thousands of grasping at straws souls, anxious for hope, for salvation. They arrived from across the country. They packed themselves into vans, SUVs, and buses like sardines in a can. Families and singles, the newlyweds, the young and the old, the infirm, and people of every ethnic and religious denomination flocked to those fields outside Clarksdale, Mississippi.

Again, thanks to Betty, they were prepared. She had mega outdoor HD screens in 3D with surround sound positioned throughout the homestead's fields. She turned it into a full-on eye-filling event.

All this drew in the national media and they descended on tiny Clarksdale, crowding into that old barn Freeman had originally converted into a church when he began his own spiritual journey so many years ago. Every pew filled. The denizens of the politically powerful, the cream of the entertainment world, directors from the Board of Twenty and every hanger-on-er that could wrangle an invite, attended.

Almost all arrived clothed in the diaphanous type material that had come to epitomize a CRS church outfit. It wasn't the color that mattered, but its transparency, the lightness used to sheathe one's body in, as if to say, "See, here I am, as light as air, as ethereal as the heavens to which I aspire to one day ascend." It was an impressive show as these American lions entered this humble makeshift church, single file, in Clarksdale, Mississippi singing the CRS's traditional opening hymn.

It all worked out as Betty predicted. CEO Berberi came and, well, wowed them all.

A short man, trim, greying hair, square jawed, sure of himself despite an obvious Napoleonic complex which stuck to him like shit to a pig, he mounted that podium like Mohammed reaching the mountain top. Clothed in one of those weightless white suits streaked by barely perceptible gossamer lavender threads, he planted his feet firmly, stretched out hands to the Keeper and the Ten and declared: "Hallelujah! We are home at long last!"

He fell to his knees, arms still extended, head bowed, tears streaming down his cheeks. The church's in-the- being audience, as well as those watching on the screens in the fields, spontaneously did the same. The Keeper rose from his seat and with three quick strides reached Berberi, lifted him to his feet and embraced him. For a moment it appeared that Berberi, who stood a full head shorter than Freeman actually disappeared, simply vanished under the folds of Freeman's raiment...

Moments later, he re-emerged appearing to the audience as a man reborn, a man clarified by the *Book of Darwin.* It was as if he had gone to Heaven, been anointed by the Lord himself and returned to serve with a renewed vigor and purpose. Freeman and Berberi rippled in the shards of a late afternoon sun, which passed through the cracks in the old barn's roof. There was not a dry eye in the house. Not a dry eye in the nation.

Freeman mounted the podium.

"No more. No more. No more proof is needed. What more could we ask for? What more could the Corpus cast down at our very feet? Yes, my Beloveds, yes right here- right here I tell you- in this most humble structure, stands next to this son of the South, not just a man of God, but one who personifies the Corpus itself. Yes, my friends, corporations are people with a heart, a soul... with the need for salvation and redemption. Like you, like me, the Corpus seeks the divine in its daily existence.... except unlike you or me, the Corpus is eternal. And WE can feel comforted, yes truly comforted by this. It is God's great and generous gift to us, to the WE.

Today the circle of prosperity begun but a few short years ago is now complete with this unmasking of our one and only eternal Revealed Saint here on earth. Yet, as powerful as the Corpus might appear, pity it, as it shoulders its burden into eternity. Yes, have mercy on the Corpus who, unlike you or me, is chained to its earthly toil, on our behalf, forever...So I close by urging that when you go about your daily lives, keep these words from the *Book of Darwin* in the fore: 'Do good, by doing well.'

Now SAY AMEN!

Now give the Corpus your thanks!

Now give the Corpus your backing!

Now give the Corpus your loyalty!

Now rise... rise to your feet and say with me just one last time: AMEN!"

The whole country was whipped into a religious frenzy, like starving creatures running wildly here and there trying to eat from a small pot of bubbling stew. Revival seeds scattered across the nation's receptive soil, sprouting ripe rows of corn waiting for harvest. America saw its rich and powerful, along with its average and struggling, joined in Holy Communion, hoping to be proclaimed one of the Revealed Saints or, at least, able to join the CRS to put their feet firmly on the path towards salvation

Women with their children, grandmas and grandpas, men who had not stepped foot in church since childhood, fell to their knees praying that they too would now, or at some point, receive guarantees of their own salvation.

And, well, you all know the story, don't you? You know why such fervor to join the CRS was sparked when the Corpus joined?

Sure you do! We've come to believe that if the billionaires think something is correct or worthwhile, it must be. [Come on now don't deny it, you know you believe it too] How could a billionaire be wrong? That would be an oxymoron, wouldn't it? They're billionaires because they know best and we believe their knowledge extends into all areas. In our world money imparts automatic expertise and competency.

Think of all the things we have permitted billionaires to opine on and push on us with no indicium of expertise. They've dictated the country's educational policy; no matter they've no particular expertise in the field. We let them control the media, the message, and the political apparatus. Why? There's an unspoken consensus that money equals wisdom. Money equals expertise. Money must be followed. For generations now, it's formed one of the few remaining American hardcore beliefs. All else has been tossed into the gutter, along with the broken USA. So if the Corpus, the eternal Corpus who sets our fiscal table, is admitted into the CRS as a Revealed Saint, as one of the Elect, well, who are WE to question their choice?

Now say amen!

Finding the Muheakantuck [GTE 45]

The Second Keeper pondered the CRS's future. He fretted over its relationship to the Corpus. They were entering a new phase, all thanks to a plan set in motion by long gone Betty. How should this physical "joining' between the CRS and the Corpus unfold? Truth be told, he was not sure. In fact, if it had been his choice, he believed he would not have agreed to the plan at all. Even as a child observing the parade of representatives from the Corpus in and out of the Savannah center, he was always uncomfortable with them. He knew the Corpus was a Revealed Saint. The Corpus, indeed all the One-Percenters, were referred to in the most reverential terms. Yet, for all that, Ice Freeman never felt a connection to these most important parishioners. He was far more comfortable amongst the WE. He loved meeting them, traveling to preach at one of their church's located in an ordinary neighborhood. He much preferred that to the sleek structures that typically graced the economic toppers' communities.

He considered the CRS' edifice; it now dominated the CCU's campus even overshadowing the Freedom Tower. He pondered their decision to permanently headquarter TC and not himself in New York City. It was, he believed, a good decision, a perfect choice. TC was just the man to reap the JC harvest. True, TC was more flamboyant than his understated mother, but he shared many of her best qualities. Most importantly, like Betty, he understood the Corpus' critical role both in America's salvation, as well as in God's restoration to the public square.

The Book's young Keeper turned once again to scan the New York landscape. He could make out most of the Cathedral of Commerce's main tower ready for its dedication, undulating in a kind of MC Escher manner so that the observer was not certain where one line of steel and glass ended and another began.

He knew he was going to have to spend more time in New York than previously. He steeled himself to laugh at their jokes, attend their parties and functions, preach a few in-the-being sermons not only in the Cathedral, but in some of their local CRS churches. It was, he thought miserably, all a show. Unlike TC who loved, actually absolutely adored being in New York City, Ice couldn't wait to return to Savannah.

He had insisted his residence was sited in the smallest, though tallest spire. His only request: a sweeping view of the Hudson River. His staff was somewhat amused and bemused by this request. One assistant once asked him why he had insisted on this.

"No special reason. I just find it calming in this great city."

The real reason, however, his staff would have found even more perplexing, indeed down right disturbing. What he didn't say was that when he looked out over that river he saw the past not the present. He imagined a distant time when the Native peoples were the sole proprietors of Manhattan Island and its environs. He had never shared this thought, this inner-space with anyone, though many knew he was a bit of a history buff. They chalked it up to his "calling." As the Keeper of the Book, of the unseen, unmasked truth, his attraction to history seemed natural.

Few people, anymore, were truly interested in history. It was so yesterday, so days past, with little, most agreed, utility. People today are content with whatever content had been downloaded for their consumption at their respective learning centers. Indeed, the old history as written before the Great Transformation was largely discredited, considered the partisan rantings of a failed society. No one except historians or, on occasion, other professionals, ever read it any longer. It was never destroyed, of course not, the First Amendment was still enshrined in the CSA Constitution, but it was no longer published or readily available. It was only not accessible through the remaining few extant in-the-being libraries, like the Library of Congress in D.C or the great 42d Street Library in New York City [the "public" long ago excised from its name], which the general population toured mostly via virtual tours as one would a museum. Their vast collections were accessible only to a handful of pre-approved scholars.

The Book's Second Keeper was one of the privileged few with instant access to in-the-being books because he was the owner of an extensive private library. It turned out the Prophet was a bit of a bibliophile; in particular a collector of books on American history and had amassed quite a collection.

On his death, Abraham Freeman became their custodian. In truth, his father had little interest in these. He never once cracked open even one of those sealed crates to peruse its content. He simply dutifully stored them in airtight containers to protect their fragile paper pages from the environment and promptly forgot them. There they remained, untouched, in a large storage room in the Savannah compound, which became a favorite play area for Ice when he was a child.

All manner of artifacts were stored there. As a child this was his favorite spot in the Savannah compound; it was his secret sanctuary. Ice's mother had fueled his love of history and things long gone by reading to him a few old books she had inherited from her grandmother. His favorite was Robert Louis Stevenson's *Treasure Island* and it was in that storage room where he reenacted Stevenson's classic tale over and over. His many forays uncovered old clothing, telephones, old TV screens, and all manner of crusted artifacts. But what most intrigued young Ice were those tightly wrapped, sealed large crates. Try as he might these resisted all efforts at unsealing. He could have simply hacked the boxes open but that would have been unthinkable. Ever meticulous, he was always careful not to damage the treasures. Once playtime was over he carefully and precisely returned everything to the same spot where he found them.

No surprise that after his revered progenitor passed from this world, one of the first things Ice did was open those sealed crates. On unpacking them, Ice realized that this was truly the storage room's real treasure- hundreds and hundreds of old books- some novels, but mostly histories. Ice not only unpacked them, but also built that very private library in his sweeping Savannah residence to house both the original *Book of Darwin* along with the complete collection he inherited.

Certainly, Ice couldn't claim to have read them all, or even digested many completely. Instead, busy man he was, when he retreated to his oh so private, secret sanctuary he would pull a volume off the shelf, sometimes quite randomly, and read a chapter or two. He was particularly fascinated by early American history. Most recently he had taken to reading chapters on the Native peoples' encounters with the early European colonists. He was surprised by what he read.

Diverging from the prevailing "restored" history, these books portrayed the Native peoples as comprised of a multitude of groups, each with their own unique way of life and culture; many quite sophisticated, but all meritorious. At least that's what the old history claimed. Even more surprising, the Europeans were not depicted as purveyors of Christian charity who watched in horror as the Native people rejected the **Truth** and literally devoured themselves with greed and debauchery. Quite to the contrary, these old histories claimed the Europeans unwittingly infected a heretofore-pristine land and people with all manner of infectious diseases while brutally driving them from their domains.

At first he was shocked to read this. But little by little he began to doubt the restored history. He thought most about this when in New York City. Perhaps it was the view of the Hudson River, which imparted such thoughts. Even on this visit for the dedication he couldn't quite stop himself from thinking about this. Shading his eyes to its final closure he imagined the Hudson River's original glory. In his mind it flowed free and uncluttered. No PCBs, no man-made junk and sewage eating away at its majesty marred its course. It was an all-giving mother to every living thing that touched its banks and waters. This, he thought, must have been what Henry

Hudson saw when Halve Maen tumbled into that river's magnificent headwaters in its futile attempt to find a non-existent Northwest Passage across the continent to Asia.

The Lenape, the region's original inhabitants, fittingly called it the Muheakantuck, "the river which flows both ways." How the Muheakantuck must have teemed with fish; the fowl swooping in for an easy supper, Algonquian canoes laden with the river's bounty drifting down river to their awaiting families. What a marvelous life that must have been, he silently told himself.

As he opened his eyes taking in the glass and steel structures that framed the former Muheakantuck's banks, the rush of traffic, along with the multitude of small delivery drones that now displaced the flocks of birds once so numerous they blocked the sun's rays as they passed by, he asked himself, how anyone could have despoiled such a landscape?

To this picture he added the miniature human dots more than one hundred stories below from where he stood that moved in an undulating assembly-like fashion. It reminded him of the ant farms he used to love to watch during their frequent visits to Clarksdale back when he was a little boy. They'd go to the local pet store and Ice would immediately rush over to the case that held the ant farm. He would stand so still he looked like one of those wax figures in Madam Tussaud's, observing the endless stream of worker ants going round and round and round the farm's tiny paths so fast, so abundant, they formed a solid strong black line becoming one with the path. Yes, he murmured to himself, the workers, the path, and even the river was one. It must, he reassured himself shrugging off a tiny tugging feeling in his gut suggesting that maybe, just maybe, something was not quite right, be God's plan for them all. That very notion made him shiver in discomfort, made him glance longingly for just the briefest instant at the Muheakantuck River. He forced his eyes closed. When he looked again all traces of the past were gone and it was nothing but the same as ever Hudson River.

"Say Hallelujah," he shouted into the air, turning to walk confidently back into his life.

Chapter 19: Handler

One Hand Washes the Other [GTE, 45]

Assam Handler, the recently appointed CCU Chancellor, stepped back from behind his desk and turned towards a very ornate, rococo style mirror hanging on the wall to his right. He stared hard at the reflection, critically eyeing every detail of his paper-thin looking white suit shot through with silver-gray and violet threads, the school's colors. He actually hated wearing those CRS *I'm a goin' to church* garments. He worried these might suddenly tear away leaving him exposed. He loosened his white tie; it looked too tight. Only the insecure walked around with tight ties- everyone said so. Not a good image. Next he picked up the suit sweeper passing it over the garment. No creases, no lint, no hairs, he needed to look perfect. He was about to turn from the mirror when he picked up a wide handless hairbrush (reminiscent of the kind for horse grooming) using it to smooth back his full head of slick black hair until it resembled more a deep, dark puddle of oil than hair.

Just about ready for my big day!

No doubt today was Chancellor Assam Handler's big day. A year ago he thought he had ascended to his mountain's highest peak, but now he realized that was just the beginning for him. There was another one on his horizon just waiting for him to scale. All he needed to do was keep climbing steadily with a sure foot. He'd get there, no doubt.

In just an hour he would receive the Reverend Isaac Freeman, head of the Church of the Revealed Saints. In just an hour he and Ice would be hand in glove. They would be intimates. He would seamlessly glide, as he had done within the STD, through that pipeline, into the CRS's inner circle.

Yeah, I'll be calling him Ice soon enough! Just do what you have always done Assam. Watch carefully, don't leap precipitously, know all the players, and position yourself for success.

That's what he had done all his life, from his humble start as a Content Facilitator to bumping off that SOB Darkit who had it in for him, he was ever at the ready to grab new opportunities, to vanquish those who would stop him. His meteoric rise through the ranks of the CCU system distinguished him as a premiere Maker. He was even reclassified as a top tier PROFFIE, all thanks to careful planning, preparation, and execution. This was where he excelled. Praise Darwin, he was truly one of the finest examples of "survival of the fittest."

The dedication of the CRS Cathedral of Commerce was a national event. Now, only sixty short minutes away from being projected onto every screen across the CSA, even around the globe. The Corpus had declared this as a "National Hour of Screen Time." Screens in every office, in every work site, in every corner of the land were tuned to it. All eyes glued. No looking away! No vacay time deducted for viewing. That's how important this was.

And why not? This was no ordinary structure. It was the CRS's new, official spiritual center located right in the heart of the CCU campus. It completed the circle of private interests- education, religion, and business - all sited in Wall Street. Consolidation, consultation, coordination; could there be anything more appropriate, more conducive to the CSA's next great leap forward? Even self-assured Handler, ambitious Handler who did not believe in luck but in hard, determined work combined with genetic aptitude, couldn't believe his good luck. He actually used that phrase but, of course, only to himself. When he stood at that mirror he mouthed at his reflection: *You are one lucky SOB! That's right, one lucky guy!* Everything he had achieved, had plotted, worked, and schemed for was materializing on this one day. Yet he had no hand in this event at all. It had just fallen into his lap. Like manna from Heaven. And who was he to turn down Heaven?

The highlight [at least for Handler] would occur right after Freeman blessed and sanctified the new structure. At that time he would lay hands on Handler as well. Handler reflected how things had changed from those touch and go days back at his old Learning Center when the Head Programmer Darkit went after him like a mongoose goes after a rat.

That soon to be rag sharpened his teeth and went in for the kill. Or so he thought. But Handler's deft rebuttal to Darkit's report condemning that in-the-being trip as a massive waste of resources- attempting to label him as a "Waster"- backfired on the old fox. To Darkit's absolute astonishment Central Systems loved, absolutely adored, how Handler was able to impress his WEs in -the –making with the importance of living a fully commodified, value driven life. Central Systems positively gushed over how he drove home the perils of non-conformity, of raising one's eyes above one's ordained station in life. It was all so subtle, yet so effective, that Central Systems actually turned this little lesson into a virtual trip for the standard curriculum.

"Fucking, unbelievable," Darkit had fumed, "Well, I am not done with him yet. Yes, he's one of the best I've had to confront, but it's not over between us- not yet. I'll have him busted down to a TAKER by the time I'm done with him."

Darwin tells us that society is based on "survival of the fittest." Darwin teaches us that, with few exceptions, at some point in life your time in the sun is over. Like the Rise and Fall of the Roman Empire; like the decline of the good ol' USA, all things and people will ultimately be replaced by something better, more efficient, smarter. Someone, somewhere will, one day, build that better mousetrap. In other words, "every dog gets his day." And, yes, one day every dog has to be put down. Yet even as that day approached, Darkit never saw it coming. He simply couldn't or wouldn't accept the fact that he was about to be put to sleep. No matter. It was already written in the stars ready made for Handler to catch and rise.

These thoughts gave him pause. Told him to reconsider his fancies about luck. Luck went contrary to all he believed, had imbibed in this blessed new realm. Maybe it wasn't luck after all, but the revelation of Grace, his Grace, his salvation in this world and thereafter. And then it hit him; he was a fucking Revealed Saint.

Chapter 20: Paul

CCU [GTE, 45]

Paul seamlessly transitioned into his new position at CCU. It was all so easy he was actually caught off-guard. Astounded more like it. There were numerous facets to this new life he genuinely liked better. True, this new position paid a bit less, but it was also less regimented, more convivial. He had never associated conviviality with work, an altogether new experience. And that wasn't his only revelation. The Social Media [SM] department expected him to not only design graphics but also help plan the underlying campaigns. It was an eye-opener to him that he was much more versatile than he ever imagined. Certainly more than indicated by his SAT and routine assessments. *Paul don't go there,* he reminded himself. So he moved onto safer thoughts.

He glanced around the office. It was a large open space for the most part, with screens and holographic projectors filling the wall. A few partitioned areas, the Team Leader's larger office with its wall of windows permitting him to scan, with a single glance, the entire office, a number of desks placed throughout the space equipped with a Time Keeper, and several conference tables completed the office. In reality, Paul had never seen such a jumble. At first, it disconcerted him, unnerved him, and even triggered a momentary panic attack. On seeing Paul's look of bewilderment as he stepped foot into the office, Team Leader Bill Symone took him by the arm, calling the others to gather round.

"Look up. Yes, actually give me your eyes. This here's your new teammate, Paul Gaugin. He comes to us from that mega SM firm, *Trendytrends* right up on Madison Avenue. Some of you might remember the Botanical campaign from a season ago- Paul here created those stylin' graphics [murmurs of approval]. So when I received his CV, well, I snapped him up. Let's welcome him, show him around. I think our physical layout is a bit different than what he's used to. And remember, he's got to get integrated into our collective hustle vibe. But hey, it's an award winning method, so I am sure Paul here will fall into line with us real quick."

He turned to Paul with one of those tooth whitener grins, signaling he expected an answer.

"Yeah, sure. Sounds great to me. I'm a team player. You'll see!"

"So glad to hear that Paul." [Nod, Nod] "Hey guys, let's give him a round of applause and a big ol' CCU welcome!"

[Applause, Applause. Woofs, Woofs.]

"Now get back to work before I delete you all. Ha, ha!!!!"

At least he had a desk- right over in the northwestern corner of the office, but he didn't sit all day, as in his former space grinding away. Yeah, there was a small Time Keeper on his desk, but it didn't loom over him as it had at his last gig. Instead, he and the others, tended to spend most of their time gathered at the large round table centered in the office. Team Leader Symone referred to it as the "Brain Trust." Only when they were in the last stages of finalizing or turning an idea into a completed campaign and he needed to polish the 3-D part did he spend much time at his desk.

When he first arrived this whole method of production confused him. "How," he inquired, "could the Time Keeper monitor and verify his productivity if he was wandering around like this all the time?

"Don't mess yourself. Since we move about all day you'll be equipped with a remote Time Keeper as your primary tracker. The Time Keeper in the center of the room is for undifferentiated productivity, which we use to substantiate our team activities. Then it's divided up using an algorithm the Commodifiers have devised to individually credit the participants with the activity. It sounds complicated, right? But we've never had any complaints. Nope, no squawks! No quejas. It's true that initially our methodology was widely questioned. There was doubt. Sure there was! But we collected the initial data, presented our system to the CCU Board for approval to go forward with it as a pilot program. They agreed. After two years the CCU director placed it in front of our local STD board and they gave it the nod and moved our proposed method up the food chain to the BoT – the big Board of Twenty. They granted us provisional dispensation to move forward for another three quarters. A year later we were fully pardoned and given permission to permanently implement. And get this: the idea is spreading to other sectors. You might say you are now a member of a pioneering organization."

"I am impressed. So glad you brought me on. I promise to give you all the time owed and more."

"That's what we like to hear," Symone exclaimed while back slapping him in a gesture of familiarity, "No slackers only producers on the go."

At least I'm not stuck all day in a windowless cube with only that damn Time Keeper as my constant companion.

He was up and about during the day visiting the many departments that comprised the behemoth CCU campus. Actual in-the-being visits, not just Palm Pad-to-Palm Pad meetings. He found these quite enjoyable. Imagine that!

So, no surprise when one morning his Team Leader told him to, "Hustle on over to the History Department. Talk to Anita Triquot – she's the Chair - you know that, right? Anyway, tell her we need to get her enrollment numbers up so, we are planning a big SM campaign for her. Just go and dope it out for us. You know what I mean- right?"

"Sure, sure I gotcha.' But remember my graphics from the Botanical Garden campaign…"

Symone cut him off, "Listen; there's no credit in our bank for that. And anyway, you know what they say, 'Your credit is only good for now.' What you did may have gotten you here, but to stay and surge, you need to ride the current production wave or you become one of those *Where Are They Now?* people." He chuckled at that. "Well, I do love that show, don't you?"

"Ahh, yeah, sure…"

"You know, what I really love about that show? How the Remi first puts up on the screen all the highlights of these now losers' former glories, then sneaks up on those has-beens and confronts them with it. Shows them their descent into whatever pit they've fallen into. We get to watch their utter horror and embarrassment as they are forced to watch their epic fall, then, bang, it ends with the message: 'You are either a TAKER or a MAKER. It's all up to you!' It's the theory of the Just Universe personified. Get it?"

"Gotcha," Paul proclaimed with great enthusiasm running out the door humming, "I'm a MAKER, not a TAKER, I'm a MAKER not a TAKER, I'm a MAKER not a TAKER..."

Paul was humming this little ditty when he literally ran right into Layla. He had just entered the History Department sector using his Palm Pad's third eye as his guide to Triquot's office when the accident occurred. He literally knocked poor Layla to the ground. Not an unusual occurrence. These days it is a common source of pedestrian accidents. You know how it is: you are in a rush, got to get to that appointment, be on time or lose those credits. You're being guided to your destination by your third eye and simply don't see the other person when, wham! Down someone goes. Will the transgressor stop? Will she make amends? Does anyone even care? Answer: usually not. Everyone understands, each to his own world, each to his own needs, but all in the service of the Corpus without which there are no MAKERS only TAKERs. It is the Corpus [blessed be the JCs] that is the ultimate MAKER and all trickles down from there. So the working assumption: such accidents simply result from each person's cherished need [truly more akin to a right] to keep their clock. The parties struggle to their feet, regain their equilibrium or whatever recalibration is required and off each goes. No apologies needed. And anyway, that would simply have wasted more precious time.

Layla, however, raised behind the Projects' walls was not always as observant of such niceties. In the Projects you watched your back, let no insult go un-contested. Theirs was **not** a fully commodified world, but something more akin to the Wild West of comic book lore. Sure, everyone was assigned to some type of labor. You wanted food- you worked at your assigned task. You wanted to keep your Pen- you performed some type of labor. But behind those gates TAKERs routinely exchanged shifts, traded items, credits and anything else of value on a kind of ad hoc black market. The Projects' dwellers made use of every scrap of crap that could be pillaged or scrounged from whatever source was readily available. Theft, not surprisingly, was rampant. Some thieves were so artful it was rumored they could steal the socks off their victims' feet without removing their shoes.

And the guns, well these were everywhere. Shootouts, drive - byes, gangs, and revenge murders were rampant. But God, did it make good screen. I mean really good 3-D screen. Sometimes, entire sections of a Project were drawn into these blood feuds. Better staged than any movie. It was jam packed with copious amounts of blood, civilian causalities and simple horror beyond human comprehension, all projected for Outsiders' viewing pleasure.

As a rule the Project Peacekeepers stood idly by for much of the carnage. Sometimes even rooting for one faction or another, placing bets. At a certain point however, they'd moved in, stop the bloodletting, and call it a day. Let sufficient numbers of these TAKERs live to fight another day – the ratings were, after all, fantastic!

When the dust and din of the explosions finally subsided the Project maintenance squads moved in with their zippered black body bags to unceremoniously shovel them in, tossing those dusky jackets into huge trash incinerators. The message conveyed by the use of these mobile furnaces: TAKERs are human garbage.

The "Outsiders" as the TAKERs called those living beyond the Projects' walls, are the real audience for this regular dose of carnage. It's both repellant and compelling. The best way to watch- or really virtually participate in these bloodbaths, is to don your U-R- Dare and drop yourself into the action. The WE, in particular, lap this up. They get to shoot and kill those lazy, good-for-nothing TAKERs who would, if given the chance, drag the rest of them down into the shithole that are the Projects. They'd destroy that warm blanket the Corpus provides. Send them all back to the bad ol' days. Beyond that, the audience got to experience firsthand the horrors that lay within the Projects' walls. No one really wants to go there in- the-being. No one really wants to lose the ability to disengage from that U- R –Dare. *May the Corpus forbid*, all intone crossing themselves!

All told, it was great advertisement for towing the corporate line on the Outside. What sane human being would ever risk consignment to such a life?

Raised in that environment, Layla, understandably, didn't suffer unwanted or casual rough touching readily. She tended to react defensively. Once sprawled on the ground she instinctively reached out grabbing Paul by the ankle sending him to ground beside her.

"What did you do that for?" he countered looking at her dead in the face. Even this was a somewhat new experience for him as everyone is now so much in the habit of looking down at a screen or into a third eye which redirects us to something only viewed in our own mind. It has, arguably, resulted in the habit of never looking anyone directly in the eye, never holding anyone's gaze. Nowadays, eye-to-eye lock is something to be avoided. It happens only as an acknowledgment of power positions. Like in, *look at me when I am speaking to you.* No rejoinder expected other than acquiescence with brief words or a gesture. Eyes lock onto mechanical devices such as third eyes and screens. And yes, eyes lock onto the incomprehensible in that brief second before we pass from this world to whatever awaits us... but not, as a rule, on each other.

The least eye lock adverse are the JCs who spend their 365s accepting submission, while the most eye lock adverse are the WEs who spend their 365s submitting and pleasing almost everyone. WEs have become so accustomed to looking down that even in bed WEs rarely look at one another too directly. A WE will look at almost any other body part and even at different parts of the face solely to avoid the eyes. Otherwise, eyes tend to be in a constant state of roaming. An instant giveaway that a person is an elevated WE is that tendency to look away. This was something Handler worked very hard to discard, spending many hours in front of a Third-Eye holographic projection holding imaginary conversations where he stares intently into those virtual eyes. Ironically, it was, his most difficult challenge.

TAKERs do not suffer from this disability. Theirs is an in-your-face community. A cut-the-shit community. No Third-Eye mediates their reality. No Palm Pads steer their vision continually downwards. Screens are, of course, installed in every TAKER Pen as they dub their nano-apartments, but these simply engender resentment and anger. A bit like the scene in that ancient movie *Doctor Zhivago* where the heroine, Lara, a member of the humble proletariat in Czarist Russia, stands outside a glam restaurant, nose pressed to the window.

It's nighttime in St. Petersburg, the snow is falling fast while she peeks through a frosty window revealing a festive, luxurious gala; exotic hothouse flowers provide color contrasting the exterior's wall of white, chandeliers dazzle, candles blaze, a gigantic hearth provides warmth in stark contrast to her situation. She sees the man she loves, the rich, privileged and oh so very handsome Dr. Zhivago. He is laughing, drinking champagne, eating caviar, and dancing with his pretty and equally privileged wife. And at that moment, Lara knows that world can never be hers, any more than her lover can be. The socio-economic chasm is simply too great.

Dr. Zhivago, originally a novel, was hailed as one of the great love stories of the twentieth century. The story spanned from Czarist Russia through the Russian Revolution and into its communist era. Poor Dr. Zhivago, even after the revolution he wants to observe the niceties. He can never adapt to the new order the 1917 Russian Revolution deposited on his doorstep. But Lara, born and bred in the bowels of working class Russia, is a survivor. She gets it. Always got it. Knows how to make it in whatever reality she's dropped into.

Our Layla is a bit like Lara. Place her in the Projects she will survive. Place her as a PROFFIE in CCU she will survive. So when Paul landed almost face- to- face with Layla, she locked eyes demanding: *what do you mean by knocking me to the ground?*

"I didn't mean anything," he meekly responded while getting to his feet offering her something he never did, a hand up. She grabbed his hand, hauling herself upright so they were again eye-to-eye.

"Where I come from when you do something like that you're looking for something. Are you looking for something?" She demanded.

But before poor Paul could interject she exclaimed, "And you ruined my sheers as well! And I just bought these," she pointed at her magenta and black striped sheers ripped, but still clinging to her legs.

"Where you come from??" he queried. He couldn't fathom what she meant by that, but almost didn't care. He was, for the first time in his life, suddenly arrested, struck by another human being's presence. He actually wanted to look at her directly. Not just communicate via a woof or pictogram. He wanted to exchange actual in-the being words, thoughts with her.

The feeling was so overwhelming, yet so unknown to him, that it was more stunning than the physical collision.

"Yeah, well, forget it. Just watch where you are going," she warned him while brushing herself off and continuing down the hall.

"Wait," Paul called out to her," I need to ask you something.

She stopped, pivoting towards him, "What now? I am already late for a meeting and look like I was dragged through a body disposal truck. Isn't that enough for one day or do you want me flagged as a Waster as well??"

"No, no, of course not. It's just that, well, look what I did to you. Let me take you for a bite. Maybe after work? It's Friday after all, so no rush for the next. Oh, I'm Paul Gaugin in SM. We could meet at the main portal. How about at 7:00 pm? What do you say?

She eyed him warily. Looked him up and down. He wasn't bad looking. In fact, he was quite striking. He had a slim but nice build – maybe around 5'10 - his heart shaped face was framed by wonderful loose sandy brown curls, a honey complexion, full mouth and grey-green eyes. Yes, he was nice eye candy at that. But SM? What could he possibly have to say to her? Yet, she did find him attractive and no, she wasn't seeing anyone either in-the-being or virtually so, why not, she told herself.

"Ok, 7:00 pm at the main portal. Don't be late. I can't abide Wasters. It's my off time after all."

"Of course not. I understand. Maybe we can get a drink and some convo? Ok? Is it a meet?"

"Ok, and since you didn't ask, I'm Layla," she called out while turning her back to him, promptly disappearing down the corridor.

Tick, tick, tick, the day dragged for Paul. His meeting with Triquot went fine. His report back to the team was ok. She understood what was needed and agreed to give them her full cooperation. Whatever they required was at their disposal. Of course, she didn't want any department deletions [certainly not her own position!!!]. She got it, despite PROFFIEs' reputation as individuals whose heads were up their asses. Did SM really think she had gotten to her position by being oblivious to life's realities? She understood the lay of the land quite well, thank you so much. In fact, she asked Paul to deliver Symone her personal, in-the-being message that she totally, absolutely, appreciated SM's efforts on their behalf.

When Paul delivered this part of the message to the Team they broke into loud laughter and even applauded.

"Got the PROFFIEs on the defensive!" called out one team member.

"She knows whose gonna' butter her bread," called out another.

"I bet we win the CCU Big Booster award this year," cackled one of the older team members.

"Yeah, yeah," Symone rejoined holding up his hand for Team silence. All getting a bit ahead of yourselves, aren't you? We gotta' produce the results. Triqout's success from this moment forward til' the campaign is complete is our success as well. So, let's get going on it."

He turned to Paul directing, "So, stretch it all out for us. What do they have going for them that we can hook onto and sell to the knowledge consumer?"

Here was something Paul was still getting used to- being asked to proactively lay out his opinion before a group. Bit by bit he was growing accustomed to it- but it wasn't easy. Over the years of trackings and assessments his education had been steadily narrowed, fine-tuned they would say, towards a career in the arts generally and eventually the graphic arts. The result? Paul's educational exposure increasingly became ever more constricted and tailored as he moved through that educational pipeline.

Of course, Paul was not alone in this. Americans had become convinced over time that education should be narrowly focused on employment acquisition and retention. "Workforce ready" as they say. They gave up on the notion it was or should be anything more. So, there was little resistance when STD enacted such policies in the interest of resource conservation. Why expend time and money trying to stuff math, for instance, into the head of a student deemed not adept at it, or the verbal arts, or whatever subject the Assessors declared a given student had little aptitude or need for? The collective wisdom: don't waste resources; don't risk student failure. Instead the new goal became to push, push and push each student into an occupational box early. The result was that Paul's prior exposure to expository writing or even speaking, was fairly limited. Placed in his current situation he was playing catch-up. To fill the gap, he had enrolled in an online oral communications course. It was worth it, but costing him a pretty credit!

Paul dashed out of the SM office precisely at 7 pm.

"Where are you off to in such a rush?" one of his teammates asked.

"Nowhere really, just meeting a friend. I don't want to be late."

"Well, she must be some friend. Just palm her. Tell her you'll be a few minutes late."

"No, gotta' be there in-the-being- face time only- no palming, no holo images. See you Monday." Out he dashed.

Paul arrived precisely at 7:00 pm, yet by 7:16 pm Layla had still not appeared. Should he wait? He couldn't palm her since he didn't have her number. She was in such a rush; their meeting well, so precarious, he hadn't even thought to exchange contacts. Maybe she was blowing him off? Forgot about him? Payback for ruining her sheers. All these strings unwinding in his brain like pulling a dangling yarn from a sweater.

Another ten minutes elapsed before Layla walked through the portal. When she saw him, a surprised look spread across her face- had she forgotten him after all?

"Hey you," she called to him, "Still here? You actually waited? My, how unusual for one of you people."

"Why do you keep referring to me like that? You people? Like you're from somewhere or something else. What's up with that?"

She grabbed him by the arm, pulling him from that spot.

"Shut up. Let's go."

She led him down into the subway's first class entrance swiping her palm access twice- once for her and once for him. He now eyed her differently. Who was she? He assumed she was a Secrey or low-level instructor at CCU on a renewable contract. No WE he knew would waste their credits on first class. He could hear Trudy Evermore chanting, "More is more, more is more... so save those credits for something more...." She obviously wasn't thinking about this, so who was she?

He hesitated to go down with her. He paused, but she urged him on.

"Come on. What are you waiting for? The fare is paid. Let's go."

He followed putting one foot in front of the other, slid his body through the turnstile and into a new world.

He marveled at the difference between first and ordinary class. These subway cars were luxurious; comfortable plush seats, screens lining the car walls advertising exotic in-the-being vacays and events, and there were even seat belts. Clearly someone was concerned for these passengers' safety. No one stood; all were seated. This, more than anything, amazed him. *How could they know how many people would board?* He simply sat there saying nothing. He was grateful Layla left him alone. Once she had informed him she was a PROFFIE he didn't know what he would say to her now or when they got to their destination. As the train moved seamlessly to wherever they were headed, he was beginning to regret this little foray

Into the Weeds

Layla nudged him gently. "We get out here." He obediently rose from his seat following her out the door, up the moving stair conveyer that he usually sprinted up, but that he noted she and the others simply let deliver them to the street. All around him were well-heeled people who were clearly not WEs but POLs, EASYS, JCs, and all manner of economic toppers. He suddenly realized he had never fully experienced these people in their native habitat. Sure he saw them on the screen, in the workplace, barking orders, delivering ultimatums, in the digital mags at their glam parties, walking the red carpet, and in so many other settings. But never, never, in such a large and unscripted in-the–being setting. Of course, he knew the top tiers travelled first class. They were all living first class lives. They earned it, they deserved it; the natural order of the world dictated this result. But seeing it unmediated by a screen or the formalities of the workplace was something else altogether. He smelled their distinctive odor, felt the purified air they moved in and he suddenly realized, perhaps the first time in his life, theirs was a world not simply filled with more consumer goods, but its woof and warp was completely different from the world the WE inhabited. They might as well live in different countries.

Why in the world had he asked her out? Just like his other attempted forays into the world outside the WE, no good could possibly come of this. Too late now he thought, as he meekly permitted the conveyer to spit him out into a perfect fall evening.

Layla led him to an exclusive weed bar. Of course, he had never been, but like most WEs he followed such venues' openings and closings on "What's Trending." He might not be a PROFFESSIONAL, but he was no newbie either. He may never have stepped foot in such a place, but thanks to the wonders of 3-D screen he was fully conversant with the layout, with the scene. *So, pull up your big boy britches, act like you belong and you will.*

Layla was known. The compère, a stunning blonde with the silkiest straightest blonde hair imaginable punctuated by shimmering lavender tips and eyes and lashes to match, slid over to Layla grabbing her two hands, kissing their palms exclaiming, "Welcome back dearest Proffie. It's been, Hao jiu mei jian! Haven't seen you in mad long! What's kept you from us? Not another weed bar I hope?"

The corners of her lavender soaked lips puckered into an enchanting pout as she raised a few strands of her hair hitting Layla on her shoulder to emphasize her disappointment.

"Of course not Marta, you are my one and only toke proffer- as least for now," she laughed brightly.

"Understood. 'Til the next big thing comes along. But I'll be in on that too. For sure I will."

"Of course you will. Who understands our needs better than you my darling?" she cooed to Paul's surprise who, up to this point, had not seen this softer side of Layla.

This compliment plastered a broad smile on those lavender lips. Satisfied she still had one of her regular consumers in tow she gestured to Paul. "Who's this new tidbit you've wound in?"

She flicked her tongue in his direction to signal she'd devour him if she could. Paul was, after all, a total package. A perfect blend of that combo beauty so prized these days. Something many paid to obtain, but which was so apparently Paul's by birth: the latte blended skin, large grey-green eyes with just a hint of a tilt, bounteous mouth simply ready for anything, that ever popular aquiline nose, and a slender metrosexual build which Layla found particularly attractive.

So what if he was a WE? Layla thought, as she looked him over again, *I've been with far less.*

"This is Paul," she informed as she pulled him towards her in a rather possessive gesture. Then leaning into Marta she whispered in her ear, "He's a WE, poor thing! But who could resist. Just look at him."

Marta tittered, "No doubt, no doubt but he's eyelightful! Where did you find him?"

"Oh," giggled Layla, "you might say I simply ran into him."

"Well, good for you! Ah! The perfect table for you two has just opened up. Please to follow me." She picked up menus and moved into the bar's interior.

Marta seated them at a small, but centrally located floating table from where they could take in the entire scene. It was truly glorious. It totally lived up to the hype. A large steel bar framed the space so the servers could access the product effortlessly. Patrons sidled up to the bar standing three deep while the fortunate few found seating on lavender lined stools - yes, the color of the moment.

They were texting their orders "Crave," "Bursting Bubbles" "Always Gold" via finger-bugs which electronically signaled to the budtender the desired jay size and blend. Those seated at the bar were given small, elaborate, colorfully decorated bongs with mouthpieces shaped like animals- leopards, lions, ospreys, and flamingos. So charming! So retro! The room itself seemed to float thanks to the miracle of holographic design that permitted restaurateurs to continually update their venues without physically demolishing a space. So cost effective!

Paul, keyed into design as he was, chatted away about the design of the bar, the nature of the software employed to create the setting, the estimated costs of production, the time spent in its design and so forth.

"Why Paul," commented Layla, her voice drenched in boredom, "I hope you are not going to be so dull all evening. Do I really give a good god damn how this space came to be? No."

He closed his mouth and simply blinked at her. She was a PROFFIE after all, what was there to say? Nothing, it appeared. They sat in silence, each staring down at their Palm Pads for quite some time until [Praise be to Darwin] the bongs went down on the table.

"Here you go," their server motioned as she set two very large, very elaborate water bongs on the table, "Sopresatta and Kush," some of the house's best. Goza!"

Layla motioned to Paul. "Take a hit and let's try that convo again."

Paul obediently leaned forward and took a deep hit of Kush. His curls enveloped his face intertwining with the bong's mouthpiece so that the bong's tube appeared a natural extension of his mouth. He breathed in deeply falling back against the plush semi-circle banquette. Layla followed suit turning to Paul brushing his hair from his face musing, "What lovely eyes you have."

"You really think so? Or is that the Kush speaking?"

"The eyes, the lips, the teeth, the nose, the hair...should I go on?"

"No, I get the idea. You just want to get laid. Fuck a good looking WE. Better than an average one. At least you can excuse this slip to your friends. I can hear it now: *What was it like? Why did you do it?* And you'll answer: *I thought of it as research; a little Darwinian experiment. And, anyway, he was drop dead gorgeous.* That's how that convo will go down."

"Is that what you think? I am some PROFFIE amusing myself with you? Conducting some cross-tier experiment or dalliance? Yeah, you're good looking, but don't think there aren't PROFFIEs or JCs or EASYs- particularly EASYs – who couldn't fit that bill if that's all I was looking for. You're right. I could just fuck you tonight and that would be that, or we could take our time and try to get to know each other. Your choice."

Choice? Paul hardly knew what to make of that word, that idea. So few real choices or options had ever appeared on his plate in his brief life. His entire existence had been so assessed and tracked, so pre-ordained; that the notion he could make a significant choice came close to filling him with dread. Moreover, a PROFFIE was putting this on the table. Was it even possible, it suddenly occurred to him, to have a "relationship" with a PROFFIE?

"I think I have to know something before I can say, or maybe I should say you should know something about me," he answered as he placed both his hands palm down on the table extending them, then braided them into the shape of the bong's mouthpiece, a swan.

Layla placed the tip of her index finger over his hand tracing the outline of the creature. "Hmmmm...interesting," she mumbled, "like your fingers were made of plastic. I wonder what else you can do?"

He gazed at his fingers for a few moments then disengaged them, impulsively grabbing onto her index finger. "I really **do** need to know what I am doing here before anything else happens."

The mood broken, she looked up at him, a bit of irritation showing. At that same moment the waitress approached to take their food order, but Layla waved her away.

He began hesitatingly, almost with a stutter, "Well, you see Professor Saenz it's just that well, well, you are, you see…"

"Just say it you jerk! And my name is Layla."

"I'm just a 3-D designer. I mean you're a PROFFIE, a big shot with a fab future. And I am well, just a WE. I don't get it. Why'd you agree to meet with me if it's not, as you claim, just some type of game for you? What do you want from me?"

"You really are an asshole, aren't you? You ran into me. You held me up. Then you asked me out. I said *yes*, and now you want to know why? Ok, so here's why: yes, you are unbelievably attractive. I dig your type, you asked me out and I thought, *why not*? More than just the initial attraction, I wanted to see who you are, yes, get to know you. And I even considered this: *Maybe he won't bore me the way most PROFFIEs do.* But I am already getting the feeling that I totally misjudged you. You're just a typical Outsider."

"A what?"

"A typical Outsider."

At this point their server returned to take their food order.

"So," she asked grinning broadly, "I don't mean to break your convo, but it's munchie time! What can I get you?"

Layla waved the menu under her nose, "Oh just bring us the Selection. That should do, right?" she turned to Paul not so much asking as telling him.

"Sure, sure," he agreed. "Bring us the Munchie Selection. Sounds fantastic."

The waitress sensing the tension palmed in the order scooting away wordlessly.

"Outsider," Paul repeated, "the only people who speak like that are TAKERs. And you're no TAKER. So what are you talking about?"

"Put your dog ears on and listen up. I am telling you that I am a TAKER. Born and bred. Just set free 'cause I tested out. But a TAKER I remain. So, if ya' have a problem with that, well you can get the out now. Don't worry. The weeds on me."

"A TAKER. Wow! Tested out! I'm impressed. You must be amazing. I wanted to test out- to be an EASY, but nada. I remain as you see me, a WE."

"So, you're not disgusted? Do you think I am a fraud?"

"No, you tested out. Proved the system's merit. That it works. When I complained, put forward my appeal, thought my classification was a mistake, I came close to being flagged, busted down to a TAKER before I even got to my Career Center."

"You complained? Really? You didn't?"

"Yeah I did. Stupid thing to do and then after getting into NCC I asked if I could go into the City and take a real art class. That didn't go over well either. Almost flagged me again- this time as a Waster. I've kept my mouth shut ever since. No point. My assessment stands. I will never be an EASY, a creator."

Layla looked at him with fresh eyes, began to reassess him. Pretty boy, yes, but there really was something behind those good looks, perhaps her first instincts about him were correct.

"So, go on, tell me the whole story."

And he did.

Later they drifted off to her apartment in Battery Park City. She opened the door. He nodded, "Nice place." She grabbed some fruit from her fridge and off they went to the bedroom, but did nothing except talk. Like in the *Thousand and One Arabian Nights* he spent the entire night telling her his story and, as in that tale, he spoke until the sun rose.

Chapter 21: Paul

Find Your Dreams [GTE, 45]

On Monday morning Paul rolled into the office an hour early. He had just experienced the best few days of his entire life. It was like something on his U-R-Dare. He had never seen the City as he had with her, had never eaten so much **real** food or been to and in so many in-the-being places and events. She even treated him to a live concert of the hottest band out there. But on Sunday, after an amazing brunch on her terrace overlooking the Hudson River, [O-M-G his brain screamed, can this be real??] they went to the Khoke Metropolitan Museum of Art. One of the many perks of her job at CCU was easy access to all the cultural institutions in New York City. She was a professor after all, and such places were considered their native domains.

Before entering they sat down on the museum's high wide steps, near to the top, to watch the entering throng. He was amazed at how many people could afford to enter. One thing Paul was sure of, there was no chance he'd bump into a friend, co-worker, or even a FB acquaintance here. After all his disappointments and rejections he never anticipated returning to that place which birthed his dream. He had given up on that years ago- or so he thought. Yet, here he was again, and he wasn't sure if this was a sign of something wonderful to come or a warning that he was about to embark on another misstep in his taxpaying career. He just didn't know, but as he sat there he realized it was too late to reconsider.

He shook his head for a moment like a dog shaking off water before speaking to her.

"Here again. My dream, or maybe better put, my delusion all began right here, only to pop like a balloon. My granny used to speak of dreams, *have dreams,* she'd say, but that always seemed so impossible. We were always told, *don't dream, that's for wasters and those destined for the Projects.*"

He worried he was being too candid. After all, who was this TAKER turned PROFFIE? Maybe she was just playing him after all? He'd never had anything but bad experiences when he spoke candidly about his dreams.

Layla, sensing his distrust tried to put him at ease, "In the Projects we are not even called 'students,' simply 'trainees.' It says to us: don't aspire. It tells us there's limited space on the Outside and that if we exit, we must be content to remain at the very bottom."

He started to interrupt her but she stopped him, "I know what you are thinking: 'look at her, she's a PROFFIE.' But I am nothing more than a bit of promo for the CSA That is all. If I step out of line or it suits them, they'll send me back. I am under no illusion about what this is all about."

"Yeah," Paul interjected rather brusquely, "I'm sure it was rough for you- the Projects and all. But you know, at least you knew the truth. But WE never know anything. WE think we have something to lose. WE actually believe it's all about merit, objective. But now... now I am beginning to think it's all been a lie. I don't need to tell you again how my dreams crashed and burned. Sometimes I think they totally mis-assessed me. Sometimes I actually believe it wouldn't have mattered how good I was, they were never going to reclassify me and then I think again, could that really be true? It's hard for me to believe, because that would make the CSA just another lie- you know what I mean? And what about the CRS? *The Book of Darwin?* [He quickly crossed himself] It would mean we've all been jerked around by a bunch of rich and powerful people, that the whole USA to CSA metamorphous, rebirth, genetic predetermination as God's earthly revelation, all of it, just a lie."

He paused for a moment, shrugged, capitulating to his true fear, "Maybe, I'm just a total loser trying to find excuses for my own genetic inadequacies. I mean, why would anyone **not** want the best, the brightest, the most talented to advance, to shine? Anything else doesn't make economic sense, does it? Don't waste your time on me."

"No, don't think that way. You just can't accept what's going on. What's staring you in the face." She hesitated; wondering if bringing him here was a good idea after all.

"You know, after listening to your story I thought it might be cathartic for you to come here again. Sort of like PTSD treatment. I kinda' thought if we came here that walking again through the place where you discovered your dream would help. I mean it was here you discovered it, only to have it shredded, torn from you stillborn. I think it's really gutted you. Maybe you can lose yourself in these halls, in all this art, and then find yourself again."

She stopped the lecture- Layla had a tendency to explicate past the point of getting a good return on her efforts- well; she was a PROFFIE, after all. She tried to gauge his reaction but he seemed impassive, his face revealed nothing.

"If it's too upsetting for you, we don't have to go in. We can do something else. Your choice."

That word again he thought. *Why is she always offering him a choice?*

"No, no," he said emphatically reaching for her hand, looping her fingertips into his. "I want to be here. It's amazing. You have no idea what this means to me."

"Good," she smiled. "Let's go find your dreams. They are in here somewhere. I'm sure."

Home Again, Home Again, Jiggity Jig

But now he was back to his reality. Back at work. Back to the WE existence he always intuitively felt he had to escape. How long would Layla, a TAKER born, but clearly pre-destined to be a PROFFIE, want to hang with him? You might say he hardly knew her, yet, ironically, he had spent more real time with her than with any other human being outside his immediate family. Yeah, he'd had some brief relationships, one even lasted six months, but most of these were Palm Pad expedited. A few meetings mostly to get it on, but otherwise much of the contact was techno mediated. How could it be otherwise? WEs were always so fully engaged. Busy commuting. Busy working. Busy keeping their heads above water.

Even when he attended NCC he was rushing between class and work, work and class, and then homework, then helping his grannies as they began to decouple from this world.

Of course, his parents could have sent them to an Oldies Life Pad where they would have quickly expired. Most everyone disposed of their old rags like that, but they wouldn't do it.

One day, when his Ma was helping to clean his granny before running out to her bleak shift at the local diner, he asked her about it.

"My friends say we're crazy to keep our old rags in the house. They say most people these days just send their old rags out."

"Would you really want us to do that to your grannies?" his Ma inquired looking at him carefully.

"No, I love the oldies, really I do. The poor things had hard lives, right? Came of age before our Great Awakening so they never really got it. We just have to do our best, right Ma?"

"Yes, we do our best...that's all we can do."

The grannies fully decoupled, at the exact same time, about a decade ago. It would be easier now as their neighbors and friends all assured them. They were, after all, just old rags and no one ever understood why they had kept them around for so long. Still, Paul and his parents had wept anyway, when the disposal unit came and took the bodies away.

These, he reflected, were his closest relationships. Other than that he realized he had no real enduring connections. Everything was focused on being and maintaining one's status as a MAKER. It seemed to crowd out almost everything else. Sure, he'd eventually hook up with some other WE, move back out to the suburbs, have a kid- no more than two- and spend his life as his parents had- commuting, getting by, taking the occasional vacay, grateful he had a job, but always, yes always, on the brink.

His Team leader tapped him on the shoulder. Paul turned. "What's up my man? How's conceptualization of the History Department sell going? Ready for the team meet up, or do you need to further digest?"

"Yeah, yeah it's all in. Got lots of ideas to throw on the Table."

"Good. Take five and see you there." He turned towards the center meeting space for emphasis.

"Sure, be there in five."

Paul swallowed hard. So hard he had to check to reassure himself he hadn't swallowed his Adam's apple. He hadn't given this latest SM project much thought at all over the weekend. Hadn't prepared for this meeting. Had no plan whatsoever. This was his harvest for deviating from his classification's demands; he would be deleted for sure, by the end of the day.

But just like in one of those old twentieth century films, a champion interceded to save the day. His Palm Pad buzzed. He answered. Layla popped up on his screen.

"Paul, Professor Triquot would like you to hop on over here now."

"Well, I have a meeting in about three minutes. Can I touch base with her later?"

"No, she wants to chat you up now. She already notified your Team Leader. He said it's ok. See you in a few..." The screen went blank.

He stood. Looked around and caught Symone's eye. He waved to him calling out, "Will reschedule for later. Be prepared to incorporate your convo with Triquot into your proposal."

"Sure, no problem."

Paul now knew how a condemned prisoner felt when receiving news that his execution has been stayed. His mission: to get his head off that chopping block.

Touching the Past

This time Paul had no problem finding Triquot's office. No accidents impeded his arrival. Going through the History Department's doors he was met by Layla -or rather Professor Saenz- fully cloaked in her professorial role from which she never wavered. No whiff of acquaintance clung to the proffered open hand or in her greeting to Paul. No one would ever have suspected she and Paul were even passing acquaintances, never mind they had just spent the past three days together.

"Please thank your Team Leader for rearranging your group's meeting so that you could congregate with us. Chair Triquot is anxious to speak with you again about the upcoming campaign. In fact, she's arranged for a number of us to join her. We have some ideas before SM finalizes its plans."

She cocked her head at him as if to cue him to answer.

"Sure, sure, I'd love to hear your thoughts. It would be really helpful. We haven't finalized anything yet."

"That's good. We may be PROFFIEs but we think we can offer some insights, ideas even, to help your department plan our campaign. Of course, we will defer to your expertise."

She motioned him to follow her, leading the way to a conference room. He looked around. He wasn't surprised by its formality. The space he now worked in was uncommon, while the History Department's offices were more in line with what he'd been accustomed to: chocolate and cream walls, large windows, wall screens. But there were some peculiarities in this set-up as well: the desks were elegant in an old-fashioned way constructed using ornamental metal designs and wood along with something he had never seen; bookcases crawling up the walls, housing in-the-being books. Row upon row of those old relics; the department must have housed thousands of books.

He stopped for a moment to peer at these. "Professor Saenz would you mind if I touched a book?"

"Huh? A book? Touch a book? Well sure. Why not?"

She opened another door leading to an unoccupied office and more bookcases and books.

"Which one would you like to examine?" She waved her hand towards the books inviting him to select one.

"I don't know. I've never handled a book before. I mean a real physical book. I didn't realize anyone actually owned these things anymore. One of our Content Facilitators mentioned these were only preserved in some of the large private in-the-being libraries, like the Library on 42nd street but, of course, they're only open to the public with special permission."

He paused, hesitated as if he were actually afraid of them. She nodded.

"I guess you can tour it right? But I've never bothered to buy a ticket. Too many credits."

"Didn't you see the offices when you were here the last time?"

"No. I just went into a small conference room just a bit past your main meet and greet room."

"I see," she said as she turned to select a book for him to peruse. After a quick scan of the rows of books she selected one and handed it to him.

"Here, take a look at this."

She tossed him an old paperback. He was surprised at how casually she treated the old relic.

"It's Howard Zinn's, *A People's History of the United States.* It's been out of fashion forever. Not suitable reading for the masses or anyone for that matter. Just old style liberal bullshit."

He was so startled she'd handed him such a book he released it, letting it fall to the floor, the spine splitting down the middle.

"I'm so sorry. I didn't mean to drop it…of course I expect to be charged. Held accountable," he gasped picking up the damaged book attempting to restore it.

She grabbed it from his hand, stepping over to the nearby desk pulling some type of adhesive out applying it to the damaged book's spine.

"Hey, don't sweat it. All fixed. Here, take it," she ordered putting the book into his hands. "We have a few copies. Take it and read it."

He looked down at the book regretting he had ever asked to see, never mind hold a physical book. How could he refuse it now? Even worse, how could he accept it? Walk with it? Bring it back to his office? Take it home with him?

"I couldn't accept it," he pleaded, holding it out to her.

She only laughed at the fear so audible in his voice. She pushed back against the proffered book.

"Of course you can accept it. Consider it a gift from the History Department. In fact, why don't you share it with your colleagues in SM? Bathroom reading perhaps?"

Paul groaned, "Layla, you can't be serious? Not only will I be deleted, but most likely immediately sent to the nearest Project!"

"For Darwin's sake! Don't be such an asshole. Just take it home and read it. I have. Everyone in this department has read it. It's what we do; read and analyze history. It's not illegal. Where did you get that idea?"

"I don't know. I guess because I never see these things anywhere I just assumed…then why don't WE ever see these?"

"Because much of these old tomes go against the new, restored history. The one I gave you is considered the rantings of an old lefty historian. There used to be lots of them. No need for you to consume outdated or discredited info. Right? At least that's the theory.

"Then why have you all read these? Queried Paul now more confused than ever.

"Well, as historians we can only write the truth, the restored history, by examining the past, understanding how Americans were misled by those so-called liberal elite intellectuals. Then we synthesize and write the truth."

He didn't answer so she continued, "Makes sense?"

"Yeah, I guess so."

"Anyway, read it. Let me know what you think."

He still hesitated.

"Listen, I won't tell anyone I gave it to you if that makes you feel more comfortable, ok?"

"Ok," Paul assented as he tucked the book into the inner breast pocket in his jacket. "I've never read an in-the-being book. I'll give it a try, but don't expect too much from me. I wasn't much of a history student even when I was at my Learning Center and that was years ago."

"Hey, you can get your revenge on me another time by asking me to draw a dog or something."

Relieved, Paul grinned. "It's a deal. I guess we should get to that meeting."

By the time Paul returned to his office his head was a veritable beehive. His meeting with Triquot and three other PROFFIEs, including Layla, gave him a totally different take on history and consequently the campaign. Triquot was warm and gracious at first, but then got right down to business.

"Paul, what kind of sell do you have in mind for us?"

He simply froze. He had no idea how to respond. Here he was with four PROFFIEs expectantly waiting for him to provide the vision. How was he going to sell something so dated like history to a student clientele? CCU students wanted forward-looking professions.

Other than getting a job at a university like CCU, what could you do with a history degree? CCU's consumers were all provisionally classified as PROFESSIONALS. These students if interested in education didn't graduate to teach at Learning Centers or Career Centers. If teaching and research was their avocation they entered the Academy, other elite universities like CCU, but it was not exactly a growth industry. So, how to pitch it? How to attract customers to courses that, for the most part, led nowhere? Gaugin, he told himself, *if you don't want to lose this gig you better think of something right now!*

He looked at the assembled, counted to three and began:

"I think this campaign needs an unexpected angle. As soon as the word 'history' pops out, the audience tunes out. We have to somehow present history as fashion forward not trending backwards. Let's be honest, your profession does focus on the past and, well, let's face it, that's not exactly of the moment. And aren't we all about that?"

The assembled professors nodded, but remained silent, so he plowed ahead.

"I've given this a lot of thought. Given it mucho hours – and, of course, this campaign deserves that and more. But what we really need to do, as I've said, is make history more of the moment, something that can push forward, not just back. It's got to be more accessible. Also to really sell it, the campaign has to include some grab you by the throat graphics..." he paused to look at these PROFFIEs' reactions whose only feedback was to lean in towards him.

"Don't worry about that part of it- graphics is my specialty. I'll figure out and design that angle of the campaign once we've mapped out the strategy- you know, formulated the vision we're selling. Once the concept is set, the graphics will follow."

Again no response so he plunged forward.

"So, here's what I'm thinking, Professor Saenz was just showing me your new career path called 'Prognostication.' My understanding is it will teach students to use knowledge of the past to predict the future or guide us towards the future we want. Am I correct?"

"Yes, yes, you might say that," interjected Triquot, "but it's a bit more complicated, nuanced I should say than that, but that's the general direction. If you want to thoroughly comprehend the complexities involved with Prognostication I would direct you to the literature... "

Layla interrupted her. "Chair Triquot so sorry to interject but Mr. Gaugin is a graphic designer by vocation. The intricacies of the discipline can't be of interest or even helpful to him- it will only confuse him. As the originator of this new direction for our field you understandably want to share its innovation, but Mr. Gaugin here, simply needs to distill it for one of those SM campaigns."

Layla turned to Paul. "I am sure you will somehow work into this campaign our dear Chair's role in this, correct?"

"Sure thing. Of course we will. And you are right," he emphasized turning to Triquot, "it's all too complicated for a graphics guy like myself. That's why you are a PROFFIE and I'm a WE- each to our own spheres, as they say. You can't teach this dog, young though I am, to prognosticate, but I can sure help sell the public on it! And I would love to do that for you Chair Triquot and, of course, for your great department."

Triquot beamed at him, pawing his arm "And you will Paul, I have faith that you will."

Then, so very pleased with the meeting, she magnanimously urged Paul, while patting Layla's hand, "And don't forget to mention Professor Saenz as well- we worked closely together on this. It's as much her baby as mine."

Chapter 22: Layla and Paul

Everyone's Happy [GTE, 45]

The campaign progressed. Everyone from Chair Triquot, to the head of CCU's SM Division, to Chancellor Handler, was thrilled. It was vibrant they said. It was innovative. SM was putting history back on the map. Enrollment was soaring. Everyone wanted to prognosticate. It was truly of the moment.

Layla's stock soared. So did Paul's. His campaign was just so now, so forward, so popping, so trendy, so, well, so everything it should be. And those 3-Ds based on Nostradamus were so very deck!

It was the weekend and Paul and Layla were sitting on the terrace eating brunch. Layla put down her fork and grabbed Paul's. "Stop chewing!"

He shut his mouth laughing, mumbling, "Ok, no chewing."

"I have a serious question: How in Darwin's green earth did you know about Nostradamus? It wasn't in your download was it" asked Layla.

Paul grinned, "You're not the only one who knows about history Professor Saenz. My Grandpa used to talk about Nostradamus all the time. He was fascinated by his predictions. Thought he'd predicted everything- World War II, 9/11, you know, all the important events. He predicted them all, or so said my Grandpa."

"So, when I started thinking about the sell, the tie in to Nostradamus was obvious. It provided the basis for the graphics – you know, it's not so easy to translate history into imagery."

"Hmmmm…indeed it's not."

She changed gears. "I really want to see where you live."

She waited. He did not respond.

"Really, Paul, I want to see where you live. I get that it's not as nice as this place, but it's important to me to get a sense of your surroundings."

Still no response.

"And anyway, your are sitting here with a TAKER."

"Ex-TAKER," he finally muttered.

"TAKER, draped in a PROFFIE's cloak, that's all. I grew up in far worse than you currently live in or will ever inhabit. And I don't need to prognosticate to know that."

"Ok," he was on his feet pulling her to hers. Let's go."

The Writings on the Wall

They were walking in Canarsie, a fairly non-descript neighborhood. Its streets dominated by large, high-rise apartment buildings. Years ago, as Layla expounded, Canarsie contained small homes, old-style apartment buildings- a mixed bag of housing. The rapid rise in New York City's population starting in the late twentieth century continuing into the twenty-first century resulted in a severe shortage of affordable housing. To address this burgeoning crisis, the City embarked on building more vertical, affordable housing in the City's outer ring. Mostly, they turned to micro-apartments like the one in which Paul resided.

Concurrent with the explosion in New York City's demographics, which became increasingly younger and wealthier, its suburban communities fell into a steep decline. Nassau County, the former queen of suburbia was no exception. Years of deterioration had left the typical Nassau County neighborhood nothing more than a hodgepodge of small cookie-cutter boxlike houses designed to lodge WE families, its adult inhabitants making the daily trek into the City.

Paul, who had grown up in one of those dreary neighborhoods, like so many single WEs, moved out as soon as the opportunity presented itself. And, similar to his current neighbors, he leased one of those micro-apartments in an outer ring neighborhood where he'd remain until marriage, children, and the need to find a larger, more affordable residence and, as importantly, a Learning Center he could afford for his children, drove him back to Nassau County. There he and his spouse would take their places as quotidian commuters into the great city. He was well aware of this and the very thought sent waves of nausea washing over his entire person.

The apartment was exactly how he had described it to Layla- a typical micro-apartment, fourth floor walk-up [exercise is good for you- elevators service was from the 6th floor up only]. He had warned her not to expect much; nothing like her comfy, relatively large apartment in Manhattan. To that, she countered yet again, "Hey, I grew up in a Pen, remember?"

"Yeah, well you're accustomed to a lot better now."

"Tell you what, I'll get us a couple of passes to the Projects and give you a tour of my old stomping grounds. Show you the Pens, which are smaller, meaner than this. Would that satisfy you?"

"Whatever. That's not the point. It's not where you live now."

He waved his hand over the snap lock pushing open the metal door so she could step in. There it was: small kitchen to the immediate left- a one person space separated from what passed for a living room by a three foot counter with two little stools pushed under. It was spotless. She guessed he never really cooked in it. Who could blame him? All it contained was a miniscule under- the - counter refrigerator, a two-burner cook-top, a recessed microwave, which Paul used daily, and two wall cabinets. That was it, the complete kitchen. The developers of these micro-units touted their efficiency. More, they maintained, was not needed. Whatever.

The rest of this cozy set-up was dedicated to living and sleeping. Paul had furnished it with a bright blue loveseat covered in a suede-like material alongside a similarly upholstered chair, a 2x2 round coffee table all crammed into an 12x12' area. The biggest thing in his living room was the enormous screen that filled the largest wall. Like a lion's maw threatening to swallow up everything, it was on night and day.

"Hey, turn that thing off," she motioned to the screen.

"Can't. I can only turn it down or mute it. I didn't want to spend the credits to buy the turn-off package"

"Hmmm…like in the Projects only we had no options at all and fewer channel choices. It was unbearable as far as I was concerned." Chuckling she continued, "Hey, maybe that was my real incentive to get out of the Projects as a PROFFIE… the ability to turn that thing off!"

Since there was no separate bedroom every evening he shoved the small love seat and coffee table aside to pull down the bed recessed into the wall. WEs had taken to calling these apartments "Murphy" pads as it all seemed patterned after that twentieth century space saving invention, the Murphy bed. Paul comforted himself with the knowledge that at least his was a double. The "en suite" bathroom was equally efficient.

"Not too much to look at, but it could be worse," he mumbled to Layla ashamed despite himself.

Layla peeked into the bathroom to examine its all too familiar all in one set-up: a pull down toilet seat, wall sink and a showerhead in the middle of the room. "Not so bad, I've seen sadder places than this."

But what really struck her, made her step back for a moment, were the walls and ceilings. Every single wall and ceiling, every centimeter, was covered in drawings, some finished, some in a state of completion, some apparently destined for extinction about to be covered over in whitewash. Only the perimeter around the screen wall was spared or, in Layla's mind, deprived of these renderings. She took a breath and began to carefully examine these depictions walking, moving forward and back from the wall coverings, peering in closely at a particular detail, returning to some after a first look, moving quickly on after glancing at others. Neither spoke while Layla conducted her inspection as if she were experiencing an in-the-being visit to a museum.

Finally, after nearly an hour she turned to Paul. "I'm stunned."

In a panic he grabbed her hand in a pleading manner. "Please, Layla, please, don't tell anyone about this. I know it's destruction of property, a violation of my lease, but I swear that when and if I vacate this apartment I will whitewash it all over. Return it back to its original state. I always do this. Have since I was a child. No one ever knows, so no harm done, right?

"Harm," she echoed, "Harm? You speak of harm?"

"Yes, yes, I will clean it all up. I always do. I always have. It started when I was little and my old Grandpa used to bring me paints from this home store where he picked up odd jobs. He'd even rescue old pencils and brushes from the trash. My Dad and Ma let me draw all over, covering the walls and ceilings. When there was no room left Grandpa would whitewash it all and I would start again. So, you see I've always done this- just a kinda' habit I guess. Like a hobby. So, please don't tell."

"Tell?" she echoed his words again. "Tell who? Why would I do that? But I will tell you something. You are a magnificent artist."

She continued to scan the walls for a few more minutes then turned to him, hands on her hips, a stern look on her face. "How did they mis-assess you? What the hell are you doing designing 3-D graphics? You should be an EASY."

Paul's expression went from deep concern to glee. He grabbed her and kissed her. Not a romantic kiss, but a kiss of simple, pure joy.

"OMG- you see, you see!!!! Right? Like I've been telling them all for over a decade but no one would listen to me. But all along I knew I was an EASY. You see it don't you? I can't believe it! Finally someone sees it. So, what do we do? You're a PROFFIE. You can tell them they made a mistake. Get them to fix it. Right?"

"Chill. I am not an Assessor. I have nothing to do with assessment and have not a clue how classifications are changed."

"Well, yours was."

"I was given a provisional classification as a result of my SAT and evaluations. It was standard procedure, part of the same process that classified you a WE. How you get reclassified once a permanent classification is affixed is another issue. I know it happens. Not often, but it does. Chancellor Handler started as a WE and look at him now; a top tier PROFFIE. But I don't know the steps or who makes such a decision. Plus, what do I know? I am not an EASY but a PROFFIE. I was expressing my eye to brain reaction. Not giving you an educated or trained opinion. Perhaps I spoke too soon, out of turn. "

A deflated Paul turned and plopped himself down on the loveseat covering his face with his hand. "So, I'm still fucked. That's great. Just great."

Chapter 23: CCU

The Brain Trust [GTE, 45]

Paul's Team Leader had gathered his tight little team around their central meeting table. The hub of all things productive, the Brain Trust that kept them moving up and onwards and not down and out. Each team member was there, on time, their eager beaver faces plastered in place, Palm Pads open, fingers poised to record each and every pearl about to drop before their swine. Recently, Symone was one happy camper. He had personally hired their star performer, Paul Gaugin, now the darling of each and every CCU academic department. All hopeful that Paul, in conjunction with the entire SM team, could perform the same magic for them they'd done for History, that former laggard of a department.

The Big Mirror

Until that campaign, along with that brilliant new addition to its curriculum, Prognostication Studies, History was a dying department. Up to that point, Handler himself had been in discussions with CCU's Board of Trustees about eliminating it altogether. What to do with the History Department had become a constant refrain at those meetings. Of course, they'd retain some history courses, keep a few of its faculty on staff, but did CCU really need an **entire** department devoted to dead stuff? That was the question. What was its proper place and how to implement? Before this campaign Handler was pressing the Trustees to consider folding History into another department as a kind of junior member retaining only about a quarter of its current faculty. Yet there was some hesitation. Some of the Trustees were skeptical. Didn't their customers require more history than the usual WEs? It was all well and good to set such a strict limit at the Career Centers, but here? At CCU?

The Trustees remained unconvinced, but Handler pressed on. He pointed out that Bill Golightly's company had recently developed and introduced an all-encompassing history fully digestible in a single semester. It was called, *The Big Mirror.* Perhaps, Handler suggested, CCU might adopt something similar. Really, Handler insisted, unless a student was a history major, what more was needed other than a *Big Mirror* type course and one CSA specific history?

"Trustees," Handler cajoled, "if the History Department can't produce, why should the CCU shoulder the expense of so many history professors? The truth is, hardly anyone wants to major in it so why waste resources on it? Yes, of course, CCU needs to keep some historians onboard. But equally important we can't overproduce history majors. Our institution's cred was built, in large measure, on producing graduates who go on to excellent paying positions and not spitting out grads who will be perpetually under-employed. If we go down that path our stats will suffer! Don't forget our institutional Report Card based ranking depends not only on student completion rates but also on our graduates' future incomes. Don't doubt but that the History Department is adversely impacting our bottom line and something has to be done about it."

Handler, snake charmer that he was, had moved the Trustees this close to adopting his plan, but the History Department's clever new major, Prognostication, combined with that catchy SM campaign, blew that idea out of the water. No downsizing, no dismantling it. No dispatching three-quarters of its professors back into the work force. Handler was forced to abandon his proposal. He was a disappointed man.

As he admitted, only to himself, it would have provided him with enormous personal satisfaction to observe those stuck-up, useless intellectuals trying to survive outside their Ivory Tower. He suspected many, if not most, would not land on their feet but begin the long downward slide. He had planned to keep track of each and every one of them. He calculated that many, within the year, would be busted down to TAKER. In preparation he'd even chatted up the CCU's Chief of Security about how to orchestrate this little drama. In his head he replayed what might have been.

The CCU Security Chief would track the released PROFFIES and coordinate with the Projects' Security Commissioner to insure a big show whenever a former PROFFIE was escorted to the Projects' gates. Handler promised plenty of positive screen time for their involvement.

In anticipation of this, Handler had struck up a relationship with the Remi, the host of that still so popular show *Where Are They Now?* He exchanged exclusive access to each and every bust for it first flashing live across all CCU screens before it appeared on the program's regular time. A twofer for all involved. Plus, imagine the STD's and other top JC's positive reaction when they saw that he, Chancellor Handler, knew how to create a continuing loop of educational events reinforcing the CSA's meritocracy and its core ideal: everyone from high to low **must** stay relevant and remain profitable. No individual or group is permitted to offend the bottom line. *Accolades,* Handler imagined, *all around.*

Well, pondered the disappointed Handler, *that's not going to happen now. Nope, that damn stuck-up Triquot's riding high again. Well, I'll just do what I gotta' do - grab that board and ride that wave with her. It's **my** damn university so the credit really belongs to me.*

Chapter 24: Paul

Always On the Move [GTE, 45]

"Ok team," Symone bellowed clapping his hands, "what do ya' have for me today?" He looked around at their faces - anxiety, eagerness, and downright prayerfulness were reflected. One by one they reviewed what was up, what was front and center, how they were working on campaigns that would grab shine time for the SM department.

Standout!

Be recognized!

Be indispensable!

After listening to each tick off his/her accomplishments, plans and goings ons it was time to get down to business.

"Listen up team! We've got a live one. Something hot, something that will keep us on the CCU map. And it comes courtesy of our current favorite department- History! They are rolling out a new book. And it's going to have a hard copy edition. Imagine that! That's how important they think this is. 'Course there will be the normal E- and A-versions but we are going to push the consumer to buy in-the-being. [the Team gasped!]. Yeah, I know, it's unprecedented, but if anyone can market this we can- yes we can! Now say it with me:"

YES WE CAN, YES WE CAN YES WE CAN!

"YES, WE CAN TEAM- so keep that vibe first and foremost in mind. We are going to convince the consumer this is something every MAKER needs to own, needs to display like in: put it on your coffee table. Now there's a quaint idea."

He looked towards Joelle, a pretty, dark haired, petite woman just six months into her first yearly renewable who seemed to spend a good chunk of her credits on sheers. Sheers that glowed, sheers advertising the latest screen show, or EASY of the moment, sheers that seemed painted to her very flesh rippling lights and colors. There was even one where tiny chameleons crept up her ankles to her calves and from there made a beeline for her thighs disappearing into that nether region.

Her male and female gay colleagues swore their very noses detected its distinctive whiff as the little creatures slid back down to her ankles only to begin their arduous journey anew.

That day, Joelle's little creature comfort sheers made our eager Team Leader pause in mid-sentence until it disappeared. Shaking himself awake he addressed her, "Joelle, I want you to work closely with Paul here who's going to take the lead on this campaign. But all hands on deck. Understand? Just because Paul's on the job doesn't excuse the rest of you. We can't rest on our laurels. Remember, credit's not deep. So, as they say, *if you think of something, say something.* Got it? This is an unusual product. An in –the- being book, a history, no less. Only Darwin knows the last time anyone really read a history book! The consumer will be perplexed, so the sell has to be creative. Gossip alert! I hear the CCU BoT itself is interested in this rollout, so let's get going on this and produce!

One Team member rose to his feet crying out: "WHO ARE WE?"

"CCU SM"

"WHAT DO WE DO?"

"WE SELL CCU. WE SELL CCU. WE SELL CCU."

"THAT'S RIGHT! NOW AND FOREVER CCU!!!!"

Symone clapped his hands. "That's it! That's it. Get going on this. We can sell it. We can do it. DO IT FOR THE GIPPER!"

[In unison all crossed themselves]

How Can We Serve?

Paul walked into the History Department. He glanced up at the Secrey sitting in her perch looking down, mouthing to him to enter, her Third- Eye focused on a large info screen while her Third- Hand waved him in. As he went through the doorway she'd opened, she swiveled toward his disappearing back singing out, "Pa-awl, back again? Ca-air-full they don't eat you for lunch!!!!"

Was she laughing at him? Warning him? Did she know something he didn't? He wasn't sure. He looked back to give the bye-bye wave and kept walking.

Well here you are, he thought, back for another round with the History Department. They were an odd collection. In some respects very practical, but in another they lived in an alternate universe. Layla was a bit different. Perhaps because she was raised in the Projects; but he wasn't certain.

Like the other history PROFFIES even Layla had this academicyness he simply didn't get. One minute he'd be having a perfectly normal convo with them and the next moment they were tumbling into an abyss of words and ideas, splitting hairs and generally engaging in what can only be characterized as flights of fancy. So if you told them the sky was blue, the whole lot of them would begin to discuss the meaning of "blue." In his HO they were big **Wasters,** yet it appeared the powers that be turned a blind eye to their tendency to tumble into quicksand. Even the more pragmatic Layla was prone to this. But maybe that's why they were PROFFIES and he was not. Whatever, right? Of greater importance to Paul was that right here in this very office was where his CCU career took off and it was where it could just as easily end.

I'm only as good as my last campaign, he ruminated. *If this tanks I could be a has-been, a "whatever happened to him object." I've got to produce something as good as, or better than that last campaign.*

As he entered the conference room he saw Chair Triquot sitting with Layla along with a number of the other PROFFIES. They looked up at him expectantly. He murmured his hellos.

Triquot, on the other hand, was delighted [simply thrilled] to see him. "Here's the young man that helped put us back on the map," she trilled introducing Paul to some of the unfamiliar faces. Among the attendees was CCU's Provost, Dr. Vasquez. Why in Darwin's universe is the Provost here his heart pounded out to him?

"Well, sit down Paul. Don't stand there. We are anxious to get started. You're not a Waster are you?"

As usual, that word made Paul blanch. "No, no Ma'am of course not. Sure, let's get started, of course. You're all busy, busy people." At that last utterance he glanced at the Provost who appeared visibly bored, hunched over examining her Palm Pad.

"What can I do for you? How can SM serve?" Paul asked.

Triquot, who had just chastised him as a potential Waster, took time to tighten her collar and rearrange an impressive gold pendant hanging round her neck before addressing Paul.

"Didn't your Team Leader brief you?"

She either didn't see or ignored Paul's bobbing head. She simply kept going, explaining to Paul and those seated all about the History Restoration Project and its product: *The Restored History.*

And she droned on and on and on explaining how this would be the seminal history about the fall of the USA and rise of the CSA ...Paul thought she'd never conclude and judging by the Provost's total inattention and squirming, she clearly felt the same.

After another indeterminate amount of time passed, the Provost finally [blessedly] interjected, "Chair Triquot." That immediately put Triquot's voice on hold while the Provost admonished, "I think we have all heard quite enough about the project and the book."

Triquot looked stricken, like she'd just been smacked in her face, but she stammered forward.

"It's just that this is more than a book. It's but one piece of our major project- you know CCU's push to restore the true history to the public square. I thought it important to fully brief Paul. He needs to understand its essence, its mission, and its potential comprehensive impact on the population. He's not a PROFFIE. Not educated on these matters. If we don't instruct him on its significance how can he design a successful SM campaign for us?"

"If you really need to expatiate in this manner then send the guy a talkie. That's all. I assume your staff, sitting here, are all fully briefed and conversant with this piece of your oh so important project. Yes?"

The Provost's voice dripped with sarcasm as she canvassed the assembled: "Who here knows about this project?"

All hands, including Paul's, went up.

"And who is familiar with this book?"

All hands, including Paul's, went up.

"Who here has actually read it?"

All hands, with the exception of Paul's, went up.

Smirking, she turned to Paul. "So, you are the creator of the Nostradamus campaign, correct?"

Knowing better than to take full credit [surely that would get back to his Team Leader] he responded blandly, "Yes, along with my Team led by Bill Symone. Great guy. We couldn't do any of this without him"

"Good answer! Now let me ask you: did you ever study Prognostication before?"

Paul shook his head.

"But you were able to design a fab campaign anyway, correct?"

Again Paul nodded his head indicating agreement. Clearly the less said the better.

"Your Team Leader sent you here to take the lead on the new campaign, correct?

Jeez, Paul thought, was Provost Vasquez or a lawyer? Again Paul nodded his assent.

"And did your Team Leader brief you on the project's details?"

"Yes, he briefed the entire Team."

"Tell me about your training.

"I have a Vocational Entrepreneur Degree, a VED in 3-D graphic design from NCC and have worked in SM for nearly ten years specializing in large campaigns such as these."

Provost Vasquez turned to Triquot, her hands falling on the table in a thud. "There you go Triquot. Do you understand? He doesn't need your chapter and verse. He's been trained to digest the essence of what's required to successfully design your campaign. So now that I've effectively schooled you in STD training pedagogy, let's get to the heart of the matter, the meat and potatoes, the gore and guts of why we're here. I'm not here to listen to you pontificate about the wonders of this book or your project for that matter. Save it for your students. Let's discuss the campaign. Let's sell this book. Make it a CCU cornerstone. Let's show them all, yet again, why we are the leading university in the CSA Yeah, screw Harvard and Yale. Their time at the top is over. Let them eat our dust."

A number of the assembled faculty had clenched their fists, pumping them up and down. Suddenly, the entire room bust into cheers and chants of 'CCU, CCU, CCU, CCU!' Paul glanced over at Layla. She was the only one not cheering. He wondered if he was the only one that noticed?

Chapter 25: Isaac

GTE, 45

The Reverend Ice Freeman was, as we now all know, an avid reader. He was, you might say, something of an anachronism for his day and age. Even at the highest levels few claimed they loved to read, to spend copious amounts of leisure time so engaged. Yeah, they read reports or information needed to advance their careers or, simply put, keep a job, get that new employment contract, but Freeman read for content, for knowledge, for enrichment of mind and soul and, remarkably, the sheer pleasure of it. It had become such a passion for him that he had taken to travelling with a number of his in-the-being books. On trips he would sit for hours ensconced in his private jet simply reading books.

"Now who does that?" his staff wondered. "What could it mean?"

A quick peek at these works revealed these were not the latest best sellers in physical copy. Sure, many One-Percenters had taken to purchasing the latest best sellers in that form. These were quite a bit pricier than your average E or A book but, then again, it said something about you. Indeed, purchasing hard copies was suddenly quite trendy amongst the upper, uppers. Consumers of these expensive volumes extolled the pleasure of feeling the weight in one's hand, the joy of turning paper pages using one's fingers, the tactile sensation of flipping through a book at will, the pleasure of manipulating, seemingly controlling one's access to information without a mediating device. Moreover, its inaccessibility to the masses further transformed these into "must haves."

It was not the fact that Ice carried around hard copies that unnerved his staff but that these were **not** the latest best sellers, or even some foul old novel some Rag had left lying about, but

159

histories written before the coming of the CSA Nasty, dangerous old relics, whispered his staff, which should have been discarded long ago. So, naturally, this odd proclivity of Reverend Freeman to read discredited histories was a mystery to his staff.

Of course, there was some chatter, some buzzing, but the unspoken consensus: best not to dwell on it. Their very livelihoods depended on their boss remaining on top, so why spread gossip that might jeopardize his standing?

Opening the Book

Freeman was flying back to New York on a private CRS Airstream Jet, this time to bless the CCU's roll out of its, *The Restored History of America from 1492 to the Great Transformation*. He sank back into his plush seat, a good stiff drink on the tray opened to his right. The attractive flight attendant leaned over to offer him a selection of sandwiches. He waved her away. He needed to at least skim through the book before arriving in New York. He was attending its Red Carpet. Word on the street was it would be a best seller not simply in its E-text, Audio and Halo versions, but the commemorative hard copy, though pricy, was expected to sell briskly. It was being marketed as a prestige item, a patriotic buy. Something every MAKER would want to display on a coffee table or as the lone book on a display shelf. Imagine owning a real in-the-being book. A hard copy chronicling the rise and fall and then rise again of the American people! American exceptionalism reified yet again.

Since it was authored and published by CCU they wanted him there. Give it his blessing and all that. He really didn't feel like attending. Hadn't he just been in New York? Why couldn't Chin do this?

"Can't bake that cake Ice," he told him. "It's got to be you. I'm just the finance guy, not the spiritual leader of the CRS. Goes with the territory. You know it. Anyway, New York's a great place. Shake that ol' dirt from your shoes and enjoy."

Yeah, just enjoy. That was easy for TC to say. He wasn't racked by doubt. There he said it to himself. Doubt. He opened his folio computer [he really couldn't do serious work on a Palm Pad] randomly selecting a chapter and steeled himself to plow through a few chapters of what appeared to be just a standard textbook:

The Restored History of America from 1492 to the Great Transformation, Chapter 35, The Founders Action Party Takes Shapes

In 2016, six years before the Great Transformation, the Republican Party, the Grand Old Party, collapsed. The immediate trigger was the failure of its presidential nominating convention to reach consensus on a candidate. In reality, its descent into oblivion had been building for years. True, the Republicans had done a fantastic job in the early decades of the twenty-first century capturing local statehouses, the Congress, blocking progressive legislation and the like, but despite these victories they continued to lose the presidency. All agreed that if the Republicans could not take the presidency, the New Deal's calumnies would never be fully turned back, a new direction for the nation never fully undertaken...

Ice closed the screen for a moment. He knew this. What was "restored" about this history he wondered? Most histories anyone read these days were revised versions of the old liberal dribble that had poured out of America's universities after the 1960s. So, this was restored to whom? Restored to the WE? Perhaps. It was written in a very accessible manner, really wondrously simplistic. Well, he'd better familiarize himself with it anyway. He opened his screen to continue reading:

There were two front-runners that year: a young, charismatic entrepreneur from the Midwest, Benedict Ganar, and the darling of the far right, Governor Frank Pasternak from Minnesota.

Ganar's slogan: "Let 'em decide." He wanted to give corporate America full reign and set the Job Creators free from all the regulations that bound them. But he also wanted the party to move away from its invasive stance on personal liberties.

"Yeah," he admitted, "I am personally repulsed by abortion, and sure I want us all to be church going, God fearing Americans, and of course, I am revolted by men marrying men, but... [And this was a big "but"] we've got to let the American public, the individual, decide for themselves. Either we want smaller, less obtrusive government or we don't. Either we want to beat back the Chinese, get rid of all those illegals gobbling up our national wealth or we don't. Either we want to set capitalism free to do what it does best and create wealth for us all or we want to bicker over what the government regulates and what it doesn't. So I say: Let 'em decide!"

Many Republicans rallied to this appeal to set the Corpus free, to set the individual free, for American business to rise again on the world stage so it could create good American jobs, but many still clung to their ill conceived desires to dictate private behavior. At the convention both sides dug in. Frank Pasternak simply refused to budge from his platform as Ganar did from his. No one was willing to compromise. Negotiations between the two factions ground to a halt after the first ballot. Still many hoped a resolution could be reached.

By the second ballot it was clear to all. There would be no compromise. Even though a mere ten votes stood between Ganar and the nomination. Go-betweens hurriedly shuttled between the parties, text messages flew across the floor and as tensions mounted recriminations grew louder. Finally, the Pasternak supporters floated a compromise candidate in the guise of Delaware Governor McCastle Stone. Many grasped this solution to the deadlocked convention and Stone, a likable guy and an old-time Republican stalwart, emerged as its standard bearer by one vote.

Appeals were made to Ganar to get behind Stone. He refused. Pandemonium erupted. Ganar supporters alleged the establishment Republicans were obstructionists, possibly in league with the Democrats. Fistfights broke out; guns were drawn and the convention collapsed. The Ganar people decamped to Houston, Texas where they vowed to complete the nominating process. Meantime, the Pasternak people stayed, throwing their support to Stone.

Once in Houston, the Ganar faction not only refused to endorse McCastle but also rallied around the standard raised by Texas Governor Pablo Cross who led them out of the moribund Republican Party. From its ashes the Founders Action Party emerged...

The screen suddenly flickered and a new message flashed across the screen:

What Really Happened (accessed only by a special password)
What in Darwin is this?? But before Freeman could apply fingers to the keyboard another message appeared:
Would you like to access?
Impulsively he tapped out, *Yes.*
Do not touch the keyboard again. A password will appear. You have 15 seconds to commit it to memory. No further opportunities will be forthcoming.
Almost immediately the password appeared and, as promised, dissolved within 15 seconds.
Why am I doing this?? Leave well enough alone, he cautioned himself. But ever curious, he couldn't resist and entered the password.
Instantly this appeared on his screen: *What Really Happened* (accessed only by a special password)
Again, he questioned why he was looking at this but his curiosity overcame his common sense and he began scrolling down the screen, reading through it rapidly. It appeared to be an alternative history of America that followed the CCU's *The Restored History* chapter for chapter, but providing a very different version. *How could that be?*
He quickly scrolled down and randomly began to read:

... in its attempts to roll back the New Deal, the Republican Party needed to win over an important block of Democratic Party support: working and middle class white men and their willing wives. Starting with Richard Nixon, the Republican Party made a calculated decision to relinquish a piece of its soul to get the job done.

The seduction of choice: resentment and fear. They began a campaign designed to convince these marginal MAKERs that their way of life was being compromised, about to be eradicated by the Democratic Party's support of civil rights for African Americans. Then came busing, Affirmative Action, women's liberation, legalized abortion, and the gay rights movement. The fear that America was becoming a godless country, along with what seemed to many as an endless tide of illegal immigration of brown people, particularly Mexicans, made some white folks mad. They believed their slice of the American dream, though small, was about to vanish into the mouths of the undeserving 'other.'

Collectively, these clashes were known as the 'Culture Wars.' Over the decades, the Republican Party fueled its flames until it burned so white hot, even they could no longer control it. Those ignited by these issues slowly, but inevitably, began wielding power, demanding the Republican Party do more than pay lip service to their worldview. But even as they moved the party to champion these issues the country, as a whole, moved away from these. By the early twenty-first century, the vast majority of Americans had no problem with women being equal to men or women controlling their bodies. They accepted gay marriage and taking a hit of pot for pleasure. All in all, most Americans wanted government to stay out of individual lifestyle choices.

Yet the Democratic Party continued to lose local level elections and couldn't keep control over Congress. Many blamed it on a lack of party unity driven by their conservative wing, the "Blue Dogs" [Woof], others on their utter neglect of local politics, which permitted the Republicans to employ a bottom up strategy. By taking control of state politics one school board at a time, one town council at a time, and one state house at a time, the Republicans were able to control the state apparatus that drew the state and Congressional district lines. In this manner, with little objection from the Democratic Party, and with only occasional and ineffectual oversight by a compromised judiciary, the Republicans successfully gerrymandered state after state, giving them permanent control of both the House and Senate and sufficient statehouses to block and then reverse, most progressive change. Yet, because the presidency, the USA's only national office, tended to galvanize the true silent majority- the young, the old, minorities, and those who simply only turned out only when the presidency was up for grabs -the GOP with its out-of-step social agenda, appeared permanently shut out of the White House.

This failure set in motion a great debate within the Republican Party as to how to achieve its goal. The result was that the GOP became a house divided... "

Freeman read through these first few paragraphs. From his initial reading of this purported history he gathered its author saw it all as part of a vast on-going "Right Wing" conspiracy, going back to the New Deal. It depicted the real struggle, the real agenda since the time of FDR, to resist the march of corporate control over America. The author seemed to view FDR as a hero. He could hardly believe this book was depicting that old villain as the "savior of capitalism."

As he continued to read he lapsed into perplexed silence. Finally he closed his screen. Drew in a deep breath. Closed his eyes as if to keep out what he had just read. He was disturbed, deeply disturbed. He fancied himself a student of history. He was certainly, even by yesterday's standards, "well read." He consumed copious amounts of materials, both old and new, and had access to things even most JCs did not. He thought of all the history books in his private library and elsewhere he had read. Nothing, but nothing he had ever digested, had ever hinted at what he was now perusing. In all his intellectual wanderings he had never encountered such, well, how to put it, blasphemy.

He didn't know how this had made its way onto his screen. He shouldn't have entered that password. It was just one of those *oh no seconds* everyone has and regrets. What popped up could only be the work of subversives; some hackers burrowed deep in a Project somewhere, godless creatures with no hope of salvation in this life or the next, trying to wreak havoc on the Corpus and on God's word as revealed through his Prophet Charles Darwin. Well, he, the Second

Keeper of the Book, would certainly not be their instrument. Best to simply ignore it, put it out his mind and stick to the restored history.

But two minutes later he found himself opening his computer, returning to that alternate history which was still available on his screen.

Yet, I'm curious what else this author has to say about the Founders Action Party. Last look:

...the hoped for Republican unity never materialized. Stone never even got through his acceptance speech before half the delegates walked out and reconvened three days later in Houston. Led by Texas Governor Pablo Cross and Tennessee Senator Randall Carey, who gave a fiery welcoming address to the assembled, they immediately voted to join with a small, mostly unknown political party, the Founders Action Party, "FAP." They vowed to "take back" the nation and remake it as originally envisioned by its Founding Fathers. To that end they nominated businessman Ted Ganar as the first FAP presidential candidate.

The Republican presidential candidate, Stone, remained on the ballot but to no one's surprise, went down to defeat. Ganar, while unbelievably, popular fared no better because the FAP was unable to get on sufficient state ballots. No matter. The FAP was actually elated to see the country repudiate the last standing Republican. The Democratic candidate, Emily Harris, won handily due to the disarray of the Republican Party and the FAP's presence, but her victory was truly short-lived.

Right after the presidential election the FAP, led by primarily by Governor Cross and Senator Randall, immediately undertook to pull together the disparate wings from the now mostly defunct national Republican Party. They imposed on their followers a discipline heretofore unseen in American politics. Moving "faster than a speeding bullet" [the slogan adopted by the FAP] this new political powerhouse immediately urged the still existing local and state Republican leaders to renounce their former party affiliation and join the FAP.

All the southern and most of the mid-western and Great Plains Republican state parties joined. Particularly critical to FAP's immediate future was pulling in the key battle ground states of Ohio, Wisconsin, Michigan, and Pennsylvania. There they quickly won over the former Republicans and FAP counted these in their column. By the following November FAP candidates found their way onto nearly every state ballot, taking over a majority of statehouses and claiming majorities in the House and Senate. The Democrats howled in protest but there was no stopping the FAP. They knew how to manipulate the levers of power and did not hesitate to do so. The soil in which the Great Transformation could grow was finally ready for planting.

How, many have asked, could this have happened so quickly? It was not quick. Compadres within the Corpus had been planning for this event for some time, decades really. The FAP was formed back when Bill Clinton was president in 1992. A minor political party, it languished at the bottom of the political food chain, unseen and unheard of by anyone. In 2008 the Tea Party exploded on the scene, grabbing the headlines, but it failed to either break from or totally remake the Republican Party. The FAP, on the other hand, funded by billionaires, sat in the shadows, quietly recruiting, waiting for its chance.

"Reverend Freeman," the young flight attendant tapped him on the shoulder. "Could I ask you to buckle up? We are coming into JFK."

No response.

She tapped him again on his hand and he startled to attention snapping the screen shut.

"Reverend Ice you need to buckle up." She moved her hand down to his lap barely touching the tops of his thighs, drawing the belt around to his front, snapping it securely.

"There now, safe landing and thank you for flying with us. Have a blessed day."

He flashed his famous smile at her, both seductive and comforting. How he managed this is unclear but it produced the desired effect- alternately seducing, man or woman into the fold, while inducing a feeling of the utmost well-being. It made the recipient wish to spend eternity in the company of this rising young scion.

God bless the gene that produced this magnificent man, she mused adding for good measure, *and he's caliente! Smokin' really.* She chastised herself for that little bit of self-indulgence but then shrugged it off. *It's not like he's some priest who's off-limits.* She couldn't wait to tell her friends about her little brush by with the Reverend. She scooted back to her jump seat, buckled up, and opened her Palm Pad to broadcast...

Take a Magic Carpet Ride

Ice exited the airport to his waiting limo surrounded by throngs of admirers, the press, and, of course, TC. TC stepped forward, detaching himself from the crowd and fell into the embrace of a smiling Ice. They hadn't seen each other in about four months, an eternity by their standards. They grew up together in Savannah, though all the children of the Faithful Ten **always** spent their summers in the old Clarksdale compound. They were a tight little group, more like siblings than mere friends or business associates.

In fact, one of the CRS's big draws was the coziness of family, the promise of community in a world so commodified that each movement from the twitch of an eye to the amount of time taken to munch on a C-snack was quantified. The CRS exuded something both otherworldly and hominess simultaneously: justification in this world and salvation in the next. Some, mostly from the top tiers, were immediately recognized as Revealed Saints, their ascent directly to Heaven assured. For most, however, their road might take years, near a lifetime to achieve. However, under the supervision of their local CRS "Guide," along with the support of their CRS community, sufficient "signs" of their salvation would eventually become visible and the hoped for guarantee of salvation declared. Of course, this required constant vigilance, constant searching for signs of salvation, God's grant of Grace.

The Book of Darwin teaches us that the best indicator of that grant of Grace is material success; so it was understandable that the vast majority of JCs were revealed Saints. *The Book of Darwin* also contains a caution: from time to time God tests us by sending a wolf in sheep's clothing to fool us. It is up to us, ever heedful, ever alert, to sort the wheat from the chaff, to uncover the deceiver. There have been instances where even a JC has been unmasked and sent down to the Projects. This is the beauty of God's design. As Darwin explained: *The divine "blueprint" is clearly laid out, you need only open your eyes to see its manifestation.* [*Book of Darwin, Chapter 22: 167*]

"Hey man," TC mumbled into Ice's shoulder as they embraced, "so great you're here."

"Same. It's been too long. Way too long"

Microphones, reporters, screaming fans, all clustered around them while TC attempted to quickly usher Ice into the waiting limo, three burly bodyguards at the ready if needed. The Keeper, born to his position, moved reluctantly towards the limo. He paused to wave, quickly laid hands on the hopeful, blessed a babe in arms reciting the standard: *Pray with me this child is one of the Revealed and give her the wisdom to follow God's differentiated plan for her, amen.*

If TC had permitted, this could have gone on for hours. He knew he'd have to insist they move along if Ice were to get to the Cathedral on time. After giving the Reverend Isaac Freeman a few more minutes of blessings, touchings, waving to the devoted, he finally put his hand on his friend's arm whispering in his ear, "Ice man, we really have to go. The ceremony starts at 3 pm and it's already noon. You need to get ready, get revved and be on your game."

"Ok, let's go. It's just I hate to leave the hopeful still wanting. Look at them. So many came to hear the **Word,** the **Good News**, the…"

TC cut him off, "Yeah, I know, but we've really got to go," and wedged Ice into the waiting limo.

Three hours later the Reverend Isaac Freeman found himself once again standing in the CRS' magnificent Cathedral of Commerce preparing to bless CCU's, *The Restored History of America from 1492 to the Great Transformation.* It was a typical Red Carpet event, the paparazzi, the fans, the devoted, all wanting to be in on this major in-the-being event. *How lucky*, many of the waiting WEs thought, *I live in New York City and can experience such a thing for only the price of a subway ride.*

"Reverend Ice, Reverend Ice," called out the CAN news reporter waving his mini-corder in the air for emphasis. "Just a question, just one."

Despite his handlers, Ice stopped for a moment stepping ever so slightly off the Red Carpet to the left. Instantly, a human sea crowded round trying to get that exclusive.

Ice's bodyguards pushed back on the throng, warning them they'd all be dispersed unless they kept the appropriate distance.

"You know where the line is," Ice's imposing head guard admonished them.

With that, they all fell back a few steps. But his head man knew, from having served in this position since Ice took up the Keeper's mantle, there would be no moving forward, no ceremony, no blessing, until the Reverend Freeman answered questions, waved to the devoted both on hand and those at home. This was his touch, his appeal, and his gracia; there was no deterring him.

"Why are you blessing a secular book? It's never been done before." cried out one reporter.

"So that must tell you how special it is," Ice chuckled as the gathered media laughed with him.

"But, why have you decided to do this? Give us the details, the blow by blow."

"CCU is a very special parishioner. It's the educational heart of the CSA, more JCs graduate out of its halls than from any other institution. It sits on hallowed grounds, right here in Wall Street. That's why God moved us to site our main cathedral, this Cathedral of Commerce, here. Naturally, when the CCU asked me to read this book [he picked it up to show its cover] I gave it due consideration."

"But what made you decide to bless it?" interjected another voice.

"Dele a su sello de aprobación," asked the reporter from Latinosocial.

"Easy, I recognized it as an important synthesis of our history. It doesn't merely explain, detail, and lay out the events but takes the reader through our journey as a people and as a nation. Once digested, you will understand how and why we arrived here, today. If we forget the mistakes of the past, if we don't understand where we deviated from the path the Founders and the Lord laid out for us, we will surely lose our way again. This book, this "restored history," serves as that constant reminder. That's why I urge all the folks out there to order it today. Like our sacred *Book of Darwin* keeping a copy by your side, on your screen, visible in your home, will help keep you, keep us all, on the straight and narrow moving steadily forward here in this world and into the next."

He stopped, looked intently at the crowed and roared, "Now say, AMEN!"

"AMEN, AMEN, AMEN…." the crowd answered in a growing crescendo.

Ice's bodyguards took that as their cue their boss was ready to precede into the Cathedral. They pushed back the reporters guiding Ice back onto the Red Carpet. Twenty seconds later he vanished into the Cathedral leaving behind what many onlookers swore was heaven's shimmer.

It all went off as planned. The blessing, the homily, the audience reaction was absolutely stupendous. The invited arrived in the most gossamer CRS garments imaginable, almost all Revealed Saints, mind you. The vision of hundreds drifting into the Cathedral of Commerce in such garments, so other worldly, gave the onlookers the sense that these folks were indeed about to embark on their journey to heaven to receive their just rewards.

The Chancellor got his day in the sun. The History Department, along with its Chair, seemed cemented into the very walls of the Cathedral of Commerce and thus into the CCU [at least for the foreseeable future], and the Book's Second Keeper increasingly looked like a powerhouse, someone who would shape the contours of the CSA for years to come. Only a serious misstep would derail the CRS' rising star.

The after party was held in the Cathedral's event space located in Spire four. The festivities spanned numerous floors but only VIPs were given access to its top floor and the terrace with commanding views of the Hudson River. Of the History Department PROFFIEs in attendance this "treat" was only extended to Chair Triquot and *The Restored History's* co-author, Professor Layla Saenz.

Much of the festivities were screened live for the masses. From home, WEs and others not privileged enough to attend, donned their Third-Eyes providing them with the illusion of being right there in the middle of the action. They could virtually touch the Reverend Isaac Freeman, converse with the CCU chancellor, and even have virtual sex with any number of the most popular EASYs present. It was really as good as being there. [Well that's the truth, isn't it?]

Ice stayed on the lower three levels for a while, pressing the flesh, dispensing a blessing here and there, making all the required small talk, uploading digital contact info for a just- in- case encounter before he drifted off to the top tier that was completely closed off to virtual viewing, and to all in-the-being guests, except designated VIPs. Most VIPs did their time below before, like Ice, drifting upwards. Once there, Ice chatted up his VIPs for a respectable interval before moving to a cordoned off distant corner of the terrace.

As usual, the lights in New York and from across the Hudson River were very bright. The illuminations never seemed to dim. The hum of the traffic below and in the sky, incessant. Nothing ever appeared to stop. Unlike most people, he had the blessing of retreat, of solitude from this 24/7, fully commodified world and he thanked God for having designated him to reap such a blessing.

He heard a noise behind him. He turned. It was Layla. He recognized her from that day's ceremony.

"Professor Saenz, how did you get past the guards?" [He had a wonderful memory for names]

"Oh, they were momentarily distracted by other things."

"I see, well now that you are here. What can I do for you? Do you seek a blessing?" He automatically started to approach her, but she backed away.

"Thank you, but no. I am not a member of the CRS. But so kind of you to offer."

He instantly put his hands down to his side feeling much as he had when, as a young child, his father would take him to task. He recovered his composure quickly.

"Please forgive me Professor Saenz, I just assumed..."

"Of course you did," she replied cutting him off, "you just assumed that I am a CRS member but I am not now and, I promise you, never will be."

He was so unaccustomed to being spoken to in this manner he hardly knew what to say next. Should he turn and leave? Absolutely not he decided, this was, after all, his cathedral, his terrace. Instead he took the, "I am amused" tact.

"I see. Well, it's all part of the Lord's design. You are obviously not destined to be one of the Revealed Saints. Too bad," he added for emphasis.

But she persisted.

"Actually, I am quite all right. Excuse me if I say this and you can report me to Handler if you wish, but it's just a lot of hubris."

She turned to go but he stopped her.

"That's blasphemy you know."

"No, that's my exercising my right to free speech. It's actually still in the CSA Constitution. Also, the last time I checked, citizens are not required to be CRS members, even if it is the official creed of the government."

"That's quaint."

"What's quaint?"

"The use of the word 'citizen.' You don't hear that word used much today."

"No you don't. The government and Corpus would much prefer we think of ourselves as MAKERS.

He looked at her again, this time assessing her carefully, completely. She was, he thought, quite attractive. Slim body, full breasts; but not so full they looked implanted, almond eyes, very dark brown, loose long dusky curls and a not quite perfect nose on an oval, somewhat thin face. Not a classic beauty and most women from her tier would have tweaked that nose a bit, but on her it was highly attractive. Yes, there was something intriguing about her physically and intellectually. He had nothing better to do. He didn't feel like going inside, he knew by heart the convo awaiting him, so he chose to stay and joust with this young woman.

"You are correct. We are all still citizens and no one, certainly least of all me, would insist you become a member of the CRS, although you do realize you needn't give up your home religion to do so. If you read our literature you'd see most of our members go right on practicing Christianity, Islam, Judaism or whatever religion they cleave to. There's absolutely no conflict."

"So I've heard," she curtly responded.

"What," if you don't mind my inquiring, "is your home religion? "

"Not that it's really your business, but I'm Jewish."

173

"Ahhh," he exclaimed, "yes your people have been some of the most resistant to joining. Even those who are JCs often feel reluctant but eventually we win them over as we will, one day, win you over."

She didn't respond so he continued. "You know it is not a betrayal of your home religion to join the CRS. It doesn't interfere with those beliefs. The *Book of Darwin* simply finishes the story. It provides us with the final explanation of the Lord's design. All religions are part of God's design. All have led us to where we are today."

Again, she didn't answer. Simply stood looking out over the magnificent view. She suddenly looked so lost, so very alone that it touched him in a way that was unfamiliar. As a minister he was accustomed to hearing people's problems, their complaints, life stories, the anguish of misgiving, paths not taken, poor choices made and, most often, the lament over not being one of the Revealed. He didn't sense any of this in her. What it was he wasn't sure. He took a step forward putting a hand gingerly on her forearm. She had her back to him as she looked out over the Hudson. She did not flinch from his touch. Appeared not to even notice.

After a few minutes she spoke to him, but in a tone much softer, more wistful than before.

"You must come here often. But have you ever just looked beyond this? Just cut through all this clutter, this debris that makes up our lives and wondered what it might have looked like before? I mean before all of this? Going way back to a time before the coming of Columbus, Verrazano, the settlers, the reworking of the river and, well, just everything that's here now."

No one had ever voiced that to him. Those were his thoughts, his private reflections. How could she know? Was someone from his staff talking about his private habits? He'd better look into that. He wouldn't tolerate anything but absolute loyalty and discretion form his people.

"How did you know?"

"Know what?" she queried turning her back to the view to face him.

"That I stand here thinking those precise thoughts."

"I didn't know. The thought always comes to me when I look out over the Hudson. I live right over there," she explained pointing towards Battery Park City. "I see the river every day. Of course, mine is not this sweeping vista, but even my little wedge is thought provoking. After all, I am an historian. My specialty is Early American so that explains my thoughts, but how to rationalize yours Reverend Freeman since this is," she motioned to the endless activity on the horizon, "according to CRS dogma, is all part of God's grand blueprint?"

Horrified by his own tactless admission along with this young PROFFIE's interrogation he was, for a few moments, at a loss for words. Should he explain himself to her or simply change the topic?

"My musings on the past does not imply the present was not meant to be. It most certainly is all part of God's design. I don't make a habit of discussing myself with strangers, but I'll make an exception and satisfy your curiosity. Yes, I am particularly interested in history; specifically America's distant past, the pre-Columbus era. Maybe that's why, whenever I'm here, this vista triggers my imagination. I look out over it and can't help but wonder what it must have looked like before all this. Do you know what I mean? I mentally eliminate, frame by frame, image by image, all traces of modern habitation replacing it with an uncluttered landscape."

"I see. Yes, I totally understand. I do much the same. What about history interests you?"

Ahhh... magic words to him. Over the course of the next several hours he spoke to her, in detail, about the many books he had read or perused. Since some were quite old, he was surprised she was familiar with almost all of them.

"How is that possible? Most are from a private library the Prophet left my father. I had no idea these were accessible digitally."

"No, no," she corrected him, "of course they're not. Who would ever expend the resources to do that? However, almost everything you've mentioned is either in the New York 42d Street Library or in the *Golightly Touch it for Real* CCU library. Of course, most people don't have entrée to these collections nor should they, but, as a history professor, I do. Ph.D. students and historians generally are required to read many of the texts you mention. How else could we do our work?

They sat down on two settees facing each other. He listened to her like a schoolboy attentively attending to his Content Facilitator. They went back and forth discussing the merits of the various books he had read. It was the first time he was ever able to converse with another person about such things. He found it invigorating. It was, he realized, terribly old fashioned. But then, at his core, so was he. He didn't know why, but he realized there was a part of him that rejected modernity, really didn't like it at all. Perhaps that was his affinity for Savannah over New York.

Around 5:00 a.m. in the morning one of his staff approached to tell him the last of the guests had departed and they were getting ready to close up the event space. Layla jumped to her feet; stuck her hand out towards him.

"Well, it was truly a pleasure to meet you Keeper Freeman. On behalf of the entire CCU History Department let me express our deep gratitude for your blessing. We are honored."

Ignoring her pro forma leave-taking he introduced a different topic. "I will be around for a few more days. I would love to continue our conversation. My driver can pick you up at one for lunch tomorrow. Would that be ok?"

"Ummm well, I guess so. I'm done teaching around noon and," she quickly flipped open her Palm Pad to check it, "I don't see any meetings so, ok, yeah, sure. But you must be busy?"

He disregarded that last comment motioning to a staff member standing off to the side, "Give Rick here your contact info and he'll tap you when he's at your office. Does that work for you?"

"That's fine, but really I could just meet you."

"No, Rick will pick you up. Is there anything you like or don't eat? Dietary restrictions?"

"No, I eat everything except Brussels sprouts," she stated very seriously. "I don't like Brussels sprouts."

He smiled at the way she said it. It sounded almost like a reluctant confession, "May I inquire what is so awful about them?"

"Maybe another time, Ok?"

"It sounds serious, but another time you can tell me the story and it's probably too late for such a serious discussion. Rick here will take you home."

"No, that's ok, I live ten minutes from here. I'll walk along the promenade and watch the sunrise…"

"Then let me go with you."

"It's really not necessary. And truly, I have to get some sleep. I have a 10:00 a.m. class, so I really shouldn't linger."

He smiled. "I understand. Let's go."

He walked her home, mostly in silence. Rick literally trailing just twenty paces behind them in his car. They reached her apartment as the sun began to rise.

"Could I ask one small favor?" He smiled his capturing smile.

"What?"

"Just stand here with me for a few minutes. Let me experience the sunrise with you right here on the Hudson River. I know you will see it as I do, as the Muheakantuck River. I've never gazed on the Muheakantuck with anyone. I've always been alone and I'd love to share it with you."

She leaned back against him saying, "Yes, I'd like that too."

Only then did she turn to face him. He bent in towards her for their first kiss, which lingered on their tongues and hearts requiring nothing more until the sun rose and they parted.

Chapter 26: Paul

GTE, 45

"Paul," motioned his Team Leader poking his head out from his office, "I need to see you."

Paul slowly got to his feet. He looked around. All eyes were on him. He felt them. Smelled them. Oh god, what now? Was he being deleted? He couldn't imagine what for. The book campaign was a great success. Everyone said so. Even Chancellor Handler had faced them with congratulations. And the Second Keeper himself, just a few weeks before, actually blessed the book. And it was selling. So, what could it be? He took a moment to self-assess: *Do I arrive on time? Check. Do I stay late? Check. Am I available pretty much 24/7? Check. Haven't even taken a day. Are my projects a success? Check.* He simply couldn't imagine what he had done wrong, but surely it was something. He slumped off to his Team Leader's office just a few steps from where he sat. When Symone offered him the comfy chair and not the death stool as it was commonly referred to, he relaxed a bit.

"Do you know why I have asked you in here?"

Paul shook his head. "No sir, I don't. But if I have done something wrong I hope you will give me a chance to correct before you delete me."

"Delete you? No. You've got it all wrong. I want to commend you."

"Commend me?"

"Yes. You're a sensation! Haven't you seen it? I mean what are you doing with your time? Haven't you been online? It's been all over the W3s since yesterday. It's your paintings. A History PROFFIE posted them. Everyone's yattering about it."

He shoved his Palm Pad into Paul's face. "Look for yourself."

"An undiscovered EASY," some proclaim.
'Slipped through the cracks," posts another.
"Do we need to keep reassessing?' asks the STD.
"OMG," Paul blurted out, "how'd this happen?"
"I told you. A PROFFIE posted these."

He eyed Paul carefully adding, "Are you doing a PROFFIE? Is that how this happened?"

"No, no nothing like that- she just, well she saw my paintings. Liked them."

"Hmmm...How'd this come about then? Bing her? Palming her?"

He paused a moment. Grabbed Paul by the back of his neck adding, "Well, doesn't much matter the detail, huh? Just as long as we all see the value adding up. As long as it remains a multiplier. 'Course it makes me shine too. After all I hired you, right? Gave you a chance when no one else would. No matter how high you rise you won't forget that, right?

"No, no of course not. But, I think it's just that 15-second thing; interest will be over by the end of the week. You know how these things are, here and then gone. On to the next big thing."

"Yeah, you're probably right. But let's capitalize on it for SM as much as possible, ok?"

"Sure thing," Paul agreed as he tried to ease himself up and out of the chair, but his Team Leader tightened his grip on his neck.

"BTW, have you perused HR's rules for employee fraternizing? Bet you haven't. Long policy, complicated set of rules. Well, check 'em out- you know just in case things go south."

He let Paul go who immediately shot out of his chair "faster than a speeding bullet," as the FAP would say.

"Naw," he reiterated with a bravado he really didn't feel, "no need."

"Ok, just trying to help you CYA."

Affirmative Action

Paul took his lunch break alone outside. Sitting on a bench overlooking the magnificent fountain designed by that popular EASY of the moment, Manolo. He snapped open his Palm Pad texting, "What were you thinking about?"

"Where are you?" she texted back

"In front of Manolo's fountain eating what may be my last lunch."

"Stay right there. I'll be down in a few."

Five minutes later, Layla appeared decked out in a pair of black gauzy harem style pants, tight copper shirt, her dark brown hair falling in its curly disarray, the fountain's spray causing it to stick to her almond shaped face. She was lovely; really beautiful he had to admit.

She sat down next to Paul drumming just the tip of her extravagantly painted fingernail on the bench in a nervous gesture. "I'm sorry," she murmured.

He twisted his back away from her. "Yeah, well that's easy for you to say. You'll be fine. A social experiment you'll say; a way to expand prognostication, you'll rationalize. And you know what? Your PROFFIE buddies will pat you on the back, and then give you a raise or a grant. Eventually they'll incorporate your findings into some new master plan. You'll rise and I'll be locked in the Projects. That's how this movie ends. I know it. People like me never win. We're always on the losing end. Rules are strictly applied to us, stuck up our asses like cattle prods. But somehow the rules, all the laws that so tightly control us, never apply to **your** activities. Oh, yeah, it sounds bad, doesn't sound like how it should be, but what can be done? There's no law against it. Of course not! Because you people write the laws, enforce the codes. It's the same old, same old. And you know what else?"

Layla shook her head.

"I'll tell you what else. I don't even believe those so-called assessments are fair. I think it's all a pile of shit. I think there's some type of quota. Just a few of us squeak through into the other classifications. Then once in a while they reclassify just like they did with Handler. They do it just to use as proof of the correctness of their Darwinian inspired system. But tell you what? I've seen the work of some of those so-called fine arts EASYs and I'm better than most of them. They're just there 'cause their Mom or Dad was an EASY or in one of the better tiers. Wouldn't want one of their precious progeny classified as a WE. Imagine little Johnnie JC after his privileged childhood being busted down to a WE? Living in our little shitholes, eating Cs, commuting for hours to get to his job, handing over every god dammed credit he makes just for the basics? The very heavens might open up. Darwin himself might descend to protest."

Paul's rising voice caused Layla to shake her head cautioning him to lower his voice. Suddenly, as if he realized he was in a public space, he stopped and stared, stating quietly, "Well, I don't care anymore. I'm sick of this shit. I'm not moving anywhere. I'm going nowhere. We both know it. There's nothing for me. Let them come and take me to the Projects. Flash me as an example. I just don't care. Maybe you've done me a favor!"

He turned to leave but Layla laid her hand, gently, on his shoulder. How could such a delicate touch stop someone in his tracks? But it did. So he stopped, but did not turn towards her.

"I've confided in you what I think about this system. But things will change for you. Don't do anything precipitous. Don't regret. You are not alone. Trust me and wait. "

She motioned him to face her and he obeyed.

"Will you do as I ask?"

"Yes," he murmured.

"Good," she intoned and walked away.

Chapter 27: Isaac

New York, New York [GTE, 45]

He stayed in New York longer than planned. Normally, he returned home to Savannah as soon as whatever had brought him to this center of the financial world was over. This time he stayed on. TC was amused.

"If I had known that all it took was an interesting woman to keep you around, I would have set you up earlier."

Ice did not comment. He was notoriously private about his personal life. He did not confide in anyone about such matters, not even his lifelong friend TC. He met women. Many women. He had his choice. Why wouldn't he? He was rich and powerful. He was strikingly good looking. He was charismatic.

Ice was discrete. No scandals, no babies, no woofs, palmings or anything like that. It was dinner, straight sex, and adios for the most part. Most women, most people, quite frankly, bored our Second Keeper of the Book. Why? Even he was not sure. TC suspected it was simply because he was too damn bright, too broadly educated for his own good. It made him look at things differently than most people.

He contrasted his own life to Ice's. They grew up together, each clearly pre-destined for their current role, ICE as Keeper and he as the CRS's CFO. Like his mom Betty, TC was a real financial wizard- damn but Darwin, blessed be **His** name, understood that genes properly distributed would tell! Like his mother before, if the CRS needed funds for a new project, well he'd conjure up investors practically from thin air. No sense putting their own funds in the game when others were so anxious to step forward. His keen instincts for the market guaranteed the CRS was never caught short, never took one of those market baths when the exchanges suddenly fluctuated wildly or fell into steep decline.

Unlike most people he understood that the markets were like an irrational child who'd throw a fit for the most ridiculous reasons. So, whenever something crazy and temp happened that caused investors to dump or spiral down, he'd shrug it off, because that's how you deal with a temperamental child. Give in to its arbitrary demands and you will take that proverbial bath.

TC knew his focus, he understood his destiny, and he was content. Life, he always reminded himself when even the smallest drip of uncertainty entered, was all about focus. Follow your calling, your occupational track. It wasn't hard. It was all laid out in one's individualized assessment. Run with it. Sure he had the basics and even more smatterings [after all he was a PROFFESSIONAL], but like most people, he hewed close to his narrow calling in life. Like most people he believed you left academics to the professors, politics to the politicians, and so on; each to his own sphere. That's what made society roll, guided it seamlessly through the pipeline. Anything else was clutter and like the word implied it needed to be emptied with the trash.

The tiering of America had permitted everyone to, well, dump the superfluous to free up the individual to function at his or her max. It was what made the CSA the global giant it was today. Who was he to buck what was clearly a superior system and, even more to the point, the worldly manifestation of God's will? Yes, now that he reflected on it, this was Ice's problem. Clutter. Maybe a good love interest would help him empty that bin. This Layla Saenz might be just what Ice needed. She was a professor, an intellectual who read books, the kind of stuff Ice loved. He actually hoped Ice had finally found his fit. Of course, she would have to be vetted. He'd better have security hop on that immediately.

Living on the Muheakantuck

Ice was again standing on his terrace. [Yes, he was actually beginning to think of it as **his** terrace] Looking over his now beloved Muheakantuck River. He had spent the day and late into the evening with Layla. He wanted her to spend the night but she declined. Demurred.

Said she wasn't into one-nighters- old fashioned she admitted, but perhaps being an historian so inclined her. No problem he had assured her. They had all the time in the world. He palmed Handler the next day asking him to assign her to him for the duration of his trip as his "guide."

"Handler, I have decided it's time for me to get to know my New York City flock so I am staying put for a while."

"Hmmm… yes, good idea Keeper Freeman, good idea. We are so pleased, so pleased."

"I am going to need a guide."

"Guide you say? No problem. So much to see. I will make the arrangements. Do you want virtual or in-the-being?"

"Thanks Handler, but not necessary. I can make my own arrangements. Just one thing I need from you."

"Sure, sure, anything at all. What can CCU do to facilitate your stay here?"

"I'd like Professor Saenz to accompany me, be my guide. She's an historian, knows the backstory to New York's neighborhoods and landmarks, right?

"Absolutely, absolutely, perfect choice."

"Good, but she's says it's not possible unless she's given workload release time. I thought it efficient to come directly to you instead of putting in the request to Triquot. Know what I mean?"

"Sure, sure, it's all fine with me. Whatever our Keeper wants we are happy to accommodate. "

"Great, I'll let her know." He hung up

A week later he was still in New York. A perplexed staffer ventured to inquire when they were returning to Savannah. He curtly dismissed the inquiry; they'd all be informed when he was ready to leave. His staff fully understood that this trip, supposedly a quickie, had morphed into something else. It seemed to all that the Reverend Isaac Freeman was, bit by bit, taking up residence in New York City, transferring his quotidian duties along with everything except the BOOK, which remained in Savannah, to New York.

He was, perhaps for the first time in his life, truly taken with a woman. He didn't use the word love yet. But to all onlookers he presented all the hallmarks of that quaint sentiment.

Dr. Layla Saenz was a complete surprise. She was spunky, opinionated, bright and, well, just plain singular. Naturally his people did a bit of digging about her, not much effort was needed. Just scratching at the ground uncovered all they needed to know and his staff made sure their boss knew it all.

The Digger presented Freeman with the final report- gave it to him face-to face. She was a TAKER born and bred; received a temporary reclassification some twelve years back made permanent when CCU hired her three years ago. No surprise to the Assessors who'd been carefully tracking this one. She was bright, engaged, and ambitious. Her parents, the Digger further informed Freeman and his entire assembled staff, had taken part in the Last Uprising, terrorists of the worst sort. Highly intelligent yes, but subversives killed by a RW&B anti-terrorist squad in time to stop them from detonating some home-grown explosive device intended to take down the Projects' gates. Something the Keeper needed to be aware of. Of course, so far, no one could say for sure that such proclivities for dissident tendencies was inherited, praise Darwin, the Keeper silently thought, but surely, his staff all opined in unison, it was something to keep in mind. Yes, yes, the Keeper agreed but, as he pointed out, both the *Book of Darwin* as well as the CSA dedicated as it was to true meritocracy, assigned us each according to our own abilities **not** those of our parents. Dr. Saenz's dossier also indicated she had been a model TAKER, now an able, energetic, time-oriented PROFFIE capable of turning a profit for CCU. A true capacity builder, she was the primary architect of that new field "Prognostication" as well as one of the authors of *The Restored History*. How was that for only three full years into her career? No sign that her parents' proclivities had been either passed down to her genetically or socially inculcated into her fiber.

The Digger ignored the Keeper's efforts to put a good spin on it and forged on with his report:

"Seems she got her fifteen minutes as the first TAKER recipient of a full Golightly scholarship to CCU. It was considered a real triumph of the system at the time. Demonstrated the complex interaction between genes and environment— gives a good name to the field of epigenetics. Resulted in several scholarly articles. I've included the links to these if you want to look."

Ice nodded.

"Still don't remember the buzz about her about dozen years back?" the Digger nudged.

"Yeah, now that you mention it, I do remember, just not her name. That was her? Well, she seems to have a penchant for the fifteen minutes. By my calculations she's up to forty-five."

Laughter all around. But at heart his staff was nervous. The Keeper's well-being was theirs. Anyone could fall from grace. That was well understood and accepted. Only the Corpus was too big to fail. As much as his Surrounders often urged him to stay longer in New York, get to know the Corpus better, this time all they wanted was to get him on that plane back to Savannah.

Layla Again

Dinner with Layla again his staff moaned. This time she picked the place, insisted he leave his Surrounders behind, and even made him board the subway. She wanted privacy. She wanted to see what a normal evening with him, as she referred to it, would be like.

"I'll be recognized," he told her.

"No you won't. Dressed like a normal person, without your Surrounders and all those bells and whistles that jangle in your wake, no one will identify you. Sure, some may say, 'Doesn't he look a bit like that CRS guy?' But then, someone will remind him or her, 'No way it's him. Just look at the guy -- at his clothing, and his face—sure it's similar but when you really look at him you can see it's not him at all. And anyway, what would he be doing on the subway?' They will move on and so will we. Free to chat, to eat, to walk, to be blessedly alone!" She laughed at herself for using that word "blessedly."

"So you say."

"Yes, so I say, and let it be so," she echoed as she playfully adjusted his collar on the most casual shirt he'd ever worn since assuming his CRS position.

"Arrogant woman! Always convinced you are right, going your own way."

"But here's a truthie: that's what you like about me."

"Correct, let's go."

Sure his staff objected when he told them he was going out alone with Layla, no Surrounders, no security, but he would not be dissuaded. The fucking TAKER [that's how they privately referred to Layla] had bewitched him. They hastily palmed TC not knowing what else to do.

"Send out two Security; instruct them to keep a discrete distance. He's not to know they're following him," he ordered.

Ice's staff dispatched security and breathed a sigh of relief. The Keeper would have some measure of safety and, if discovered it, well, he could take that up with his CFO and not them.

His date [yes, as old-fashioned as it sounds that's what it was] with Layla was truly extraordinary- at least for a man who'd rarely gone anywhere unaccompanied. She was correct. What he needed was anonymity, a bit of privacy. In a world that craved celebrity, valued it only behind amassing so much credit you'd never spend it all even if you lived several life times, even Ice, the introspective Reverend Freeman, had failed to comprehend that everything had its limits. His position, his celebrity was, in fact, suffocating him. He couldn't even relieve himself without someone waiting by the door. He might be perceived as a powerful man, but it was all an illusion. It was the position that was formidable, commanding. In fact it commanded him, dictated his every move. He was nothing apart from it. He hadn't created it; it had birthed him, quite literally. No wonder he was searching through those old books for answers. He was looking to the past to validate his present.

She picked him up late in the afternoon urging him to follow her into the bowels of that city to take the subway to the Cloisters. She laughed at him because of the stunned look on his face- not that of a tourist amazed by their first glance at a big metropolis, but more akin to a man from a different planet.

"Well, you are chatty today. What's up?"

"This feels, well, very alien to me."

"No subways in Savannah?"

"No."

"Never ventured down here before on one of your visits?

"No."

He hesitated for a moment. He spoke low, as if she were a Catholic priest and he a penitent in a confessional. "It's not just that I've never been on a subway, I've never been on any form of public transportation."

He stopped speaking but Layla said nothing. She knew he wasn't finished. He continued his admission.

"Never been on a bus or even on a commercial airline before. And maybe that should make me feel proud. The *Book of Darwin* as interpreted, tells me I should feel proud. It's a mark of my elevation, of who I was predestined to be, the Keeper and a Revealed Saint. That's what I was taught. I deserve it. Yet, right here, right now, I don't feel that way. I'm just wondering why I've never had this or countless other experiences. My only friends, when I think about it, are the sons and daughters of the Faithful Ten. I grew up on the CRS compound in Savannah with them. Summers were spent in Clarksdale where the CRS originated. We were kept close to our roots. I guess to those like us. And now, here in this metal car surrounded by strangers, our destinies tied to one another for these brief minutes, I wonder why I've never experienced this before? I feel, somehow, incomplete, unfinished."

"Then maybe the time for new experiences is now. There's nothing wrong with that."

She spoke it as if she had just given him absolution. Minutes ticked, but neither spoke until she announced tugging at him, "Let's go, this is where we get off."

In the Castle

"It's somewhat of an anomaly in New York City. A great medieval-like castle overlooking the Hudson River located close to the edge of the Bronx. Who'd have guessed?"

Layla, ever the history professor, was lecturing him on the edifice's construction while she pulled him up the path towards the entrance.

"It's called *The Cloisters*. It was built between 1934-1939 as a museum to house a collection of medieval art donated by some of the most prominent JCs of that era. The entire structure was brought over in sections. Amazing, right? They took pieces from five separate European cloistered abbeys then pieced them all together – like a jigsaw puzzle, right here, to recreate a medieval castle cum museum."

She turned to look at him, making sure he was paying attention.

"Have you ever seen anything like this place before?"

"Never." He admitted.

"Well, yet another first."

They wandered through the castle commenting on the art, the architecture, discussing its history. Things most people would find dull and duller. But they didn't. They pondered endlessly the JC Rockefeller's motivation for establishing the Cloisters. They chatted about the qualities of medieval art as they strolled through its vast galleries until they exited to an outside promenade overlooking the Hudson.

"So, here's the other reason I brought you - the view. The Hudson River, your *Muheakantuck*, but I wanted you to see another bend in its curve. Do you like?"

"A lovely gift Layla."

Later that night, she appeared on his terrace wearing one of his diaphanous vestment shirts. He could see the outline of her body underneath. She was lovely, but so were many women. That was not what called to him. It occurred to him he should be angry, outraged really that she had so little regard for these holy garments, but he was not. So many thoughts streamed, in no particular order, through his head. He knew he should rebuke her, tell her to return the shirt but before his lips moved in that direction she had encircled his waist whispering in his ear, "How many apparitions have you glimpsed on the *Muheakantuck*, tonight?"

He did not turn to her; but still facing the river described his vision:

"Fifteen, I think. Two were returning home in their canoes laden with fish and furs. Look," he pointed to the river, "can't you imagine the joy they felt on seeing their families waiting by the shoreline to welcome them after weeks away? Imagine no Palm Pads, no screens; no means to communicate with home during those long stretches away, only patient waiting. Imagine that? We were very different people then, I think. Oddly enough, I believe the need to "wait" made us better, stronger creatures, both more independent internally yet more connected externally. Do you know what I mean?"

"Yes, I think I do. We had to think more, ask more questions, and understand our world more in-depth. It wasn't all within instant reach."

She hesitated for a moment and then switched gears.

"I think people today are confused by the onslaught of information. It gives us an excuse to abdicate our responsibility to sift through it all, to draw our own conclusions, have our own opinions even if we're sometimes in the minority. We've all come to believe it should all be left to the so-called experts. And...." She looked away for a moment then resumed. "You know I respect your beliefs Ice, but I can't help but feel it has added to a lack of spontaneity, the loss of some of our basic humanity."

She waited for some sort of response, but he said nothing. He got up and moved away from her, but she edged towards him, changed tactics.

"Perhaps the *Book of Darwin* doesn't really mean what you all think. No, not at all."

He finally spoke, his tone defensive, "What do you mean by that?"

"Well, Charles Darwin was really just a man, a scientist actually, right? Yes, I know you think him a prophet and maybe he was that too, but mostly he was the product of the nineteenth century, a naturalist and geologist, who's true contribution during that era was the theory of evolution. It was Herbert Spencer who later used Darwin as the foundation for his "survival of the fittest" theory, not Darwin. Sir Francis Galton, ironically Darwin's cousin, in the 1880s built on Spencer's theory by conducting a study of the British upper classes, which he claimed proved their exalted position was due to their genetic inheritance.

"This led to more studies on the role of genetics and the growing popularity of the notion that "selective breeding" could refine and elevate the human population and condition. The Eugenics Movement, an off-shoot of all this, came of age in the early 20th century funded by numerous JC foundations spear-headed by the well-regarded biologist Charles Davenport." She paused for a moment to make sure he was still listening adding, "Did you know he spent most of his working life on Long Island and had a strong connection to the city?"

"No, I had no idea."

"Well, he did. His mother was a Brooklyn 'Joralemon' and he spent his summers in Brooklyn. In 1904 he was appointed as the director of the Cold Springs Harbor Laboratory on Long Island and six years later he founded the Eugenics Record Office and the movement took off from there. Eugenics based laws, governmental policies and ideologies sprouted in every corner of the country. Tens of thousands of individuals deemed "unfit" were forcibly sterilized and even institutionalized over the next forty years. Only World War II slowed down the march of the Eugenics Movement when it became associated with Nazi atrocities. Thereafter, until its re-emergence about a half-century ago, eugenics mostly fell out of favor. However, growing social and economic inequality, the desire of those at the top to justify that disparity, combined to fuel the re-emergence of eugenics' style dogma. The CRS's *Book of Darwin* was the final justification for resurrecting this formerly discredited theory, though that appellation was not recycled, and it added a new twist- our destiny was all part of God's design, HIS will.

Ice shot her a pained look, but Layla continued, she felt they needed to come to an understanding about this.

"I know this is as difficult for you to hear, as for me to say. But I have to be honest. I think you know how I feel, think about this, but I need to tell you directly. It's just that... well I've come to feel so much for you, and about you that... how can we move forward if you don't understand or accept my position on his?"

She looked up at him hopefully, expectantly, but he remained unmoved.

"My bottom line: I can't and won't ever believe that God has pre-destined or volitionally imprinted on us genetically to be the Elect here on earth or beyond."

He pulled away. "You really are an unbeliever, an apostate."

She knew from his tone it might be over between them. Yet, she had to tell him the truth before this went any further. It was not in her nature to hold back and despite this seeming, unbridgeable chasm between them, she was, for reasons she did not fully comprehend, beginning to love this man. So that despite his initial tone of harsh disapproval, his pulling away from her, she reached out to him again. She hoped that the connection between them was strong enough that he might be willing to explore with her, just a little longer.

When she spoke there was some reconciliation in her voice, in her words, "I am not saying your *Book of Darwin* is or is not a revelation from God. Why should your Golden Tablet be any less true or valid than my Moses's Ten Commandments or Christians' belief that Jesus was the Son of God? Do you see what I am saying? Faith is simply faith. It should never be, can't be questioned."

Silence. No response, so she tried a different approach.

"Perhaps, as with all religions, the imperfection lies in man's interpretation of the message. Maybe it's not God's fault but our own. Perhaps, it's always been that way. God sends and we can't hear it correctly. So **He** or **She** tries again and again. We just can't seem to get it right. We misinterpret. Isn't that possible?'

"Yes," he murmured, "maybe the fault lies with us."

She redirected his attention to *Muheakantuck*.

"Can you see them now greeting their husbands, fathers, sons who have returned? They flourished because they embraced their world and let it embrace them. Imagine a world where there was no need for a Project gate? No Bill Golightly or Corpus to vacuum up every last resource only to turn around to dole it out to us according to their whims? These returning husbands, fathers, and sons placed what they brought at the people's feet and all partook. And maybe we can't turn back that clock precisely, but does it mean we have to abandon all notions of a just society? Why do WE settle for so little, think WE deserve only what **they** think WE should have?

"And, even worse, all of us thank them humbly, yes with gratitude dripping from our tongues. We are all a people reduced, so debased we don't even realize it. Yet, when I remember the lives of those who lived along the *Muheakantuck* I can't help but see what's happened to us, as a people, as a nation. Perhaps that is why, even though you might not want to acknowledge it, you are drawn to that time just like I am."

He still said nothing. She thought, *he must be horrified by what I voiced. He's going to tell me he's done with me. He's just thinking of a diplomatic way to express it. Putting on his minister's affect.*

She couldn't blame him. He was who he was. She was who she was. For all their kinship, in so many areas, there was this gulf that would always exist between them. His position, yes she had to admit, his destiny, was written for him before he was even born. Not by genetics, but by an accident of birth. No matter the reason. It was what it was and made them something that could never be.

Yet, to her amazement, he spun around taking her hand in a gesture so tender her heart nearly broke. In that moment she realized he was still with her. She could feel it in the press of his hand, hear it in the rhythm of his heart that he accepted her for who she was, for what she believed, even though she understood that what she voiced profoundly challenged his assumptions and even his very place in society.

Pure acknowledgment was so unknown to her she hardly knew what to think or feel. And what did she feel for this man, anyway? He was, first and foremost, the head of the CRS. Of that she had no doubt. He was to the position born. He had never considered another path or existence for himself, of that she was also certain. She had just made it perfectly clear she was no believer. Not now, not ever. If someone had proposed him as a possible love interest to her, just a few weeks prior, she would have told that person s/he was insane. Normally his vocation would have repelled her. Indeed, it was the only thing that made her uncertain about him. Yet, she was enormously attracted to him in every way. She trusted that he actually understood her and liked her, might even love her, for exactly who she was. In a world where even personal relationships were commodified, one built solely on personal feelings, a meeting of the minds was exceptional. Perhaps, for this reason alone, neither was ready to abandon this experiment quite yet.

Of course, there was also Paul to consider. She felt very invested in him, felt almost responsible for him. But it was different. Sure she was sleeping with him, but it wasn't quite love- at least not the sort that made her want to devote a lifetime to him. It was closer to an act of rebellion, defiance of the system. A literal "up yours" opportunity for her. She had plans for him, but none included a lifelong commitment. But Ice was different. She could see herself with him.

Unbelievably, until this very day, they hadn't consummated their relationship. She had hesitated, put if off because she felt that if she slept with him she might never be able to turn from him. It was all so complicated…

So when Isaac Freeman, this Second Keeper of the Book, turned to face her, taking her hand in a manner so dear, telling her to *rest now,* that they'd sort it all out in time, she had no doubt but that he loved her in a way no one ever had before. She wanted to tell him that this could not be. For all the reasons she had just expressed and what she left unsaid: she was a TAKER -yes at heart always of the Projects- and he was the Keeper. How could the Keeper be with someone like her? One who was Unrevealed and would remain so. One who he would surely conclude he might love, but could never marry. She did not give voice to any of these misgivings. When he took her hand all she wanted to do was rest. Rest against a person with whom she thought she was capable of sharing everything, despite their seeming differences. Who, no matter he was the head of the CRS, did not view her first and foremost as an up and coming PROFFIE, nor commodified her in any way. She wanted to repose her trust in him. No price could be put on that in a society where people's personal stock rose and fell in an instant. Maybe it wouldn't last, but for now, all she wanted to do was stay with this man and watch the *Muheakantuck* drift by.

Chapter 28: Paul and Layla

At the Gate

"All packed like I told you? I have a surprise for you."

Layla jumped out of her sleek black convertible with its mocha leather interior. She opened the trunk for Paul to stow his bag.

"Not much of a bag really. More like an oversized knapsack. But whatever."

She ignored that comment and motioned again for him to get in.

"It's a girl's dream isn't it? Amazing what my credits will get me."

She cocked her head at him knowing full well what he was thinking. "Yes, it's great that I can say this. Great you think, I give you a little taste, a tease, but return you to this," she waved her hand dramatically at the building, "the famous micro-apartment. But, who knows, the boy's dream may be about to come true. So get your sorry ass into the car."

"Where are we going?"

"We are going to blow open the gates. You'll see."

"Why are you always so cryptic? Maybe I'm just an undereducated WE, but sometimes I wish you weren't always speaking in some sort of code or invented language. It gets really irritating at times. Makes me feel small."

She ignored that last comment. "Just get in. Let's go."

They drove out to the Hamptons, an exclusive gated district, via the Long Island Expressway or "LIE" as those conversant with it and what it held for its residents, called it. Paul recognized much of the trip as they passed through Nassau County, once one of the richest counties in America. Even years before the Great Transformation, it had fallen on hard times as the changing tastes of the rich heralded its downfall. Little by little, its rich white suburban landscape became browner and its wealthy residents exited, abandoning it to the WE.

Chapter 29: History

What Really Happened [accessed only by a special password]

At the end of WWII the nation needed to quickly and cheaply house the growing families of the returned WWII vets. The solution was found in the passage of the GI Bill of 1944, a smorgasbord of benefits providing such things as: cheap mortgages, money for college tuition plus living stipends, as well as low-cost small business loans and a year of unemployment compensation. It was this federal legislation that was the true creator of the great mid-twentieth century middle class. The so-called "Greatest Generation" did not pull themselves up by their bootstraps, but were actually the most subsidized generation ever to grace the USA.

Theoretically, its benefits were available to all honorably discharged WWII vets. But here's its dirty little secret: those opportunities were almost exclusively extended to white men and their families. Practices such as redlining, restrictive covenants contained in the deeds to those new suburban tracts, along with segregated education, all conspired to exclude people of color. Women, too, received differential treatment. It was assumed that white women would give up their jobs to returning vets, go home, have babies, and hitch their wagons to an honorable vet now husband/civilian bread winner. In reality, they had little choice. The result was that large swaths of the American people were shut out, simply left behind.

By the time the dispossessed, ever knocking at the door, were admitted, the bulk of the opportunities which might have secured for them good upwardly mobile jobs, cheap but quality housing, low-cost, quality higher education, pensions, and a nest egg with which to secure theirs and their children's futures, were vanishing.

Once those formerly dispossessed groups entered communities like those found in Nassau County, local governments had a sudden epiphany: they needed to cut back on funding the type of county services which had attracted those first waves of suburban dwellers in the first place.

By the beginning of the twenty-first century and moving forward, public schools, along with all type of public services, were rapidly defunded. Simultaneously, the descendants of the most affluent of those post-WWII settlers, began to out-migrate from these suburban plantings, never to return, further fueling Nassau County's downward trajectory.

By the dawn of the Great Transformation many of the once neat rows of tract homes and the even the larger Mc-mansions were abandoned. Zombie homes, the newspapers called them, would soon be re-dedicated as WE housing in a tattered and discarded landscape.

So, who became the WE? Mostly the decedents of the formerly modest white middle and working classes along with minorities. In other words, the vast majority of Americans. Beginning with Reagan's "trickle down" policy moving forward through to the downturn of 2008, followed by the Great Fiscal Crisis twelve years later, the middle class was marked for extinction. Yet most perceived their fall from grace as sudden. They never understood how tenuous their foothold in the middle class had been all along. To the very end, these Americans refused to face reality. They claimed they never saw it coming, but the handwriting had been on the wall for decades.

Chapter 30: Layla and Paul

On the LIE [GTE, 45]

Paul was born and raised in Nassau County. Of course, by the time he was a teen, it was little more than a disturbing suburban dream lying in ruins. Paul wanted no part of it, but as a WE, he knew it was where his future lay. As Layla and Paul passed the exits for these once glorious towns, he pulled his cap down over his eyes as if that gesture might protect him from its pull.

"Don't worry Paul, it won't eat you!" she laughed at him.

"It's funny to you, but not to me. I'm slotted to return here at some point."

"Can't you stay where you are? If you get married you could get a bigger apartment, right?

"You really don't know anything about being a WE do you? Just jumped from the Projects into that PROFFIE stuff. The good life," he spat out at her slumping further into his seat.

"Well, you needn't get all pissed. I grew up in far worse than you"

"Yeah, yeah, so you keep saying… I know, the Projects, yatta, yatta."

She swerved the car, pulling it over to the shoulder, bringing the vehicle to an abrupt stop.

"Are you starting up with that crap again? You really are a little moron aren't you? Just get out of my car, ok? And just so you know, I was taking you to the Hamptons for your CCU gallery premier. It was to be a surprise. Booked a res at Sag's American Hotel. The best in the Hamptons, but you've blown it. "

"No, wait Layla, wait. I'm sorry, so sorry. I don't know what comes over me."

"Passive aggressive," she sneered.

"Yeah, you're right. I've got a problem. I know that. That's how I almost got bounced out of NCC and, before that, close to being flagged at my Learning Center. Remember, I told you all about it."

She hopped out, opened his side of the car and practically pulled him out. He scrambled to his feet.

"You need a god damn shrink, that's what you need. But I'm done."

She turned, walking back to the driver's side shouting, "Walk back to Canarsie you stupid little jerk."

"Wait," he pleaded, "wait."

She stopped and turned to him.

"I promise never to pop off at you again like this. It was driving thorough Nassau County- made me crazy. Just looking out at that place gave me a panic attack. I just can't go back there. Honest, I'd rather just end it 'cause that's what life would be for me there, ended."

"You're pathetic. You know it, don't you?"

"Yeah, I know it. But I love you Layla. Don't abandon me."

She looked at him. Truly he was physically adorable and gifted to boot. She was a sucker for that combination in a man. For an instant Ice passed through her brain. Two such different men. Ice didn't need her help, but Paul did. Paul was as much a victim of the system as she was, as most people were. She'd promised to try to help right the injustice done him and she would. But did she love him? She felt love for him, but she didn't think she was actually in love with him nor did she believe he was in love with her. He needed her. Wanted her. Aspired to be in her position, but in love? Whatever he might think, she didn't believe it was the, "you are my soul mate and I would do anything for you type of love." Certainly, it was not the love of equals, but the type of affection you feel for a dog you've rescued and that dog feels for its rescuer.

She motioned for him to get back in the car. He clambered back in, fastened his seat belt, and looked over at her. "I'm ready," he announced like a child that's done something bad but is determined to behave and get on with it.

She nodded, started the engine, then leaned over flicking her tongue against his ear like a serpent tasting its prey, "One more outburst like that and it's over. Understand?"

200

"Yes."
She put the car in gear and drove off.

Chapter 31: Isaac

Bridging the Divide [GTE, 45]

Ice was stretched out in the back seat of his limo on his way to the Hamptons. He'd been invited to stay at Bill Golightly's estate. TC, as expected, accompanied him.

"Jeez Ice, I can't believe you are actually still here. Six weeks now, a record. "

"Yeah," Ice responded with no intention of discussing the matter further.

"I mean, I never thought we'd pry you from Savannah. That Layla woman's gotten to you."

Ice held up his hand indicating no more discussion.

"Ok, I hear you, no more on that topic. But we are happy to have you. In-the-being attendance at the Sunday service is way up and so are the contributions. And guess what bro'? The East Hampton Sunday service is totally booked- every top JC, POL, and EASY have gobbled up the tickets. You'd think we were giving something away."

"But we are giving something away. We are giving them a path to Grace, the **Revealed Word** of Darwin; the peace of mind that comes with knowing it's more likely than not one is saved. We are helping them stay their course. Isn't that worth spending a Sunday morning in church?"

"Sure, sure, we all know that. All I'm saying is that these are the cream of the CSA; they want the best and you," he said jabbing his forefinger at Ice for emphasis, "are the best. So they attend. Flock to church, to *our* church. The ministry *our* parents built from nothing. Think! Seemingly humble people from a small town in Mississippi brought all this to fruition. They were true Saints, the chosen, living proof that the cream will rise to the top. It was in their bones, their DNA. Whenever I think about it, I realize we are spreading the truth – how could it be otherwise? What they did was truly sanctioned by God."

Ice smiled fondly at his friend. "You know, sometimes I wonder if you truly believe or if this is just a great gig for you. But when I hear you speak like that I am comforted, reassured, you are a true believer.

Ice leaned forward pressing a button releasing a good-sized screen.

"Time to work on Sunday's sermon. I'd like to get it done before we arrive so I can actually enjoy myself."

"Good for you. What a novel concept. The Reverend Ice Freeman wants to have a good time. That's promising."

Ice made no comment. TC shifted in the plush back seat, stretched out his legs. "Well then I'm going to get bit of sleep. Had a late night."

"I'm sure you did," Freeman noted, but not disapprovingly. "I'll be sure to wake you when we arrive."

Freeman turned back to the screen. Pulled up his address. The screen dissolved.

Good morning Reverend Freeman. Please enter your password to continue your exploration of What Really Happened.

He glanced over at TC who was already napping. He entered the password.

A smiley-face ☺ appeared on the screen. *For Darwin's sake,* Ice thought, *this was really getting out of hand.* He should shut down the screen and reboot. He should have reported this cyberjacking to CRS' security team, but...he didn't. He entered the remembered password passing into its alternate worldview.

Embedded text, **What Really Happened,** accessed only by a special password:

History records that the last presidential election under the old constitution was indeed historic. Immediately after the Founders Action Party ("FAP") organized, it moved to and took control over more than three-quarters of the state governments. Easy enough. Most Republicans flocked to the new political party.

Its rise to power was unparalleled. Before the next presidential election of 2020, the FAP controlled critical state houses.

They finished what the defunct Republican Party had tried to accomplish for years, but could not. FAP controlled state legislatures tightened up the voting laws keeping groups who did not historically support the Republican Party from voting. That meant no college students, as well severely limiting the number of eligible elderly, African Americans and Hispanic voters.

While this was an important step on the road to the presidency the real game changer for the FAP was an innovation that changed the face of the Electoral College. FAP controlled state legislatures passed laws awarding Electoral College votes by congressional districts instead of on the basis of the statewide popular vote. The presidential candidate winning the majority of a state's congressional districts would win all that state's Electoral College votes. Since the congressional districts had long been gerrymandered in favor of the Republicans, the FAP, who had quite literally donned the defunct Republican Party's congressional district shoes, were now poised to take the presidency. There was never any doubt which party would win the next presidential election. The fix was in.

Democrats brought multiple lawsuits to have these laws over-turned. They scored some victories at the district court level, but consistently lost in the U.S. Supreme Court.

"There is little doubt but that Article 2, Section 1 of the U.S. Constitution left to the states the apportionment of their Electoral College votes. If the Founders had desired uniformity or the application of a particular methodology for apportioning that vote, they would have so provided for it in the Constitution. They did not... Where the Constitution is silent state law may fill the vacuum. This is the case we are currently presented with and we hold, unequivocally, the states many determine the methodology to tally and apportion their Electoral College votes. We sustain their right to do so. Let freedom ring!" [U.S. Supreme Court, May 8, 2018]

That decision, plus the Great Fiscal Crisis, all but guaranteed President Cross's election. He swept the Electoral College despite losing the popular vote by 5%. Experts noted that even if the hundreds of thousands of disenfranchised voters had been permitted to vote that percentage would have been to closer to 20%. All, however, agreed that due to the changes to the Electoral College, the outcome would have remained the same.

During the campaign Cross boldly accused the sitting president of conspiring with economic terrorists to bring about the crisis. Most thought this was simply typical Cross hyperbolic rhetoric. Just nasty campaign tactics. It was expected each candidate would accuse the other of everything and anything, but this campaign and its aftermath were different. Even in victory Cross's vitriol continued unabated despite out-going President Harris's gracious concession speech and promise to assist with the transformation. Cross's victory speech was laced with invectives and more accusations against President Harris and her administration:

"I caution President Harris and her administration from destroying documents contained in either private or Whitehouse computers and files. I hold here in my hand [he picked up a sheath of papers] evidence that President Harris not only conspired to bring about our present crisis but also accepted bribes from foreign agents. She is, in a word, an economic terrorist, a traitor."

The nation was shocked by this post-election pronouncement. President Harris immediately made the late night talk show rounds to deny it all. Numerous members of her administration along with the now out of power political party did the same. Cross did not back down. She held a formal press conference in the Rose Garden denouncing Cross as a demagogue. His rhetoric only escalated. She even addressed the nation in a prime time speech condemning Cross and pleading with the American people not to succumb to fear mongering, reminding them that this nation's political success was anchored on a peaceful and gracious transference of power. Cross responded by demanding her immediate arrest.

Consequently, no one was really surprised when his RW&B minutemen stormed the Whitehouse taking the soon-to-be ex-President, Vice-President, Chief of Staff and all of her Cabinet into custody. Some of the media noted that neither the Secret Service nor any U.S.A. military forces came to her defense; even her personal security detail fled. FAP sympathizers had been infiltrating the U.S. armed forces for many years, while key military officers were firmly aligned with the FAP. Even the head of the Joint Chiefs of Staff was in the FAP's pocket.

The Capitol was secured within hours and President Harris and her vice-president were confined to their residential quarters under close guard. Cross took to the airways demanding Articles of Impeachment be brought against the sitting president. Some asked, *why bother*, since she was leaving office in less than three months anyhow. No, the FAP demanded she must be formally impeached, her administration and all its policies repudiated. The FAP wanted, needed, to justify what was to come. Sure enough, one week later the House of Representative impeached President Harris along with her vice-president for treason and sedition. The Senate, hastily called back to Washington, quickly passed sentence: immediate expulsion from office. But it didn't end there. The reviled former office holder, along with her entire Cabinet, close advisors, and the vice-president, were straightaway taken into formal, military custody and held in a secret location. The FAP commander explained it was for the protection of the detainees as well as the nation.

As per the Constitution, the reins of power were turned over to the President pro tempore of the Senate who just happened to be newly elected Vice-President Randall Carey, one of the founding members of the FAP. He quickly reaffirmed the arrest of the President and Vice-President along with the others declaring, "We will let a civilian court deal with them later."

Their fate was never disclosed.

Meantime growing numbers of RW&B security forces were deployed in all major urban centers. When asked at his first news conference why he wasn't deploying USA military forces or the National Guard, he drawled smugly in his Texas two-step accent: "Why, everyone knows that private military contractors are more efficient."

Wall Street was cordoned off returning it to its antecedents as an area enclosed to protect it from the "hostiles." Chicago's Mercantile Exchange was similarly locked down, while that city's simmering pot, its South Side, was doused with cold water when the National Guard, now led by a RW&B commander, swarmed through its decaying buildings and projects confiscating guns, semi-automatics, and pistols.

Simultaneously, another military contractor, Fortified Star, threw up an electrified fence along that neighborhood's perimeter providing its residents with only one entry and exit checkpoint. When asked about this at a hastily put together news conference, the President elect's spokeswoman, a well-known right wing pundit May Halter, tossed her mane of bleached blond hair, stabbed her bony finger at the assembled media, brusquely informing them:

"You all need to understand what's happening here- it's sedition; treason from top to bottom. The woman, who's been occupying the White House for the past four years, and I mean occupying in the basest understanding of that term, was **never** legitimate. We have it all here," she declared while waving the now familiar sheath of papers in the air.

"Here's confirmation of what's been going on. That woman who calls herself "president,' is a foreign born agent placed into the heart of **our** democracy by **our** enemies to destroy **us** from within. Our great fiscal crisis is nothing more than economic terrorism, plain and simple, launched by Harris and our enemies. Harris was **never** going to step down if elected to a second term. The plan was to change the Constitutional prohibition on holding office more than two terms so she could run again, and again and... well you get the picture. But, that's not all. Oh no, not by a long shot!

The legitimate election of Pablo Cross, thank the Lord, ruined that plan. So, what were she and her cohorts to do? A new plot was hatched that would have stopped our President elect from assuming office. But Jesus be praised [her eyes rolled up to the heavens] certain patriotic Americans stepped forward to alert President elect Cross who, with the full assistance of our military and the RW&B forces, were able to quash this plot guaranteeing the peaceful, orderly, and lawful transformation of power."

She paused. Looked out over the audience of the stunned assembled media and continued.

"You think it's all over, right? But it's not. There's lots of mopping up to do. We have to sweep the streets clean. Root the vermin from their nests. Exterminate, exterminate, exterminate! And one of the biggest nests is right here on the Southside of Chicago- Harris' home base. We know there are still significant cells here as well as elsewhere across the nation. Even as we speak those centers are being secured just as they are here in Chicago."

She stopped to run her talons through her hair then chirped at the assemblage:

"Questions?"

The stunned reporters looked around. Here's what they saw: an at-the ready division of RW&B minutemen had stepped into the conference room. They took up their positions: chins high, shoulders erect, legs planted firmly in the military "V" configuration, fingers lightly pressed against their AR-15 triggers ready for use if called on. They looked every inch like commandos in those old TCM movies.

The media seemed frozen in their seats. No one spoke for quite a while. After what seemed like hours, one tentative hand went up. Communications Director Halter snapped her head in the hand's direction- more like a raptor about to eat its prey than someone looking to field a question. [Well, that's what we had come to!]

The reporter was, Inez Rosenfeld, a well-known cable news network personality- yeah let's call her what she was, a mere dolled up woman playing a reporter. She read the news, made vapid pre-canned comments, smirked and simpered on cue for the cameras and ratings. Let's face it; few genuine reporters were left by this time. It was all about celebrity.

Yet, for once in her insipid life, Rosenfeld actually shrugged off her chipper news-read persona, stood shoulders straight, prepared to ask a **real** question. A probing question, the type of question her Columbia University School of Journalism education had trained her to ask.

"Let me ask you. I see a military presence here in this room." She motioned to the armed minutemen with a jerk of her head. As she did so those men visibly tensed, but the commander standing well behind Halter to her left quickly raised and lowered his hand and the soldiers' trigger fingers relaxed.

"Why," she continued, "in a free country are they required? Are they here to intimidate the press, the public? And why is the acting president, soon to be the Vice-President Randall Carey, using a private contractor? And last, why has the National Guard been placed under its direction?"

"Well," began the simmering Halter, "I am surprised that someone from your network would ask such a question. What would you have us do? Permit an insurrection; a coup d'état against the legitimately elected president? Or are you in league with those advocating the overthrow of the government by fomenting revolution through such scurrilous accusations? Is that what you want Inez?"

"What I am suggesting," the suddenly plucky reporter responded, "is that the rule of law be respected in this country. What I am asking is why are military contractors being deployed and why is the National Guard under their command? What I am asking is why have all the nation's major urban centers – specifically the so-called ghettos- been literally walled off as if they were prisons?

"And why are what looks like – and forgive me for drawing this always controversial comparison- but for lack of a better term – storm troopers, stationed in this room armed to the teeth and clearly ready to mow us all down with a nod from that RW&B commander standing over there in the corner?"

As she finished she stood very still, clutching her cellphone [as they were called back in the day] and some papers in her hand. Halter glanced back at the Commander who crooked his finger and a shot rang out. Inez, in a final protective gesture, raised her hand that still gripped her cell phone as she fell to the floor, a bullet cleanly wedged in her left temple. As this happened the assembled media luminaries dashed for cover, diving [when they could fit] under chairs, some making for the doors, which were blocked by soldiers who intoned as if ushers at a Broadway show, "Sorry ma'am, Sorry sir, no one's to leave. Please return to your seat."

The Commander, looking as if he were arriving at a state dinner his dark blue uniform bearing the identifying red and white shoulder stripes of his employer encased his body like a glove, grabbed the mike out of Halter's now shaking hand and unceremoniously pushed her into a chair on the stage. Leaning over her while pushing back the streams of blond hair falling willfully over her face he hissed at her, "What a mess you are! Pull yourself together. We are about to move in for the kill."

Then as if realizing the irony of what he just said, grinned, "No pun intended, just stand behind me."

"But, but, don't you see what's happened," she gasped, her eyes darting here and there as if she could not fully absorb what had occurred.

"But, what?" he asked nonchalantly.

Coming back to life she looked up at him. "Not this, "she sobbed, "not this..." as she gestured to the dead reporter.

He grabbed her, pulled her to her feet spinning her around to face the audience whispering in the stunned woman's ear in what almost sounded like a caress, "What were you expecting? Did you think we were playing? Did you think this was another one of your ridiculous talk shows? Lady, this is and has always been the plan. It was all put in motion well over eighty years ago. Of course, no one had expected it to take so long. Each succeeding generation used their own tactics, but the bottom line was always the same: dismantle the New Deal, the Liberal Society ushered in by Roosevelt and his ilk. You are either with us or against us. Your choice."

"I'm. I am... with you... I just hadn't expected... I wasn't told... that's all," she mumbled while smoothing down her hair and clothes. That action caused her entire demeanor to brighten so that she was able to look up at him with that TV personality smile plastered on her face declaring in her most professional tone: "Commander, you're on in five."

He beamed down at her. "Now, that's better. We each have our part to play. Follow my lead. Just remember, rats must be exterminated."

She obediently did as instructed trailing after the Commander as he took center stage. She handed him the microphone. He put it to his lips like a child about to lick his favorite ice cream pop, but nothing sweet emanated from his mouth. He bellowed:

"Shut the FUCK up you sniveling little shits... take your seats!"

Immediately, the dazed reporters who unexpectedly found themselves the subjects as opposed to the objects of a huge media event [ahhh... how the worm had changed position] returned, zombie-like, to their seats. All except, of course, the dead reporter who remained where she was when shot, lying face up, slumped across three seats, cell phone frozen in her dead grip.

"Now, that's better," the Commander crooned at them. "Things aren't always as they appear. I know what you're all thinking. You believe you just saw one of my men blow away your colleague. You think we did it to intimidate you, to muzzle the press. Well nothing could be further from the truth."

He stepped forward toward the row of chairs where the dead reporter sprawled, motioning to one of his soldiers.

"Lieutenant Jimenez. Take the phone out of Rosenfeld's hand- mind you- remove it carefully."

Jimenez, with a show of great caution, gingerly removed the phone from the now lifeless hand and handed it to the Commander.

"NOW, ladies and gentlemen, watch and learn that appearances can indeed be deceptive."

He turned to the lieutenant commanding, "Jimenz pick up the chair Rosenfeld was sitting on. Turn it over to show these good people here what's there."

Again, Jimenez did as he was told revealing what appeared to be a plastic explosive taped under the chair. The assembled group gasped.

"You see, your so-called colleague was doing a bit of moonlighting. That chair was rigged to explode. She was an operative for domestic terrorists, a suicide bomber." [Murmurs from the audience of: "Oh, no!" "How's that possible?" "She seemed so nice, so normal."]

"This is what we are facing; like it or not. It's a coordinated effort by domestic and foreign terrorists to destabilize the country to stop President-elect Cross from taking office. Did you all believe that once President Harris was arrested all was right again in the world? Think again. She was simply a plant. The forces behind her have burrowed deep into the American political, social, economic and yes, even military fabric. That's why I'm here. That's why the RW&B has stepped up; to preserve the American way of life; to preserve American democracy. To ensure there is, as there has been for over two centuries, a peaceful transformation of power. So yes, we shot her. We shot a terrorist who was about to send your comfortable butts into the next world."

He removed his marauder style military cap putting it to his chest bowing low, "So please forgive me if we had to put a bullet through her head to protect you and the Constitution."

As he rose from his formal bow the audience began to clap, first tentatively and then it came as a roiling roar as the group leapt to its feet chanting, "Pab-lo Cross, Pa-blo Cross, Pa-blo Cross ..."

The Commander, knowing when to make his exit, turned to Halter, kissed her hand and signaled to his "boys" to take their leave.

After that, all went off without a hitch. Any media dissenters were quieted. Some got with the program while those that refused quietly disappeared. No one asked questions. No one dared.

On January 20, 2021 President Pablo Cross, along with Vice-President Randall Carey, were inaugurated. As it turned out, they would be the last president and vice-president of the United States of America. Two years later President Cross called for and got a constitutional amendment and three months later the USA was no more.

At the Gate

The limo came to a halt at the Shinnecock Canal, the gateway to the Hamptons. Only a small bridge connected the East End Peninsula to the rest of Long Island, but the imposing gate and guardhouse guaranteed only select **MAKERS** would traverse that bridge. The guard approached the limo, semi-automatic in hand at the ready, peering at the license plate and its occupants. The guard and driver exchanged a few words, an ID was flashed, an invitational code was punched into the keypad, and the gate opened. The limo drove through and the gate closed. All so very secure, so very efficient. No one enters without the required permission. Workers, except for those residing on the grounds of a Hampton's estate, daily stream in an out via a separate workers' security entrance producing carefully coded clearance badges. No chances are taken with the lives of the Hamptons' residents. After all, the CSA depends on these folks who are the top of the top.

When the entrance to the Hamptons was first gated, ingress was slow and awkward. The entering WEs complained. The Hampton's residents complained. Several security firms were hired and fired until the right protocol was hit on. Now the needed labor force streams seamlessly through its privileged portal to serve the residents. Service WEs tend to the Hampton's residents' every need. They manage their eco-scapes, sanitize their swimming pools, bag their groceries, cook their food, wait on their tables, and care for their children. It all works so flawlessly. A joy, all agree, to behold.

"Sir, Sir, we'll arrive in ten minutes," the driver's voice drifted through the speaker.

Ice closed the screen, nudged TC with his foot. "We're here-you up? Ready to go? Lights on?"

TC, a tall, slender but muscular man, stretched himself out like a contented cat about to lap up a big bowl of milk,

"Yeah man, I'm ready. Just a little catnap was all I needed. Good to go."

The driver stopped, stepped out and opened the passenger side doors for Ice and TC to exit.

"I hope you enjoyed the ride Sir," he said to Ice.

Ice beamed at him, "Yes, very nice, very efficient, as always Tom," Ice reassured.

Ice's attention was immediately drawn to his surroundings. The verdant rolling hills on which Bill GoLightly's estate sat filled his eyes. In the distance he could make out the blue of the Peconic Bay, smelled the salt, felt the calm.

"I can understand why so many New Yorkers trek out here on weekends and holidays. It fills the senses; let's you shed the city's dirt and tension. I could stay here for a while. Maybe even get a place out here."

TC looked at him astonished. The continuing turnaround he was seeing in his friend appeared to have no end. The thought occurred to him he might be serious about Layla. Sure they'd checked her out, but maybe he'd better examine her current life a bit more closely. Ice was, after all, the Second Keeper of the Book and couldn't remain unattached forever, but his choice had to be sound; not just for him but also for the entire CRS team. He discreetly opened his Palm Pad sending new instructions to the Digger.

Chapter 32: Paul and Layla and Isaac

You Like? [GTE, 45]

Paul was very nervous. This was his moment. His one and only opportunity to break out from the WE. It was now or never. In a world of small bites, tiny samplings that were quickly consumed and forgotten, he knew this show was everything. He simply could not believe he was doing an in-the-being show. This was something exceptional even for an Art EASY. Sure he'd heard of such exhibitions, but he never dreamed he'd ever attend one, never mind be its star. It wasn't even something most WEs followed; too intellectual, too elevated, not really of their moment. But the One-Percenters, those at the top of their tiers, loved these events. It set them apart, even from their own. They collected art, paid large sums of money for it. Some collectors had amassed so many pieces they actually bought multiple dwellings simply to display their collections. It's true there weren't many fine arts EASYS who created. Few individuals with an aptitude for art were granted this status. But for the designated few, life was good.

Paul's opening was in the gallery wing of the CCU Hampton's estate on Saturday night. Handler's staff had arranged it all, even giving their boss mucho credit for Paul's success attributing it to that long ago in-the-being visit to the Khoke Museum Handler had devised during his Learning Center programming days. The promo read:

*The Art World is abuzz. Are we seeing the emergence of an undiscovered **EASY**? Paul Gaugin, currently on contract to CCU's Social Media department, recently headed the team that brought us the wildly successful Nostradamus campaign. Now **his** art has gone viral. Specs are he slipped through the* *cracks provoking an Assessor uproar and controversy. An in-the-being show of Gaugin's work is set for this Saturday at CCU's exclusive Hampton's estate. Will this be sufficient to change Gaugin's classification? Stay tuned.*

Layla parked in front of the exclusive American Hotel in Sag Harbor. A bellhop eagerly bounded down the short flight of steps to greet her.

"Professor Saenz," he saluted while taking their bags, "we've been expecting you."

Layla looked the young man over carefully. She recognized him from the Projects. They were in the same graduating class. He was part of the "let's see if they can make it on the Outside" group. She remembered him as a quiet boy. His parents were not bad people, just a couple who had fallen on hard times, committed some petty crime and wound up in the Projects. He was always dirty. The kind of kid who had a perpetual bit of snot running down towards his upper lip. She always wanted to give him a handkerchief and tell him to wipe it but, of course, she didn't. He was freckled and eager to please.

A "Pleaser," as these types were called, no backbone at all. Even as young as she was she divined that about him, but he was not stupid, always ready to learn and she wondered why he couldn't do better than this. She had. Maybe it was as the Darwinists claimed, mostly a matter of genetics with just a dash of environment added in. Yet, she couldn't help but question the system every time she considered her many acquaintances, friends, and colleagues. Some were extraordinarily bright, strong, well balanced. You couldn't imagine them ever failing, no matter what. On the other hand, some were truly below average, while others were just bad seeds. But even for these, with few exceptions, a place was found for them, even if it was just as low-grade **PROFESSIONALS**. In the end, and what had become abundantly clear to her over the decade or so since she first exited the Projects and began to regularly network with the children of the upper tiers, was that most of them were simply average. They flourished sufficiently to function well in their assigned slots, but anyone with half a brain could see it was only because they were the sons and daughters of the privileged. They were bright, or just so-so, but nothing special. It seemed to her they were pushed forward more by their circumstances and the opportunities handed them, than their genetic inheritance.

That's the sad truth - most of us are "nothing special." Stick these JCs, PROFFIEs, POLs, EASYs and the like in the Projects and most of them would wind up like her former classmate, a bellhop. No, she reassured herself, for most people it's simply some genetics with a big dose of environment. Sure there were outliers, the brilliant, the driven no matter the circumstances, or the socio-paths, but for the most part, we're just swimming together in this vast pool trying to dodge the sharks because we're just the average fish, nothing exceptional. To really succeed we need that helping hand, the extra tutoring, the exposure to new experiences, that second chance that only money and position buys. And for those to the lucky sperm club born, whose parents are at the top of the "food" chain, the children of the Bill Golightlys and others similarly situated, legacy and the luck of birth is what it's all about.

Indeed, Layla, always curious about placements, got a peek at those stats not generally available. It showed that at CCU 60% of the entering class was made up of the children of alumni; top tiered families and the like. Thirty-nine percent came from your typical upper tier families, while only 1% came from the WEs. Yet, she knew many, many WEs eminently qualified for acceptance. It left her with no doubt that "assessment" and all those standardized exams were nothing but gatekeeping tricks to keep life's goodies in the same hands generation after generation. "To the victors belong the spoils," pronounced a New York POL on Andrew Jackson winning the presidency in 1828. Boy, was he right.

She looked up at the bellboy and decided not to say anything to him. No, best not to remind him or acknowledge their former acquaintance, too awkward. She blandly directed him, "Leave that bag in the car. Just take that other up for now."

"Yes, ma'am," he nodded complying with her request, efficiently disappearing into the hotel with the one bag.

"Listen Paul, I've got an invite to Bill Golightly's estate for tonight. He love, love, loves, Prognostication. Thinks it's a go forward career. Triquot was supposed to attend but she's sick or something. Really, she must be totally incapacitated-- this is something she wouldn't otherwise miss. It's instant credit in her account and she's all about the credit and grabbing it anyway she can.

"Do you know that bitch barely contributed even a sentence to the Prognostication program's design? Well, whatever....listen I'm so sorry about tonight but you'll find something to do. Just ask the CCU concierge-- he'll hook you up, ok?"

He was about to protest when the CCU staffer assigned to them bounded over. She was a long limbed, dark skinned young woman who set off her magnificent chocolate tones against a variety of vivid purple and lavender hued clothing. From the sheer lavender mesh hose to her amethyst gauzy blouse she was a CCU sight to behold.

"You like?" she asked Paul coquettishly.

"Great colors, the CCU colors. Do you always dress in those?"

"Not always, but on certain occasions I do. I am a living embodiment of CCU. It's my job. I attend to special CCU guests and events, as well act as its physical personification." She ended that solemn recitation but instantly transitioned to that singsong: "You like?"

"Yes, I like."

She was so very, very glistening and yummy that he couldn't help revealing his desire for her in his response, despite Layla's presence.

Taking that as her opportunity to leave, Layla reminded Paul, "Listen, I have no idea when I'll be back – in fact if it gets too late I'll probably sleep at the Golightly estate, so find yourself something to do, ok?"

The purple-garbed staffer, whose name of the moment was Orchid, answered for Paul as she reexamined him from top to groin, "Oh, Professor Saenz don't worry. I will have him covered. "

"Great," she waved to him then added, "On second thought, I will definitely stay over, so I'll see you at ten a.m. mañana, Ok?"

"Sure, sure, Layla. And thanks," he mumbled as Layla got back into her car. He noticed she still had her bag with her.

"Come on," Orchid indicated poking at Paul, "I'll take you to lunch courtesy of CCU. Then we'll go to the gallery to inspect the hangings- - if you need us to move anything or adjust the lighting you'll let me know and after that...well, here in the Hamptons there's so much to do. She shoved her Palm screen up to his face.

"I've a CCU expense account so we can go wherever, do whatever..."

"Yeah, great," still irritated by Layla's desertion.

"So, which is it?"

He smiled as if realizing that Layla or no Layla this was his shine time so he'd better make the most of it. He threw his arm round Orchid's waist enthusiastically declaring, "Let's go. I'm starving."

And they headed off for a meal on the CCU house.

More Gates

Layla arrived at the gate of the Golightly estate feeling anxious and just a bit guilty. True, she really did have to be there later that evening but, as she confessed to herself, she was really deserting Paul to meet up with Ice Freeman. Such an unlikely match for her, if it was even that. Nevertheless, she was determined to discover its entire content, bitter or sweet.

Security at the gate was tight. Terrorism, domestic and foreign, was something that shadowed them all since that terrible day on 9/11/2001 when Islamic terrorist brought down the twin towers, ploughed into the Pentagon while a group of brave passengers forced a third plane down into a Pennsylvania field thwarting their mission to hit our nation's capitol.

She sighed at the thought. Though it was long ago, this event was still very much alive in the hearts and minds of all Americans and she was no exception. It forever transformed the country, shattering our national delusion that those two oceans protected us from outside attacks. It was that newfound feeling of vulnerability which truly opened the door to all that was to come as we shed, one by one, our most exceptional American core values.

She shook herself. This was the peril of being an historian. Her thoughts always wandered into the past, connecting long ago events to the present. Honestly, it gave her no peace. It was like a Dickens's novel, only instead of being haunted by the Ghost of Christmas Past, she was haunted by the past itself. But now it was time for the present and maybe even for her future.

On rolling up to the Golightly estate she was greeted by a valet. She dropped her car with him and walked into a vast structure styled after the Hampton homes built in nineteenth century by one of the JCs' preferred architect's, Stanford White.

"Can I help you?" asked the Greeter perched high on the reception platform.

"Yes, I am looking for Reverend Freeman."

She scrolled down the screen glancing up at her, "Hmmm, let me tap him."

A minute went by when a "ping" from her Palm Pad directed her eyes down, then up to Layla. "He'll be down in a moment Professor Saenz, please," she motioned with her hand, "take a seat."

The Greeter returned to other matters popping up on her screen and promptly forgot about Layla. A few minutes later Ice exited the elevator followed by three members of his staff.

"It's all done. So now I'm gone for the day so, no, I don't need or want any of you to accompany me. I'll be back later for the Golightly event- see you all then. Now scatter." And they did, like three blind mice.

He greeted Layla coolly, "So good of you to meet me here Professor Saenz."

"No problem," she responded in kind, "how can I assist you today?"

"I think by first taking me to lunch. Clams? Lobster rolls? I hear there's some great places out here."

"Yes, there are."

"Well, good."

"And then?"

"We'll do a little sightseeing, I think. I've never been so far east in New York State before. In fact, I've never been out of New York City- seeing this spot is really quite surprising and has piqued my interest."

"Ok, no need to wax prosaic. I'm starving, so let's go."

She drove along the Montauk Highway stopping at one of the better clam shacks, snagging an outdoor table overlooking the beach.

"Now this is a place where I could live," Ice proclaimed.

"Yeah, well it's unbelievably pricy. Certainly nothing I could afford on a PROFFIE salary- not that I'm poorly paid but," she stretched her arms out, "not enough for a place out here."

"I see."

"Right. Now let's eat," she said as the waitress approached.

"Welcome to CLBs, what can we do you two?" the server asked while looking Ice over carefully thinking,

Sure, I'm used to seeing a lot of celebs. Place is crawling with 'em. They come and go all day long. No biggie. 'Course they get to stay, enjoy the beach, the parties, while I haul my ass back and forth from Middle Island. No use complainin' even to myself- as they say havin' a job is the greatest blessing we can receive in this life.

She smiled brightly at them asking again, "Can I get you folks somethin' or do you need more time?"

"Layla, what do you recommend?"

She looked up at the waitress carefully; she was always looking for her former in-mates- she seemed to see them everywhere, but not this woman. She turned back to Ice, "Really, there's nothing bad on the menu but definitely try the clams and the lobster."

"For sure," agreed the waitress, "those are our specialties. Won't get none fresher anywhere."

Layla nodded in agreement, "It really all does look so good...so, let me have a lobster roll, an order of onion rings, and a watermelon margarita,"

"Good choice," she warbled, "and for you, sir?" She turned to Ice her finger at the ready to send their order in.

"A beer – actually do me a Culebra with lime- a small basket of fried clam bellies and a lobster roll."

He flashed that lights on smile and handed her both menus.

"You got it." She sauntered off still pondering, *that guy looks so familiar; I know I've seen him before.*

A few minutes later she came back with the drinks. Set them down. Turned to go, then turned back.

"Hey, I know you. S'cuse me for not recognizing you right away Reverend. I can't believe you're here. I mean right here at my table! Does it mean I'm blessed? Can you give me your blessing? Will you bless my little boy?" She shoved a Palm Pad pic almost up against Ice's nose.

Layla could see this was a common event in his life as he patiently, gently, pushed the screen back assuring her the child looked healthy and of sound spiritual constitution.

"Really, you think so? Are you sure?"

He laid a comforting hand on her arm, "I wouldn't tell you so if I didn't feel it."

She instantly sank to her knees while the normally, 'I can't be impressed' crowds' heads swiveled to watch this little liturgical drama unfold as she began to shriek:

"Oh, oh, praise Darwin and the Lord! Thank you, thank you, Reverend Ice," she blabbered grabbing his hand.

Ice pushed back on his chair, raising her to her feet, while reassuring her it was all good, part of a preordained Darwinian blueprint, and that all she and her boy had to do was follow its plan for them. That meant working hard. Following the rules, staying on track. This went on for a few more minutes until the manager finally dragged the waitress off apologizing profusely to the right Reverend Freeman, assuring him there'd be no more intrusions.

"No bother at all," he reassured the manager.

When it was all over Freeman sat back down, sipping his beer as if nothing had happened. Layla giggled.

"What, Missy, are you so amused by?"

"Why you know; that whole display. I'm surprised the heavens didn't open up with angels and trumpets blaring; the whole nine yards. Does this happen often?"

The waitress was back with their order but very subdued.

"Here you go Reverend. Sorry for my outburst. It won't happen again. Here at CLBs we know how ta' respect the celebs. That was uncalled for. Do please forgive."

"No problem," he winked adding, "I'll let your boss know it was no biggie. No reason for you to lose your job, ok?"

Closing in on a whisper she mouthed, "God bless you sir," and vanished back to the kitchen.

They ate in silence for a while until Layla broke it.

"You are kind. I mean genuinely kind. No artifice."

"I take that as a sign of approval."

"Yes, but all from me."

"Yes, all from you, heaven can stay out of this one."

She smiled. "Finish up and let's go."

At the car he asked, "Do you mind if I drive?

"Drive?" she asked her voice barely concealing her astonishment, "I didn't think you could drive."

"Think again. I drive. Country driving mostly, but I definitely drive."

"Well, ok," she giggled, "but if you get into an accident you'd better pay upfront or my insurance goes up."

"I think I'm good for it. Just get in."

"Sure thing, just let me program the GPS and then you can drive away."

"Let me do it," he smiled as he punched in the directions.

"I thought you wanted a tour guide?"

"I didn't say you were the guide, did I?"

"No you didn't. Ok, surprise me."

"I just might."

Less than fifteen minutes later they pulled up to the gates of an estate overlooking the Atlantic. Ice opened his Palm Pad, waved it twice and the gates opened.

"Friend of yours," asked the surprised Layla.

"Not exactly."

Ice had parked the car in front of a modern glass and Douglass fir wooden home. It was magnificent. The ocean was visible from every angle, including through its strategically placed windows that permitted a view of the ocean from front to back of the home without giving up its inhabitants' privacy. It was sleek with a touch of retro- 1960s modern. Just the kind of vibe Layla would have chosen if the house fairy had appeared before her to grant her housing wish.

"Are you getting out or are you waiting for me to do a mid-twentieth century thing and open the door for you?"

"Not necessary," she rejoined sliding out.

"You like?"

"Of course. I mean, what's there not to like? View, water, a stunning house." She considered it for a moment. Taking it all in. "Who owns it?"

He didn't reply but took her arm shepherding her to the front door and into the house. No one else was there. The house was furnished, staged more like it, but clearly not occupied. They moved from room to room finishing up on a magnificent deck with its infinity pool emptying into the Atlantic Ocean's boundlessness.

"So, what do you think?"

"I love it! I could spend all my free time here just letting this endless horizon consume me. I can't think of a more delicious way to go out.

"I'm glad. I'm thinking of purchasing it."

"You or the CRS?"

"No, just me. It would be my private residence. My only private home. The Savannah and New York City properties belong to the CRS. I am, you might say, a mere tenant."

"Why here? I thought your true home would always be in the South?"

"Sometimes you need to reconsider. To listen and learn, don't you think?"

She nodded in agreement adding, "Of course- but still, why here?"

He leaned against the deck's railing looking out over the expanse motioning to the infinite blue and water that stretched before them.

"You know, when I stand here looking out over the water I lose track of my age, my position... I could be anyone, anywhere, at any point in time. I become a being without boundaries and I realize the universe and its possibilities are limitless."

"You surprise me- constantly. I've always believed someone like you would be so directed, so limited- as if living in some type of ideologically circumscribed box. But that's not you at all."

He smiled that warmth of the sun and the infinite promise life could hold smile and she felt the possibilities. Just for a moment she entered into his vision, but then his next words jolted her back to reality.

"There is one other motive behind this purchase."

She thought she knew what was coming. She held up her hand to stop him from speaking.

"Wait. I have something to tell you."

"Are you rejecting me before I even speak? You must be pretty sure about your prognostication skills."

"Ok then. Before I tell you something I don't have to, let me ask: are thinking of buying this house because of me?"

"I am."

"Just so. Please, let me speak before this goes further. "

"Go on," his voice uncharacteristically tense.

She took a deep breath.

"I need to explain my family's circumstances to you. I want you to understand who I am. How I got from there to here."

He nodded, she continued.

"My parents were grad students at NYU. They met there. You know, the usual, they fell in love, married- all that. But it was during the time of the Great Fiscal Crisis, the protests, the upheavals - I know you're familiar with what happened, so I won't give you a lecture."

"Your confidence in my historical knowledge is much appreciated," he quipped.

"Really there's nothing funny about this, my history, our history."

"I know, but I think you are far too worried about it and about me."

"We'll see. Anyway, my parents met in grad school and both were very active on their campus helping to organize grad students. After graduation they both got jobs at a local community college. They were very active in their union. My father was even a union officer. Of course, it was during the last years of unions.

From the beginning of the crisis and moving forward the **POLs** stepped up their attacks on organized labor, particularly on the teachers. The public, sadly, blindly followed along. And who could blame them? After all, they saw the ads on TV sponsored by the Silicon Valley billionaires urging them to hate the teachers, privatize it all. They lavished buckets of money on selling these ideas through organizations they funded. They were excellent salesmen. They sold, the public bought. The average citizen railed against everything that might have benefitted them. Sadly, this has become the American way.

New York State's Governor Lakeside, a so-called liberal Democrat, did everything he could to break the teachers' union and destroy the public school system. He took money from private foundations and corporations to push charter schools, the forerunners of the STD. He didn't stop with what was called K-12 but went after the community colleges. He played on the average family's economic insecurities and fears their children were racking up phenomenal debt while failing to secure good paying jobs. He used all these uncertainties to convince people that all they really needed was vocational training, workforce development- no real education required. I believe they never understood that what he was really doing was institutionalizing a two-tiered educational system- one for the rich and one for the rest of us."

"That's quite a mouthful." Ice interjected.

She looked out over that boundless ocean that framed their exchange, then at Ice again and laughed.

"When, Reverend Freeman, was the last time you heard the term, 'civic culture,' or 'citizen' used? Don't misunderstand. There was blame all around. Many unions had become insular, tone deaf, more interested in protecting their turf and the prerogatives of its upper echelon than in really galvanizing the **WE**. They were segmented too, private versus public unions, trades versus educators. All these divisions weakened the labor movement. All workers eventually paid the price.

Just as devastating to the **WE**, were union leaders who had been corrupted. They sold out their members without batting an eye. They walked away with their own versions of the golden parachute- of course nothing compared to the CEOs of that era, but for them it was sufficient. They got through it; drifted away to comfy retirements, while those left behind lost almost everything. Even worse, the public, the average American, lost out.

I don't believe this is God's blueprint and I can't believe you really do either. I've watched your interactions with people, there's no whiff of Darwinian superiority about you. God has nothing to do with what's happened. It all originated right here on earth. It's called greed, plain and simple. They've made sure everything rises to the top: the good jobs, the good schools, and all the breaks. No wonder their kids do well. They set the table for them. The **WE** are simply slotted to be trained for some industry, some employer, given no opportunities to learn, explore, or discover their path. **WEs** and **TAKERs** are assigned our path. If only we'd open our eyes we'd see it. It's right in front of us: if you give most of the resources to one group, their product, in this case their children, they will emerge the winners. It's obvious, so simple."

Ice put his large elegant hand on hers. "Ever the historian, but what happened to your parents?" Of course, he knew from the dossier he read, but he asked her anyway.

"When they moved to disband the unions, when they began to disenfranchise people: minorities, college students, older people, cut back on public services, and simply narrowed the American experience, my parents, along with many others from all walks of life, attempted to organize an active resistance. In my parents' case it all went south quickly. The union president betrayed them all and in return got a nice fat going away 'present.' She took it and ran. Shortly thereafter, in GTE, 15, the STD took over all the public colleges and universities and they were fired, told they'd never work again.

Anyway, they continued trying to organize, peacefully resist, but they were accused, along with others, of carrying a social contagion that required containment. They were sent to the Projects. Two years later came the Last Uprising; it was a blood bath. I was about two years old, so of course I don't really have any memories of it. All I recall is my mother putting this little copper bracelet around my wrist, hugging me and telling me she was going to do something dangerous, but that it was to preserve my future. I never saw her again. My parents were both killed, but my grandmother was permitted to keep me until I was eighteen years old. And you know the rest. Here I am. A **PROFFIE**, but tainted goods nevertheless."

Ice led her back into the home's living room and bent down to pick up the small briefcase by the side of a chaise. He put it on the coffee table and opened it removing a large folder.

"Layla, I know your history. It's all here in this dossier my people assembled. You see they are concerned about our 'friendship' so they sent me this." He motioned to the papers. "They thought it so sensitive they didn't want to send it through the Internet."

"How peculiar to see something on paper," was her only comment.

He smiled. "Yes, my staff often puts sensitive information on paper. Safer, don't you think?"

"Safer, sure," she agreed. "But on screen or on paper my history remains the same. My parents were who they were. I was raised in the Projects and for all my momentary accomplishments I am simply a paper **PROFFIE**. I am an unreconstructed Jew as well and I'll simply never really believe in the system. I could be sent down any moment."

"You sound so certain. You make it all sound imminent." He paused to give her an opportunity to reply, but she remained still so he continued.

Faren Siminoff

"Anyone can be sent down. Even I could be. And as to being unreconstructed that could change, must change. Right Layla? You can remain a Jew. You keep ignoring that most CRS members continue to enjoy their home religions. You can join without giving up any of your beliefs or practices. Eventually, of course, you will come forward for full admission as a Reveled Saint. We will examine you and if all the signs of salvation are evident, you will be fully admitted. End of story. Can't you do that?"

"I don't know. I'm not sure. And it's not just that I don't buy the whole idea that GOD selects some to rise and others not, some to lead and others to follow. I simply don't accept any of the CRS' foundational beliefs. More to the point, I don't accept the whole premise of the CSA"

"So you've told me and recently so I've read."

At that they both fell silent.

"Layla," he rose inviting her to follow him outside again before he began to speak. She took up her position against the terrace's railing, leaned over it and looked out over the ocean. If she could, she would have dived into that sea and swum away. But the water was too rough, the rocks too sharp, and besides, where was there to go?

He began again.

"I don't care about your past. I only care about our future. Think about what I said earlier: 'Sometimes you need to reconsider. To listen and learn.' I meant that, but it's a two-way street. It has to be, or we can't work."

He was hoping for some type of response so they could begin a dialogue, but Layla remained obstinately silent.

"Layla, I don't think I can be happy without you. I don't want to be happy without you. I get who you are and I think you get who I am too. And though you've never said it in words, all your actions, gestures, the moments we have shared, tell me that you love me too, despite my CRS trappings."

She turned away from the sea to look at him but only murmured, "How I wish I were a mermaid and could swim far away from here."

He smiled at this passing whimsy. She was such an odd combination of things, hard and soft, practical but dreamy, all simultaneously. It occurred to him he loved her as much for her contradictions as for anything else.

228

"Layla, my Layla, I'm afraid you will have to stay here on land and I hope it will be with me. And, as antiquated as it sounds, I love you in all ways one human being can love another. What I am saying is, trying to express...I want to marry you. It's that simple, that true. That's why I brought you here. I want this to be our home."

She turned to look at him directly. She couldn't help but smile, just a little, and he lightly touched the corner of her mouth.

"Most men propose with a ring."

"Well, I chose a house. A home. I want to offer you a home with me, with our future children if God sees fit to so bless us. I propose to give you my heart, my soul, my support, my friendship, and the best views of the Ocean my resources can purchase. All for you, if you will have me and all this."

She turned her back to him, said nothing, and walked out of the house.

Chapter 33: Paul and Layla and Isaac

Samp

Paul bounced out of bed. Layla had arranged for separate rooms, but he thought it was just for appearance. It was just as well. Last night he and Orchid had spent mucho hours in his room after they made the rounds. The best place though was the Beijing West. It was this slick new venue Orchid knew about and was simply the hottest res in the Hamptons. You tumbled in to play mah-jongg and place bets, all while scarfing down the best kao ya this side of the Pacific along with copious amounts of baijiu, a super charged alcoholic drink from China. Yeah, what a night he crowed to himself! Could it get any better? Yes, he considered, it could. In fact this was his make it or go home moment.

I am either stuck as a WE forever or I get promoted to an EASY. It's as simple as that. Either this little taste will have to stay on my tongue for a lifetime, or I get to eat the whole pie. It's one or the other. I guess I'll know tonight.

He dressed then went to Layla's room knocking on the door. No answer. He palmed her. Waited. No response. Palmed her again. It was almost 10:00 a.m., the time she promised they'd meet up. Finally she responded.

"What's up?"

"What's up? You know what's up? Where are you? I am freaking out."

"Give me thirty minutes and I'll meet you in the American Hotel for brunch, ok?

"Fine." He signed off.

Thirty minutes later she sauntered up the few steps onto the American Hotel's porch immediately going over to Paul who had

230

engaged a prime time spot. He raised his hand to greet her. She moved to the table, sat down and motioned to the waitress.

"I'm famished," she announced.

"Hi, to you too," he said.

She ignored him, motioning again to the waitress who hustled over.

"Welcome to Sag Harbor. What can I do for you on this wonderful morning," the waitress trilled.

"You could start by getting me some coffee, orange juice and a menu," demanded the impatient Layla.

"Of course. Here's the menu." She gingerly laid two menus on the table.

Paul picked one up. "Why so cranky and rude to the server? I thought you were all about the WE?"

"You're right. Just a bit tired and stressed, that's all," she responded as she swiveled in her chair looking for the server and the needed caffeine.

"You know," Paul continued truly oblivious of Layla's genuine state of mind, "I like looking at a real menu. There's something about it that makes eating more fun, you know?"

"Yeah, more fun." She hesitated, moved a curl from her face, adjusted her very cool Entokii shades recently purchased, which every one assured her framed her face perfectly and was about to plunge into conversational cold water, when the waitress returned with her coffee and juice.

"Here you go," their server trilled again, putting the needed liquid on the table, "So, what can I get you two on this glorious morning?"

Layla had on her, 'don't make me vomit' face, but managed to reign herself in to smile at the server.

"Eggs Catalon would be great. But make sure the yolks are runny. I hate rock hard yolks. And what kind of bread do you have?"

"Sourdough, cibatta, raison pecan...ummmm...silver rush laced, and standard rye, wheat, and white."

"Raisin pecan. Oh, I didn't see the samp. Do you still have it?"

"Yes, ma'am."

"I'll have that too. But why isn't it on the menu?"

The waitress leaned over pointing her stylus pen at the bottom of the menu.

"So you do. Great. Love the stuff. So Native American. So Long Island." She turned to Paul. "You should try it."

"Yeah, I'll have it along with the waffles, a side of sausages and eggs over easy."

"You got it," the server intoned punching in the order as she turned to attend to another couple just sitting down at a nearby table.

They sat in silence, Layla sipping her coffee until the waitress reappeared; chipper as ever, setting their breakfasts down in front of them.

"Enjoy!"

Layla stuck her fork into the center of the egg, dropped it, and pushed the dish away.

"Shit, the yolk's hard. I hate hard yolks. I'm not eating that."

Paul looked down at his egg, poked at the yolk, which began a slow run down the circle of white. "Eat this," he gestured magnanimously, "I don't mind hard yolks."

He picked her plate up, placing it in front of him while inching the other plate towards Layla.

"Come on, eat," he cajoled her, "you said you were hungry."

"Yeah, I am. Thanks."

She ate about half her food, then raised her fork as if she were about to face a class to give a lecture. "You know Paul, I was thinking."

Oh, God, he thought, here it comes. She's dumping me. Maybe someone gave her the heads up about last night. I shouldn't have slept with that skank - wasn't worth it."

"Wait, Layla. I have something I want to tell you too. Let me get this out first," he said grabbing her hand in his, twisting the intricate band of diamonds and tiny emeralds encircling her finger.

"No, Paul," she insisted, disengaging, "I think I know what you want to say but don't. We, you and I, we can't go on. I mean I will remain your friend and always your biggest fan, but it can't be any more than that…this is very hard for me. I do love you, just not in that way."

Paul's face had already begun to crumple. Tears ran. His mouth quivered.

"Well, of course you can't love me in that way. What am I but some wanna' be, couldn't be EASY? I'm not good enough for you. Yeah, I know that. I'm lucky you wasted the time you have on me."

He stopped, adding a bit sarcastically, "I guess I was just a pretty boy for you. A curiosity fuck, right? I hope I didn't disappoint."

Layla looked up at him, the sorrow she felt spreading over her face, but her words reflected more indignation than sorrow. The combativeness she learned growing up in the Projects always clung to her.

"Absolutely not. How dare you suggest that!"

Paul, on the other hand, a WE through and through, drew back at the least bit of verbal rebuke, conditioned by years of navigating the assessment passages that steered him clear of the Projects as well as accustomed to the continual groveling at the feet of "superiors" in whose hands his future depended, immediately changed tone.

"You won't flag me as a Waster or try to put some other dirt in my file, will you," he asked, the fear audible in his voice.

"No, of course not. How could you ask that? "

He pushed back his chair, stood up placing his napkin on the table and took a last sip of coffee. "You'll still support my exhibit, won't you?

"Absolutely. I'm your friend and biggest supporter and when you are the EASY of the moment, I'll be your biggest fan. I'll even be your first sale."

"Naw, Professor Saenz. It'll be on the house. I owe you that much," he smiled while sending a message from his Palm Pad. It pinged a few seconds' later.

"Hey, I gotta' go. Orchid's picking me up to run me around. Then I'm going to do some visiting sights before heading out to the CCU estate to check again on the exhibit. It may be the first and last time I'm ever out here, right? So I gotta' provecha."

"Good idea. Yes, buen provecha," she agreed relieved he hadn't made a scene. She was surprised he acclimated to her news so quickly and still wasn't sure he was truly resigned to what she had just told him. Paul was nothing if not hyper-emotional, but his rapid turnabout reassured her she was no longer essential to him. His biggest concern had been her continued support. That was, obviously, the sum total of her true value to him; she was not, truth be told, surprised in the least.

"You know," she continued, "I think you will become a regular out here. In fact, I know it. You're a fab artist. It will all change for you tonight. Your Grandpa was wrong; even in this world dreams sometimes come true. It's ok to dream"

"From your beautiful lips to God's ear," he grinned, beginning to lift his hand into the bye, bye position.

A car pulled up and Orchid got out looking no worse for last night's wear. Her braided hair was streaked with green to resemble the leaves of an orchid, make-up perfect, a skin tight, blindingly white shirt playing off her luminescent lavender mini, she was dressed for success.

"Hey, Professor Saenz. Thanks for feeding our young genius here. I'm grabbing this pony while he's fresh."

"Yes, I see. Well, enjoy," she said to Orchid while applying the bill to her Palm Pad.

"Thanks for picking up the bill for Paul. I could do it but I'm afraid we went a little over last night- know what I mean? Everything out here is so expensive... Well I guess that's what keeps it exclusive. Can't pay, don't play, as they say."

"As they say," Layla responded. She turned to speak to Paul who was already getting into the sporty convertible mumbling, "Love these."

"So, Paul," she called out to him, "I'll see you tonight, ok?"

"Yeah, sure," were his last words to Layla.

She got it. His words hung in the exhaust fumes. It was fitting.

In the Light of Lime

Layla left her car with the CCU valet. There were lots of media types on hand. It was a newsy event only because everyone wanted to see if Paul would rise or fall. It was all in the gossip mags. It was one of those juicy 15 minutes of... stuff. Americans loved it. The WE loved it, particularly when it involved a "from nowhere to everywhere saga." It was real, it could be you, it could be me, but always it's us. That's what life is about. Always running in place, moving up or moving down. It's the essence of existence and at its center is creation; the limits that God has embedded in ones' DNA.

A small mike was shoved in Layla's face. The toothy reporter grinned. "Professor Saenz, a question." She looked at him blankly and was about to walk through the door but he stopped her again, grinning. He turned to the camera, his toothy grin still in place. "Hey people that's a PROFFIE for you. Not interested in the limelight. Let's see if she'll respond if I raise my hand." He sniggered at Layla raising his hand.

"Do you have a question?" she asked sweetly.

"We understand you're the one who discovered Paul Gaugin's talent. If he fails to catch will you be disappointed? Feel like you failed, misjudged his talent? Will you give yourself an 'F'?"

"I asked you if you had one question, not fifty. Get it together. Maybe you just don't know how to do your job. Will you feel disappointed when you are replaced?"

She glared at him; he blanched.

"Now excuse me, I have to go inside for the opening."

"Wait," the reporter laid a hand on Layla [as you all know by now, a big mistake].

"Take your hand off me," Layla commanded knocking it away and kept walking.

"Hey Layla, Ms. used-to-be **TAKER**, rumor has it Paul Gaugin is your boy toy and U'R doing this to make him more suitable for your new station in life."

"You really are a pig, aren't you? I hope the cameras are on **YOU** when you get sent down! In fact, I prognosticate that should happen sometime over the next forty-eight hours."

She walked through the mansion's door leaving the stunned reporter choking on her words, which the cameras caught. The anchor at the studio immediately picked up on this turning to her co-host quipping, "Hey, Brad, did you catch that? The CCU's prognosticator-in-chief predicts our colleague will be at the Project's gates shortly. Do you think she was in serio or just pissed?"

"Absolutely. Dead serio. I think we need to keep our cameras trained on him over the next forty-eight. Let's see if Professor Saenz is good to her prediction. That would be a first, right? The implementation of prognostication."

He swiveled to face camera "A" to directly address the viewer: "So keep your eyes stuck to this screen. We may have an exciting bust and you'll only see it right here."

"Well, that's a wrap," the co-host announced.

"Yeah," Brad agreed. "And let's thank our reporter in the field, Mike Scottbottom, for providing us with this exciting lead-in to what may be the next big bust."

They panned back to Mike who by then had collapsed into a quivering gel.

"Oh cheer up Mike," cheeped the co-host, "Just think you might get your thirty seconds. How exciting is that?"

Layla really did look elegant that night. She had her hair piled up with little curls escaping to frame her face, long slippery gold earrings with matching bands around her wrists and upper arms. Uncharacteristically, she was in a dress, more like applied green and purple sheer tissues that covered her up with raggedly draping ends. Innovative nineteenth century it was called, fitting for a young history professor on the rise. Chancellor Handler himself greeted her.

"Professor Saenz, thank you so much for coming. Of course we were expecting your Chair as well. What in the world happened to her?"

"I really don't know. She just said she was ill, that's all."

"What a shame. I think this is going to be a memorable evening. I'm sure she will regret having missed it."

"Absolutely, but it must have been something serious to have kept her from attending."

"Yes, quite serious."

Layla excused herself and moved into the gallery. The paintings were truly magnificent. How, she wondered again, could the Assessors have missed his talent? She hoped they would rectify their mistake. He was destined to be an EASY. She flinched at the use of that word "destined." So CRS. But in Paul's case, he really was meant to be a creative working artist. It was only right.

The gallery was already packed. And there was Paul, in his glory. Numerous prominent EASYs were in attendance. Look, there's Greta Siekle the winner of the Grand Slam in tennis, Billy Budster the quarterback for the Gas-Corp Jets who'd help clinch the Super Bowl for his team and Lena Mayez infamous and renowned sculptor. True, none except for the toniest could afford her work, but she kept it all in the headlines with her antics. She proved that highbrow could be lowbrow, all to great profitability. Of course, there was the usual collection of Screen stars preening, strutting and generally looking hot. But they had to. That was their job, even off duty. Couldn't be caught by the cameras looking ragged. But really,

Layla had no interest in any of these people. She was looking for one person and one person only.

She stood for a while not quite knowing what to do. She saw no one she really wanted to speak with and in reality no one wanted to speak with her. In this most rarified spot on the earth, where the rich and famous and simply rich and richer gathered, she was a speck. She was relieved when Paul came over with his Orchid now pinned to him.

"Hey Layla, so happy you could make it." He kissed her dispassionately on both cheeks showing her he was well over it.

"You like?"

"You know I like. I am your biggest fan. The only question is which I like best."

"No need for that. If all goes well there'll be more to come. Wherever you are, I will send you a painting. Just tell me the size. It'll be delivered. "

"What do you mean, wherever I am?"

He looked at her with what Layla could have sworn was a mixture of guilt and pity.

"Oh, la, Paul, look who's motioning to you?" Orchid said as she tugged on Paul. "It's K-Tin, the biggest thing in music. His assistant approached me earlier. Said K-Tin wants to commission you to do a painting for his house, right out here in Sag Harbor."

"Unbelievable. It's all happening so fast. Like a dream," Paul murmured.

"Yes, like a dream, so enjoy," Layla rejoined.

"Well, adios Layla. See you around. You know these big EASY types can be flitty, 'cause they're always onto the next cool thing."

He turned, dashing off to speak with K-Tin, Orchid in tow.

For Layla the evening dragged on and on. She spoke to some people, had her share of cocktails and trendy bites, but all in all, she wished herself out of there.

Around seven p.m. the Reverend Ice Freeman finally showed, large retinue in tow. Tall, distinguished as ever, dark skin against white garments, he was a walking Brahmin. No one who saw him could doubt it and people often pointed to Ice as Darwinism's finest proof. Hadn't his father risen from nothing? Didn't the son not only follow in his father's large footsteps but also appear poised to surpass his progenitor? There was no doubt but that the Second

Keeper's career was a living, breathing example of the truth embodied in the *Book of Darwin,* validation of the CRS way.

His progress across the floor of the gallery was slow. Everyone wanted to stop him, chat with him, and be acknowledged by him. She wondered why he had arrived so late. The invite indicated the show would close down by ten p.m. Well, she guessed he was busy or maybe bored by it all. Now he only had to put in a few hours and then he could leave. She hoped to be out of there by nine.

A few minutes later she looked up again and noticed Ice taking his place next to Handler on a small stage that had been placed at the far end of the gallery. Behind it was Paul's largest, most impressive and expensive canvass. Overhead lights blinked and Handler took the mike asking the room to settle down and turn its attention to the back.

"Friends, friends," Handler called out, "please turn your attention to us. We have an important announcement to make. In some respects an historic announcement."

Handler stepped back motioning Paul to step forward. Orchid squeezed his hand giggling, "Oh Paul, it's your moment for sure. How exciting."

Paul climbed up onto the stage. Handler shook his hand calling to the crowd, "Let's give a round of applause for Paul Gaugin."

[Applause, Applause]

"Let me tell you Paul's story. He came to us almost two years ago from *Trendytrends* the gigantic SM firm. Sad to say he had screwed up, been dumped."

[The crowd groaned]

"But redemption, the chance to be born again, was at hand. Because he took responsibility for his failings his CV was sent to us in response to a call for a position. And guess what folks? Our very own Bill Symone looked over Paul's vitals, assessment reports and past performance and saw promise, saw hope for Paul and gain for CCU. Let me tell you about Paul's accomplishments in graphic design and SM..."

[*Yawn, Yawn*]

"But, folks, there's another twist to this saga."

[Audience finally comes back to life, perks up]

"CCU did a bit of digging and guess what? It turns out our Paul is a direct descendant of that long dead Art EASY, Paul Gauguin."

[APPLAUSE, APPLUASE]

"Imagine that! But, as the *Book of Darwin* says, *God's design will be written in the genes.*"

[Chants of: *GENES WILL TELL, GENES WILL TELL…*]

"So now, to make a long story short, here's the happy ending…"

[Woofs and chants from the audience of: *SPIT IT OUT, SPIT IT OUT…*]

"As CCU Chancellor I authorized this information, along with his body of work, sent to the Assessors for re-evaluation and guess what folks? Yes, our very own Paul Gaugin has been reassigned as a provisional EASY. He's even been given a short-term contract in the CCU Art department."

Turning to Paul he gripped his hand pumping it, "You didn't think we discovered you just to let you go, did you?"

Paul shook his head grinning, his pretty curly locks bobbing. Tears of joy ran down his face. Finally he croaked, "Thank you Chancellor, thank you. I will make CCU proud."

"I am sure you will. The consequences for failure are, well, unthinkable," he said through a crocodile grin.

[Thunderous applause, woofing all around, newsfeed sent out and Paul got his forty-five seconds]

The Reverend Freeman stepped forward, raised his hand and the crowd quieted.

"Chancellor Handler asked me to bless this new EASY and his future. But what blessing can I give, you might ask? Hasn't the All Knowing set his path, given **His** blessing? Yes, it's true. We may deviate from God's path…we often do. The *Book of Darwin* does not negate free will. What God gives, human beings can derail. But how, you might ask? By ignoring the path God has assigned us. Yet here stands Paul Gaugin, a fine upstanding **MAKER**, a child of God. He accepted his placement as a 3-D Graphic artist, and yet he quietly continued to pursue the Grace that God had placed inside him: his art. His patience paid off, his talent was revealed, and the mistake that **man** made was corrected."

He paused, looking around to place emphasis on the idea that it was people who made mistakes, did not properly interpret **His** will, **His** design, which were at fault for Paul's mis- assessment.

"So now, let's say, *Amen* and thank the Lord who has redirected Paul onto his rightful path and to Chancellor Handler who has given voice to that will."

He turned to Paul motioning him to kneel and pray. As Paul did so, the assembled crowd of the most righteous EASYs, PROFFIEs and JCs also fell to their knees praying until Ice rose to his feet dragging Paul with him.

"Congratulations Paul. It's all up to you now. All in your hands."

"Yes," he agreed, "I guess it always was."

You Said it All

About an hour after the BIG announcement Layla's Palm Pad buzzed. It was Handler's office requesting she pop in for a moment.

"Be there in two," she palmed back.

Handler's office in the CCU mansion was tucked away on its top floor. She couldn't imagine why he wanted to see her so urgently and so late in the evening. *Couldn't it wait?* But she understood this was not a request she could put off or ignore.

There was no Secrey. The place was quiet, the door ajar. It appeared it was just to be the two of them. She found that odd. She knocked on the inner door to announce her arrival. She felt uncomfortable, but she could handle it. She always did.

"Take a seat Layla." He motioned her to sit. She looked around; there was only one chair, so she sat. She said nothing.

"Aren't you wondering why I wanted to see you at this particular moment?

"Yes, I guess I do."

"So, aren't you going to ask?"

"Since you asked to see me, I assume you will tell me what's up."

He picked up a copy of *The Restored History of America from 1492 to the Great Transformation* pushing it across the desk towards her like a hockey puck gliding across the ice. She put her hand against the edge of the desk to stop it from falling onto the floor.

He glared at her. "Sassy, aren't you?"

She picked it up. Glanced at it. Put it down. Looked back at him blandly answering, "So, I've been told."

"Did you believe anything you wrote in that book," he asked gesturing towards it.

"Of course. As you said, I wrote it."

"Really, then what's this?" he clicked on the wall screen behind him and the first page of *What Really Happened* appeared. She said nothing.

"Professor Saenz, what do you have to say about this?"

"Nothing."

"Nothing? Do you think that's a satisfactory answer?"

"Well, it'll have to be, because I don't know anything about whatever it is you just flashed." She leaned forward preparing to stand up and leave.

"Hold it right there Layla. We haven't finished."

She stood up anyway bending down to retrieve her small hand bag. "Well, I'm tired. I have to drive back to Sag Harbor and tomorrow I need to get back to the city early. I have some work to catch up on."

Handler smirked. "Sit back down please. I haven't dismissed you."

Layla lowered herself back into the chair. "Is this what they used to call 'detention'?"

"I guess being from the Projects you should know all about detention, huh, Ms. Saenz? Better get used to being called plain 'ol Ms. Saenz again 'cuz it looks like ur' bein' sent down! You remember how they speak in the Projects don't you?"

"Yes Sir, I certainly do remember. Still, if it's all the same with you, I'd like to go. CCU chancellor or not, you have no right to detain me."

She got up again from the chair, grabbed her bag, and turned towards the door.

"Just remember, I know you wrote this heresy. Did you do it alone or are you part of some cell? Sure you can write what you want but you can't circulate what you want. Something like this requires Internet clearance. And you don't have clearance. Moreover, we'll prove theft of services. Your time has been contracted for by CCU."

"Listen," she told him coolly, "I don't know what you're talking about, I don't know what this is…clearly you are mistaken."

She got up and left. Her heart was pounding. There was nowhere for her to go except to return to the party.

Less than twenty minutes after that encounter Handler reappeared bounding back onto the stage.

"Quiet everyone, quiet. Let me have your attention once again." The crowd grew silent. All turned towards the stage. Layla who was deep in chat with some up and coming **EASY** turned towards the stage. She muttered, "What does that blowhard want now? Didn't he get his five with that stupid announcement and standing up there with Freeman? How much more mileage does he think he can get from this evening?"

"I don't know baby but you can never get enough, don't you think?"

"Whatever," she responded, "I just hope he says his peace real quick."

"Yeah, me too," he replied looking at her like she was a rare lamb chop he wanted to devour.

"Don't get your hopes up," she said as if she read his thoughts, "it's not happening."

"I know," Handler began, "that this evening's story has been one of celebration and discovery. The CSA has a new EASY." Handler pointed to Paul who stood at the foot of the stage.

[Applause, Applause]

"But there's another discovery that must be revealed tonight. Not a pleasant one, but a necessary one."

Layla looked around her. She knew what was coming next. She eyed the exits. Homeland Security Marshals were posted at the doors. And, just as alarming, moving forward, parting the crowd like Moses parted the Red Sea, was the Remi from *Where are They Now?* with his filming crew in tow.

"It seems we have all been the victims of a small but dangerous deception. To clear this up I'm going to ask Mr. Gaugin and our very own Professor Layla Saenz to step forward."

Her **EASY** friend began to push her forward. "You go girl. Catch the shine."

Again Layla looked around for an exit or savior, but none appeared. She had no choice but to cut through the crowd and mount the stage. Handler motioned her to stand on his left and Paul on his right side. Guards flanked the sides of the stage. There would be no escape.

"There's a bit of irony on this stage, isn't there?"

The crowd looked perplexed.

"Yes, it's true. Lots of irony up on this stage here tonight."

He motioned to Paul. "Here we have Paul Gaugin; worked hard, stayed the course. He got his just reward, from **WE** to **EASY**. Straight and narrow, following the plan even when it's not as quick or as clear as we'd like, as long as we stay the course HE laid out for us, success will come." [Applause, Applause]

He turned to his left. "On the other hand, we have Professor Layla Saenz. Beautiful. Brilliant. Started out life in the Projects. Her parents were subversives. They were killed in the Last Uprising. The report said they were the ringleaders. Yet, despite such antecedents, she was given a chance to show she was not tainted. The CSA system objectively looked at her scores, her record, and found her worthy to not only walk out of those gates, but with a scholarship to CCU and eventually as a trusted professor at CCU. Yet, she has not repaid our faith in her, our collective trust. She has engaged in illegal content uploading. She has published something, surreptitiously, without Internet clearance, without CCU permission. She has engaged in theft of time."

He flashed a page from, *What Really Happened* up onto the wall screen. It was from the book's preface.

The up and coming **EASY** Layla had been speaking with just a few moments before, recoiled in horror. He turned to his friend muttering, "I barely know the bitch. I was just trying to get laid..."

"So, Professor Saenz, do you have anything to say?"

"I am going to say to you what I said before. You are mistaken. I have no idea what you are talking about. Or what," she pointed to the screen, "this is."

"Mistaken? I don't think so Ms. Saenz." He turned to Paul. "Tell everyone here what you told me."

"Paul," she said, the alarm in her voice perceptibly rising, "what does he have to do with this?"

"Oh, everything."

Paul stood mute, looking guilty, looking unhappy. His head bowed.

"Paul," Handler ordered, "tell Layla here what you saw."

243

Paul didn't answer. Just stood.

"Go on, tell her. It's your duty to tell the truth."

Paul shuffled his feet. *Honestly*, Layla thought, *he's so pathetic.*

"I'm so sorry Layla. I didn't mean to hurt you. They said they knew I should have been an EASY the whole time, just made a mistake. They promised to correct it, but I had to tell them the truth."

"The truth," she side stepped Handler grabbing him hard, "The truth about what?"

He looked up at her. "You know, about that book you've been writing. That other history book. Honestly, I didn't know this would happen. They told me nothing bad would happen to you and I'd get what I deserved."

"What do you mean by that?"

The Remi was in his glory! What screen this would make. He motioned his crew to shoot the scene from two angles. They'd edit it later. They had so much material- perhaps enough for two shows. The ratings would go through the roof!

"Yeah, what I deserve," he spoke up becoming surly, "I deserve to be an EASY. You're not the only one who deserved to be tiered up."

"I didn't do it by screwing my friends."

"Friend? I was just some low class curiosity for you. You discarded me Layla. You know you did."

"That's enough," Handler interjected. "I'm not interested in any of this. You can settle your personal issues some other time."

Handler turned to Layla pushing his Palm Pad in front of her. "Just sign this affidavit of guilt and I'll see what I can do for you. Maybe CCU won't press charges. Maybe instead of the Projects you can become a low level Content Facilitator in some other Zone. Sign it and I'll see what I can do."

He turned to the crowd wholly engaged in the drama playing itself out, seemingly for their entertainment.

"Why are you doing this? Why are you lying about me? What's in it for you?" she asked Handler turning away from Paul.

"My duty to CCU demands this. You know that Ms. Saenz."

"Really, really? That's what this is all about? Protecting CCU? Bull shit! It's all about you, about promoting your career. Say, what's the next step from here? Oh right, head of the STD and then, maybe, a seat on the Board of Twenty, the step up to JC? Oh, happy days for Assam Handler. Do you think this little splash will get you over?"

He cocked his head. "I think I'm doing my duty. If there is a reward for that well, that's as it should be. It's as the *Book of Darwin* says, *Do good by doing well.*"

One of the guards mounted the podium approached Handler and whispered to him, "Sir, Keeper Freeman wants to approach. He wants the stage for a moment."

"By all means bring him up. Maybe he'll even bless this act."

As soon as Freeman mounted the stage cheers erupted from the crowds again demonstrating to all that the tall, handsome, silver-tongued Keeper with the common touch was an enormously popular figure in the CSA amongst all tiers, top to bottom.

Layla looked towards him but Ice did not acknowledge her. Instead, he addressed the crowd.

"Well this is an unusual ending to such an evening. I am, to say the least, disturbed."

This statement caught Handler and the assembled off guard. Handler's mouth opened to say something but Ice, anticipating this, held up his hand to silence the crowd as well as the percolating Chancellor.

"This is a serious accusation. Certainly too grave to be the subject of the show we are witnessing today. Let me remind everyone that the CRS is headquartered in the heart of the CCU campus. We have chosen it as the site for our Cathedral of Commerce. As such we monitor everything. Nothing escapes the CRS's watch. We are the eyes and ears of God- - yea, in God we trust."

He scanned the now silent crowd calling out to them: "Now say with me the motto on our ancient currency, *In God We Trust.*"

The crowd began to chant: *In God We Trust, In God We Trust, In God We Trust...* After about thirty seconds of this Freeman indicated he wanted silence and the gathering complied. The actors in the room were particularly gratified to have some stage directions to follow.

He turned to Handler, "So Chancellor I would like to see **all** the evidence against Professor Saenz because my people have drawn a different conclusion."

"A what?" croaked the astounded Chancellor, "What do you mean, 'a different conclusion' "?

Freeman motioned to a tall, thin, very pale man standing near the stage. His Palm screen was open and he appeared to have taken control of the large wall screen situated behind the stage. A mass of computer codes appeared on the screen. Few in the audience understood it, but all were impressed.

"What! What is this," an astonished Handler demanded.

"Why, this is evidence. Watch and learn how it's done." Freeman motioned to the thin man to come up on stage.

"Let's give a round of applause to one of the most highly rated computer security specialists in the business, Tim Johnston!!!"

The crowd began to cheer, *Woof, woof, woof...*

Freeman shook Tim's hand. "Tim, thank you so much for appearing today. I know you are a behind the scenes kind of guy, but tonight is your night to shine." He grinned at Tim.

Tim Johnston was, no surprise, the grandson of that same Jim Johnston who helped I.M. Coyne, the CRS Prophet, crack the Tablet conundrum. His grandson was part of the CRS' inner circle and in charge of Internet security.

"Thank you so much Reverend Freeman. The honor is mine. Shall I proceed?"

"Yes. Let everyone here know what you've discovered."

Johnston proceeded to speak for close to fifteen minutes moving from screen to screen, explaining how he had analyzed the data and the biometric markings he'd uncovered. No surprise, that most of the audience found this a snooze. They didn't snap to attention until Freeman posed the question everyone was waiting for:

"So Mr. Johnston, where did this document Chancellor Handler alleges was produced by Professor Saenz originate from?"

"From Chancellor Handler's office. Indeed, while I cannot tell if the Chancellor himself produced this document- that would be the subject of an in-the-being investigation- there is no doubt but the Chancellor authorized it. The clearance for posting on the Internet, the password encryption, the recipients to date, the biometric prints – all can be traced back to the Chancellor's personal computer."

The audience gasped.

"Are you positive?" intoned Freeman.

"Totally. No doubt. The responsibility for this lies with Chancellor Handler."

Freeman motioned to the marshals who moved to surround the stage. Handler panicked. He screamed, "That's impossible. Me? Not me! It was **her**. Paul saw it on her computer. Tell them Paul"

Freeman turned to Paul, "Did you see this?"

"Yes, I think so. I saw it on Layla's computer. I just kinda' assumed it was a book she was working on..."

"Did she ever tell you she was working on this book?"

"No, I never asked. I just kinda' assumed..."

"I think you were mistaken," he told Paul. "Yes, mistaken. An understandable misunderstanding but still, incorrect."

"What do you mean," asked Handler.

Johnston now interjected, "It appears you sent this to Professor Saenz's computer, like a virus. Paul here may have seen the program activated on the computer. He would have had no way of knowing that Professor Saenz didn't produce it. She probably never even realized it had been embedded."

Freeman again turned to Paul and queried: "Is that possible Paul?"

Paul picked up on the cue. "Yeah, sure, totally possible. I mean I'm an artist, right? I'm no computer programmer. I just saw it, that's all, and assumed...."

Freeman clapped Paul on his back. "Well, of course you did, and you did your duty by reporting what you saw. But you understand now how you were deceived, don't you?"

"Yes, yes of course. I was deceived by the Chancellor." He turned to Layla, "I am so very, very sorry. I stepped into something I have no expertise to judge. But Handler kept insisting that **he** knew what it was I saw- I never characterized it..."

"Why you little shit," Handler screamed. "I'll see you sent back to SM. Or better yet, you'll lose your contract. Sixty-days WE benefits then, who knows? No one's going to give you a job. You get my meaning?" Paul blanched at those words.

"So you say," Ice coolly stated. "I think you won't be doing anything for a while except preparing your defense. But, of course, that will be for a court of law to decide. That's out of my bailiwick. In the meantime, the Homeland Security Marshals are here to escort you off these premises." Ice nodded to the Marshals.

The Remi and his crew were filming it all – the handcuffs, the screaming, the sobbing. As the Marshals led Handler away the crowd booed while the Remi stuck his microphone into Handler's puckered face. "Handler what have you to say to this? Why'd you do it? Who are you working with? Were any members of your family ever terrorists?"

Handler said nothing.

"Come on, come on, talk. This may be your last chance to get your side of it out to the public."

Handler began to scream, "I'm innocent, innocent. Can't you all see that? She set me up! The bitch set me up!"

Freeman shot the now thoroughly dissected man a look of contempt. He nodded at the Marshals. "It's enough. Show's over. He's in your charge now."

The captain of the Marshals saluted and motioned to his men to take the bawling Handler to the waiting car.

Freeman directed the crowd to settle down, then turned to Layla who still stood on the stage, "Professor Saenz is owed an apology. She's been maligned; subjected to a terrible ordeal. While I certainly can't claim to speak for CCU, I think I can speak for the assembled here tonight when I offer Professor Saenz our heartfelt apology for what she has had to endure."

[Applause, Applause, Woof, Woof, Woof…]

Layla nodded her acceptance. The captain of the Marshals who just twenty minutes earlier was ready to take her into custody stepped forward, saluted her, and offered his arm to escort Layla from the stage.

Much applause and woofing as Layla accepted his gallant offer and walked off stage a vindicated woman, her PROFFIE status securely intact. Paul trailed behind.

Freeman, looking satisfied, turned back to the crowd telling them, "That's it folks, it's over. I think it's time to wrap this night up. It's been eventful, hasn't it?"

Yes it has, yes it has, the crowd chanted.

"Yes it has," Freeman agreed "So, let's wind it down. Finish your drinks and call it a night. And may God bless you all. May God bless the CSA."

[Applause, Applause]

Freeman bounded off the stage approaching Layla and Paul. "Paul I think we are done with you. Stay away from intrigue and you'll be fine. Understood?"

Paul nodded and scurried away into the waiting arms of Orchid who was more than happy to assist him recover from the trauma of the evening and assure him all this would be a boost to his career.

"And you Layla, let's go into the anteroom over there. We need to talk."

"Yes," she agreed twisting the ring on her finger, "We need to talk."

Freeman motioned Johnston to follow. Once alone, Johnston pulled a good-sized laptop from a briefcase setting it on the table. He turned it on and pulled up a screen that had instructions for sending the book, Layla's book, *What Really Happened*, viral. Johnston said something to Ice she couldn't hear and left the room.

Freeman pointed to it. "What do you have to say Layla, are you the author?

"Yes," she admitted, "Yes, I am."

"I thought so. You know the next time you want to write something like this you might want to adopt a different writing style. But lucky for you, I'm probably the only one who would recognize it anyway since most people don't read that closely."

He looked again at Layla who said nothing. "Oh, don't be so disappointed. Nobody reads these days, except for me," he winked at her. "Were you really planning to viral this, or was this just a little gift for me because I'm a fellow lover of history?"

"I wanted to viral it. Make people understand what really happened. So maybe they'd want change, agitate for change."

She stopped then continued, "I know, I know. My book wasn't going to change the world. No matter what, few people would have even read it. I'm a **PROFFIE.** I fully understand most people simply won't read and that when they do, it's certainly not a history book. I just needed to write the truth after contributing to that ridiculous drivel the CCU published. I wanted to correct the record."

"I think we need to discuss all this more in-depth, but some other time. I understand your reservations about the system, the need for change. No revolution is perfect. Sometimes things go amiss. And while I don't agree with everything you espouse, I agree there are problems in the system, a need for some genuine transformation."

" At least you see some merit in my perspective," the still stunned Layla replied.

"But, in the future, you might want to consult with me first. Perhaps there are more constructive ways of seeking change than engaging in theft of services or illegal uploading of content."

"Agreed, but it seems a shame to waste all my work."

Ice nodded. He moved closer to Layla. Took her hand looking down at the ring on her finger. "I see you received it. Does that mean, *Yes*?"

She smiled at him, a tentative smile, but a smile.

"Yes. It means, yes."

She reached out to him, led him over to the computer on the table, took hold of one of his fingers and together they pressed:

SEND.

Made in the USA
Charleston, SC
10 August 2016